Published by Turning Point Books
15th Floor, Concorde Building, Dunan Street
Verdun, Beirut, Lebanon
P.O. Box: 14-6613
Tel: 00961 1 752 100
www.tpbooksonline.com

First edition: March 2011

Text: Dania El-Kadi
Editing: Dina Dabbous
Layout and graphic design: Chantal Coroller
Cover illustration: Cinzia Sileo

Although inspired by real life events, the storylines, characters and most locations (most notably Rantour
and Kafarneem) in this book are imaginary.

ISBN 978-9953-0-2013-6

Printing: ●**dots**

Dania El-Kadi

SUMMER BLAST
When War Threatens Lebanese Women's Plans

turning**point**
B O O K S

BIOGRAPHY

Dania was born in the US and raised in Beirut. Her father's career in the military also took her to Belgium as a teenager. She studied History at the American University of Beirut before taking up jobs in the technology sector across Kuwait, Lebanon, Dubai and, more recently, London — including roles with multinational corporations such as Intel and Nokia.

Dania's short novel, *Un Chemin Sur Son Front*, was published in Paris by "Éditions Caractères" in the year 2000. Her short story, *Trophy Wife*, will be published in the "Words to Music" anthropology. She has also contributed articles to leading Arabic dailies. *Summer Blast* is El-Kadi's first published full novel.

Dania currently lives in London with her husband.

To my mother, cousinettes, friends
and all the fierce and fabulous ladies of Lebanon.
And very importantly, to my real life heroine, my sister Nibal.

ACKNOWLEDGEMENTS

I have hundreds of people to thank for bringing this story to life. Charlotte Hamaoui for giving me this amazing opportunity but also for bringing a breath of fresh air to publishing in Lebanon. Dina Dabbous who provided invaluable editorial input (and much needed common sense). Debi for "seeing" the story and believing it even before I did. Last but not least, to the more than 500 early readers who shaped the book through their online comments.

To my dad and my brother who have been so supportive all along and Samy Khodr, the coolest guy on Earth.

And I couldn't have finished the book without my husband Hani who put up with me working on the edits during our honeymoon.

Dear Mark,

Thank you for the support on the book & being a great colleague. Hope you enjoy it!

Chapter 1

The screech of the warplanes jolted Elyssar from her sleep, sending her running towards what felt like the safest place in the apartment: the entrance hallway. Her mother and sister followed, dishevelled and barefoot. The three of them clung to one another as a series of blasts made the nearby mirror shake on the wall. Elyssar lunged to secure it.

"What on earth is that?" she yelled.

"Only an air raid can make this kind of noise," her mother replied, trembling.

Within minutes the commotion died; the three women stood there for a while longer, too scared to move.

"I think it's over," Elyssar said at last, venturing towards the living room.

Her father was already there, tuned in to the news. Elyssar stared in horror as the TV broadcast showed columns of smoke coming out of a familiar location: Beirut airport.

"The Israeli air force raided the Beirut airport runway," the presenter announced. "All flights have been suspended." The images succeeded each other, displaying the destruction from various angles. Then the broadcast moved on to show frightened passengers rushing out of the terminal.

Aghast, Elyssar remembered that her friend Rouba was supposed to be travelling today. She grabbed the phone and pressed the buttons, her fingers fumbling on the keypad.

"I'm alive," Rouba announced as she picked up.

"Thank God! Were you at the airport when it happened?"

Elyssar's mother, father and sister turned their eyes off the screen to follow the conversation. Rouba was considered a family member; they'd known her since she'd befriended Elyssar in primary school.

"No, I was still at home," Rouba said, "I haven't been able to watch the news yet. How bad is it?"

"They've bombed both runways, but no casualties."

"Is this a one off like they've done before, or will there be more attacks?" Rouba asked.

"No one knows."

Depressed silence on both ends of the line. Elyssar had another pressing question for her friend; she left the TV room to be out of earshot.

"How did it go with your family last night?" she asked.

"I mustered the courage and told them."

"And?"

"It was more of a monologue, they barely uttered a word. And there I was, expecting to have to argue it all night. It's almost as if they didn't care."

"Divorce just isn't what it used to be," Elyssar said.

Rouba recounted the conversation. Her mother had cried so much when she'd announced her plans to marry an older Kuwaiti man that Rouba expected worse when her parents found out she was now about to get divorced. But both of them had taken a long look at her and gone on silently with dinner.

"You've lost your ability to scandalize your family. I'm mortified," Elyssar said.

Rouba chuckled.

"So what do I do now?" she said, "My plan for a swift exit to the airport has clearly failed. I haven't left my room all morning because I don't want to face anyone."

Elyssar looked through the hallway into the TV room. Her parents and sister were still riveted to the screen.

"There's nothing you can do. Just stay put for the time being," she said.

Now that business in Lebanon looked set to come to a screeching halt, Elyssar knew she would have to work hard if she wanted her employer, a multinational US software maker, to keep the recently inaugurated regional office open and her as its manager – although currently she was also its only employee.

A few hours after the bombing of the airport, she was pounding away at her laptop, wrapping up a submission for a new bid when her sister, Reem, put her head through the doorway.

"What are you doing?" she asked. "You should be packing."

With mounting threats between the Israeli government and Lebanese politicians, Elyssar's extended family had decided to leave Beirut for the relative safety of their summer homes in the mountain village of Rantour .

"I need two minutes. I have to send this email."

"Send it later, people will understand your circumstances," Reem replied.

Elyssar kept her eyes glued to the screen. She loved her family, but at times like this her domestic situation drove her up the wall. For the millionth time she promised herself to do something about it. Whether the social norm allowed it or not, she had to find a way to leave her parents' home and live on her own. She and her sister were now in their thirties and four adults in the same household was too stressful. Whereas Reem, a French language teacher in a school in Beirut, seemed to accept this situation, Elyssar found herself at odds with it. For a while, she'd even considered leaving the country. But she'd decided to stay when she found this new job: it was her opportunity to strengthen her career in Lebanon's growing technology sector.

"This is for a project in Jordan," she said. "No one will wait for me to resolve my little issue with international politics."

"Then make it quick, we're leaving in forty-five minutes."

Reem disappeared to help her mother pack the supplies in the kitchen.

An hour later the family took to the road, their two cars filled with a month's worth of clothes and wartime supplies: canned foods, rice, sugar, salt, powdered milk, candles and matches. Elyssar drove behind her parents' SUV as they joined the heavy, yet unusually orderly traffic. They drove along rows of tightly packed building blocks. These were 1970s eyesores in terms of design, but their reinforced cement walls saved many lives in the war and were still bullet ridden, several carrying gaping holes caused by shells and bombs. This part of town, with the Hippodrome at its centre, hadn't been fully reconstructed after the civil war ended in the early nineties, but, testimony to the recent economic boom, brand new modern banks had been erected in between the shells of bombed offices. Sadly, this area remained a far cry from other districts of Beirut where old souks had been renovated to their former glory, or modern towers lined the wider, cleaner streets.

"Running away like this reminds me of the civil war," Reem said. "It's 1989 all over again."

Elyssar gave her sister a wry smile.

"*And* 1984 *and* 1982 *and* a few others..."

"At least this time we're of driving age."

"Yeah, but our metabolism is slower, we're worried about wrinkles and it's much harder to get dates."

Reem smiled. Elyssar switched on the radio.

"What about the Madonna concert?" Reem asked.

"What about it?"

"If the war continues we'll never make it to Paris to see it."

"I'll swim there if I have to," Elyssar replied. "We can't keep putting our life on hold war after war."

She knew her admiration for Madonna bordered on childish. It had started in her early teens and never gone away. Maybe it was because, growing up in war torn Beirut, she had looked for a strong female role model and the pop star of the moment had been the right fit, or maybe she had related to Madonna's well publicized rebellion against her conservative upbringing. Today, Elyssar remained a fan but to her the real importance of this concert lay in the fact that it was a long time dream come true: attending a pop concert had felt so out of reach to her when she was growing up.

As the traffic cleared, they soon left the city and started on the winding mountain road.

"I'd forgotten how nice this road is," Reem said. "I always take the sea road and turn at the Khaldeh crossing because it's faster."

"Dad came this way because the sea road is a prime bombing target," Elyssar replied. "Glad you're enjoying the view."

Reem sighed. "We only *really* look at this country when something terrible takes place."

Elyssar nodded in agreement. She tried to look around as she carefully steered the car. Typically for this part of the Mount Lebanon chain, oak trees and pines surrounded the narrow and winding two-way road on both sides. To her right, beyond the hills, she caught a glimpse of the Mediterranean sparkling in the sun; a quick calculation told her they were now at around seven hundred meters above sea level. Her old geography schoolbooks came to mind; they referred to Lebanon as a "green jewel" in the vast desert of the Middle East...

OK, she was getting too sentimental now. She turned the radio up. "I'm glad the cousinettes will be there," she said.

"Yes, it will make things bearable," her sister replied.

Bearable was an understatement. The sisters shared a special bond with their female cousins, built over the many holidays spent together in Rantour.

Elyssar sighed in relief when they finally took the turn into Rantour. It felt safe to be in the village that her family had inhabited for more than six hundred years. They drove along Rantour's only road, a two-way street devoid of side-walks but lined by small shops and low rise residential buildings. In this rural part of the country, building a house sometimes involved two generations. The father laid the foundations for a multi storey structure that could house several apartments for his children's future households, but he could only afford the full construction of the first floor, leaving room for his children to build on top of it, if and when they were able to afford it.

Elyssar's grandfather built their first house on land owned by his ancestors and, later on, his sons had each added their own homes. Now the extended family occupied what could be described as a compound: four summer houses that shared common gardens. Although as a female it wasn't expected, Elyssar had made a pledge to herself that she too would one day build her own house in Rantour.

She slowed down as she negotiated a turn behind her father's car. This was one of her favourite locations: the place where the road takes a sharp curve and the rows of homes on each side give way to the sight of the almost untouched valley beneath the village. Outside their front gate, her father stopped the car and stepped out.

"The power must be cut," Reem said when he didn't use the remote control to open the gates.

Elyssar shook her head, power and water cuts were common in Rantour like in most rural parts of the country. Even telephone landlines had only been installed a few years earlier. Of course by that time most people owned a mobile phone, but the village had still celebrated the installation of its first switchboard.

Reem helped her father push the gate open, their mother got behind the wheel of the SUV and drove it to the garage, followed by Elyssar. A look towards the villas next door told her no one else had arrived yet.

The rest of the family started pulling up shortly after she finished unpacking: the cousinettes but also uncles, aunts, male cousins and their children. The property filled up with chatter as they took turns helping each other unload the cars and settle in.

Uncle Najeeb and his French wife, Aunt Bernadette, arrived towards the end of the afternoon, the latter reeling from her phone call to the French embassy.

"They said they don't have evacuation arrangements in place yet." She sounded scandalized. "You'd think they have emergency plans for a country like Lebanon."

She continued to complain as everyone helped carry her luggage inside the house and was still grumbling when she finished unpacking and joined the group for coffee. "It's a disgrace to France," she said. "The embassy is too busy spending our tax money on cocktail receptions."

The cousinettes tried not to smile. Aunt Bernadette loved referring to her money being misspent by the French government although she'd been in Lebanon her entire adult life and had never paid a cent in French tax.

"I'm sure other governments have already organized everything," she continued. "But ours..."

Her husband, who'd had to suffer this rant all day, ran out of patience.

"Look at all of us," he said pointing to the dozen family members around them. "Do you know what *our* government is doing to help us right now? Nothing. So find something else to complain about."

That night, Elyssar woke up to the sound of voices outside. She grabbed her mobile to check the time: three a.m. Heart thudding, she pressed the light switch but the room remained in pitch darkness: the power was still off. She clasped the phone, using its screen to light her way as she rushed downstairs to find everyone gathered around Cousinette Maya and Aunt Hala both looking frazzled and scared, having just arrived from Beirut.

Aunt Hala wore a dressing gown over her nightdress while Maya flaunted a pantsuit and high heels.

"Is this the new dress code for dodging bombs?" Elyssar teased.

"A shell exploded so close I woke up thinking it was in my room,"

Maya replied. "This is the first thing I got out of the closet. I didn't have the time to find a shirt."

"So you're wearing the jacket with nothing underneath?" Elyssar whispered.

She looked closer in the near darkness. Her cousin's blazer barely covered her cleavage and midriff. "You're lucky the power's out." She glanced at Uncle Najeeb. "If *he* sees you showing skin in the village, we'll have our own nuclear blast to worry about."

Chapter 2

The following morning Rouba couldn't think of an excuse to stay in hiding, so when her mother announced breakfast she gathered her courage and stepped out. Her grandmother, uncles, aunts and cousins stood around the table, some already munching on *hummus* and *labneh*. Silence fell and everyone stared at her as she walked in.

Rouba wished she hadn't waited so long to fly from Kuwait to Lebanon in order to break the divorce news to her parents . If she'd arrived a week earlier, she would have caught them in their home in Beirut, with the rest of the family at a safe distance. But by now they had moved to their summer apartment in the town of Kafarneem where her grandmother and the rest of her father's siblings occupied the other apartments in the building.

She cringed at the sight of her father, the shadows under his eyes and his unshaven face were evidence that the news of her divorce had taken its toll. The political developments didn't help either; Rouba had followed the updates on the radio in her room: overnight the Israeli air force had targeted the infrastructure, destroying bridges and key roads, and announcing a blockade of Lebanon.

Her hopes of a smooth divorce in Kuwait had collapsed alongside the first of those bridges. She kept her eyes down as she ate, praying that people would have the common sense not to broach any uncomfortable topics. But her grandmother had other ideas.

"Rouba, child, what is this news I hear?"

Teta's sweetness made it difficult to be upset at her. The world order as she knew it dictated that women stay married no matter what, otherwise they would lose face in society and would have to depend on their father or brother for livelihood. Yes, she understood that today's girls were educated and had jobs that allowed them to support themselves, but they still needed a husband to protect them and give them a social status.

"Yes, it's true."

Those around the table did little to hide their interest in the conversation as all eyes turned to Rouba. She avoided their gaze.

"Majed is a wonderful man, you'll be miserable without him," Teta said.

Rouba summoned all her patience.

"We reached a point where it's impossible to stay married. I guess we're not destined to be together."

"You will miss Majed's children and they will miss you." Teta made the statement as if Rouba hadn't thought about that.

She pushed the tears away. "My relationship with the kids will not change," she said, pushing the tears away. "We'll always be part of each other's lives."

The other family members rolled their eyes in disbelief. In a silent prayer, Rouba asked God for his help in proving them wrong.

In Rantour, Cousinette Maya sat on the patio in deep thought. By sticking to her plans she had persuaded herself that she would be sending a positive message to the universe and the conflict would finish in time for her wedding to take place as intended in September. She had started preparations early and employed a good planner. She'd already set the menu, agreed the floral layout, selected the design of her custom-made shoes and booked the first dress fitting for next week. Ziad, her fiancé, and her parents had already bought their outfits and she had "approved" most of her close friends' dresses.

Maya felt satisfied that all was on track... until her mother decided to turn up the drama. She walked onto the patio, the knot between her eyebrows giving away her emotional state. "I couldn't sleep all night," she said as she settled in a chair next to Maya.

"That humming drove me crazy too," Maya replied. "What is that?"

"It's *Emm* Kemel."

Maya smiled. Who knows where the old habit of giving nick-names, as with 'mother of Kemel', to dangerous weaponry came from, but it had become part of Lebanese culture.

"Is this a new nickname for a weapon? I remember *Abu* Abdo the cannon from the old days."

"It's the MK spy plane," her mother replied.

"You'd think they'd make a spy plane a little more discreet."

Her mother sighed. "I'm not talking about the noise. I couldn't sleep because of the wedding."

Maya lifted an eyebrow. "What about it?"

"What if this insanity continues until September?"

"It won't. It will be over in less than a week."

Maya's confidence didn't seem to convince her mother. The twist-ing and turning all night must have made her consider every pos-sible worst-case scenario, and a few impossible ones. "We thought the same in 1975," she said. "Then the war went on for seventeen years. Your father and I never had a wedding."

"You've told me that story so many times, Mama. But we're not in the seventies anymore."

"Nothing has changed," her mother replied, "except that they've all got more powerful weapons now."

She looked so sad, Maya's heart flinched. "Stop worrying," she said, "we *will* have this wedding."

"Yes, God willing, we will." Her mother tried to sound positive but ended her speech choked up. "It's just that I don't want to give away my beautiful daughter just like that. You deserve a big celebration."

Maya hugged her. "Stay positive, OK? It could be a lot worse."

Her mother nodded and left for the kitchen still fighting back the tears. Maya decided to join her cousins next door.

As she walked through the garden, she remembered the old days when they would organize play dates here with other children in the village. As they turned into teenagers, they'd become immersed in their social life in the city and reduced their Rantour stays to a few weekends a year or short holidays. Little by little they had lost contact with their friends from Rantour; Maya promised herself to take the opportunity of this extended stay to rekindle the relationships. Her father and uncles kept strong links with everyone in the community; they'd be more than happy to help her track down her old buddies.

She found the cousinettes slouched on their seats looking bored. She took a seat next to Reem on one of the sofas.

"Could they have made this spy plane any noisier?" Maya said.

"They want us to know that they know that we know they're spying on us." Elyssar replied.

The cousinettes laughed.

"We need to brush up on wartime entertainment," Maya said. "Any suggestions?"

"Backgammon?" Cousinette Lara proposed. She used to beat everyone at it when they were kids and had won a lot of free ice creams that way. No one seemed thrilled.

"I brought *Sex And The City* DVDs," Elyssar said. Relief all around the room.

"Good, men and shoes are exactly what we need to cheer us up," Maya said.

"Talking about shoes, do you think the world knows Elyssar's collection of Manolos is under bombardment in Beirut?" Reem teased.

Elyssar snuck a side look to ensure her mother was out of earshot. A pair of Manolos cost more than some Lebanese families' monthly income. "Of course not. The UN would have enforced a cease fire to airlift the shoes to safety," she replied.

Maya admired Elyssar's independence; at thirty-three, her cousin was focused on her career and enjoyed the lifestyle that her professional success afforded her. Although she'd had a few disappointing relationships, she never seemed bothered about the pressure to get married and settle down. Maya on the other hand, had just finished her training as an associate lawyer and, at twenty-five, couldn't wait for her life to start with Ziad, her high school sweetheart and the only man she'd ever loved.

The power was on so Elyssar zapped to CNN. "Look who's covering our war!" she said. "Anderson Cooper, he's my favourite journalist. He's based in New York, and it's the first time I've seen him cover a story about the Middle East."

"You make it sound like we should be flattered," Maya said.

"He's reporting from Israel. If he'd been in Lebanon we could have tried to meet him."

"Turn yourself in at the border as a prisoner of war. Maybe he'll interview you." Maya said with a laugh.

"Naaah, I'll just wait for the next war. If we're lucky he'll do us the honour then."

Maya's heart squeezed in guilt. "We shouldn't joke about this, just because we're lucky to be in a safe area."

"Say that to the ones waging the war. We're victims like everyone else, we've had to leave our homes in Beirut," Reem replied.

"And our jobs are at risk," Cousinette Dana added. "The economy's all but dead."

Elyssar's giggle broke up the miserable silence that followed. "If we don't make jokes, the other option would be to moan all day," she said. "But that's not fun and it gives you frown lines."

In Kafarneem, Rouba stood by the window watching a group of children play in the apple orchards. The scene reminded her of her own childhood when she enjoyed these forced stays in the mountains because they meant school was out for weeks.

Her phone rang. Majed's third call today from Kuwait. "The violence is escalating, things will get worse."

She could tell from his voice that he was more concerned than he wanted to show. He frequently visited Lebanon – not only because he'd invested in various businesses but also because he liked the Mediterranean weather and lifestyle. Since the start of this war, he had followed the events closely and knew more than she did because she avoided the family TV room.

"Please don't say that." she replied.

"I hear that power cuts are increasing."

"Yes, we've dusted off the generator. We use it for a few hours in the morning and the evening to keep the fridges cold and the shower water hot."

"The fuel supplies will also run short because of the blockade," he replied.

Rouba knew it was wrong to talk divorce at a time he showed such concern for her and her family but she couldn't help herself.

"What did you tell the court about my failure to show up for the hearing?"

"I wasn't there. The lawyer asked for a postponement."

"Have they set a new date?"

"Not yet."

She didn't reply. It had taken so long to come to terms with the idea of divorce that now she couldn't wait to put it all behind her.

"I'll call you later," he said and hung up without waiting for her reply.

Rouba went back to the window. How did they get here?

She was twenty-six years old and fresh out of the breakup of her college romance when she and Majed met on a flight from Kuwait to Lebanon. She'd received a free upgrade to first class on her way back from a business trip and was already seated when he came in wearing a traditional white *deshdasha* and *Ghutra* head cover.

As soon as they left Kuwaiti airspace a flight attendant circulated with a tray of champagne. Rouba hesitated, sneaking a peak towards the man sitting next to her; was it disrespectful to have alcohol in front of him? But the sight of the golden bubbles got the better of her. She couldn't wait to get a drink after the week she'd had, meeting with the firm that invested in her start-up press relations agency. To her surprise, her companion also accepted a glass.

But before he even took a sip from his glass, Majed opened a bag and took out... a large pizza. Rouba had never seen anyone do this onboard a flight.

"I had a craving and grabbed it on the way," he said, slightly embarrassed. "Didn't get the chance to eat it before we boarded."

It was packed in a thermal box. It smelled heavenly and was piping hot. Rouba absolutely loved pizza. "I won't tell on you if you give me a slice or two," she replied.

He shared the food and they chatted over dinner, ignoring fellow passengers' envious stares. Many stood up to check where the smell was coming from and the hostesses gave them nasty looks for upstaging their first class catering.

Somehow Rouba and Majed jumped from commenting on pizza toppings to a deep conversation about the meaning of life and the two and a half hour flight felt like a minute. Philosophy and social sciences fascinated Rouba, and Majed had read a lot about the theory of knowledge, a favourite topic of hers.

They barely noticed the landing announcement and she disembarked a little disappointed because he hadn't asked for contact details.

But like any Kuwaiti who wants his woman, Majed found her number and called two days later. "I'm flying back to Kuwait in a few hours and absolutely have to eat a good pizza before the trip," he said. "But I can't go without my partner in pepperoni crime."

Although she had assumed they'd never meet again, she'd been curious enough to research him and had learned that he was one of the most respected businessmen in Kuwait – a father of four who lost his wife a couple of years before in a car accident.

From thereon they found themselves engulfed in a beautiful whirlwind. It felt as if the stars had aligned to have them meet at that point in their lives. He a recently widowed single father, and she, unsure what life would be like without the only relationship she'd ever known.

Although Majed came from a very conservative culture he somehow *got* her. At the same time, Rouba discovered in him a broken man. Shattered by the untimely loss of his wife, he doubted his ability to be a good parent to his children, who ranged in age between six and seventeen. He opened up and told Rouba of his worries and insecurities – and like two naive kids they decided to take one another's hand, believing fully in the future and in the power of love, convinced that they were destined always to be together.

Maybe it was this excessive confidence that made them unable to pull through when real life set in. The daily troubles of raising children and the pressures of trying to conceive a baby had caught up with them. Bit by bit, they'd lost the ability to enjoy each other; getting to a point where they only spoke to have an argument. One day Rouba had broken down in tears after an especially bitter exchange and asked for a divorce; Majed had only been too happy to agree.

While Rouba was hauled up in her room, trying to avoid her family, Elyssar and the cousinettes were playing cards by the light of a battery powered lamp in Rantour. The radio had just announced that new air raids had taken place in several spots in South Lebanon but no jets came to disturb the stillness of the cool summer night in Rantour. The window opened wide onto the garden and Elyssar could smell the jasmine tree, which always released its fragrance at this time of day. As a kid she used to believe this scent had magical powers.

Their stock of Smirnoff Ice was holding up well, but the blackout meant they'd had to replace the microwavable popcorn with mixed nuts.

"Let's record these moments for all posterity," she said, clasping her camera phone. "Come on, ladies, share your deepest thoughts and emotions with the world."

Cousinette Dana, a manager for a cosmetics brand stood up. "I have something to declare," she said in an inebriated voice. "Several of my containers are blocked somewhere in the waters near Cyprus. Is that fair? How is that *fair*? Couldn't they have told us that they wanted to start a war before we placed our orders? Now who will buy my make-up? The fish?" She pleaded so passionately that the other girls couldn't stop laughing, oblivious to the fact that people could probably hear them at the other end of the village.

Then Maya took a turn. "I propose a truce," she said. "There's a very important segment of society who needs it: these are all the people whose weddings are planned this summer. We're starting families to ensure the future of this country and this is what we get. We've made down payments, commissioned the dress, invited hundreds of guests. What are we supposed to do now? I'm sure the politicians who started this war didn't have any weddings planned in their families this summer!"

The girls raised their glasses to her appeal, giggling uncontrollably. But as she captured the scene Elyssar sobered up. "Guys, this is terrible," she said, turning the camera to herself. "We are laughing when our own people are dying and being displaced. We should be ashamed of ourselves."

Drunk or not, she was right and this was enough to quiet everyone. The laughter abruptly ended and the cousinettes fell into an atypical silence. Now, all Elyssar could hear was the timeless chirping of the crickets.

The next day Rouba received a call from Elyssar bearing good news. "I just found out about organizations that specialize in wartime evacuations," she said. "They take people by bus to the Syrian border and from there straight to Damascus Airport. Try this number; it's a friend of a friend, he's leaving tomorrow with his family so maybe he can help you get a seat."

Rouba lost no time in calling the man in question. He gave her a few more names and numbers but none of them were reachable.

Her father didn't try to hide his irritation when she told him her plan. "You shouldn't even think about this," he said. "Haven't you seen the news? Scores of civilians are being killed on the roads trying to flee the country."

"Western countries have started calling for the fighting to stop, it won't be long now," her mother added. "Just wait it out."

"Why are you so keen on leaving immediately?" Teta interjected. "What's the rush?"

Rouba scowled. She clearly couldn't win with her family. She went back to her room and decided to call Majed for moral support. After all, this was his divorce too.

"Are you sure you want to leave right now?" he asked. "It's unsafe."

"We can't wait forever. Who knows how long this will take?"

"I don't mind waiting."

Rouba flipped. "You don't *mind*!" she retorted. "What, you don't think this divorce is important enough for you to *mind* what happens?"

"You know this is not what I meant."

"Nothing about this relationship ever mattered to you. You don't care whether we're divorced or married…. Whether we have a baby or not!" Her eyes welled up. Damn him, just when she thought she didn't care anymore he found a way to hurt her again.

"I just don't want you to put yourself in danger," he said.

"Thousands of people make it across the border alive everyday.

I'll be just fine."

The line went silent for a few seconds.

"Fine," he conceded. "Just let me know when you can be here."

Chapter 3

Elyssar was starting to have sleepless nights. They were on the fifth day of the conflict with no sign of respite. The media now openly called it a war. Luckily, she kept the business ticking over by phone and email, but with no end in sight and with the country nearly sealed off from the rest of the world, it looked like she wouldn't be able to leave on time for her long planned vacation, and most importantly, the Madonna concert.

Since Reem was also planning on attending the show, Elyssar decided to go to her for ideas. She left her laptop open on the desk in her bedroom, and went looking for her sister. She found her reading a novel on the balcony.

"Let's not make any decisions now," Reem proposed when Elyssar shared her worries about the concert. "The show is in six weeks. We still have time."

"Not really. Even if the war finished we're not sure the Beirut airport will be back in service because of the damage. And if they did reopen it, we may not get plane seats."

"Then we could try to go by sea and get a flight from Cyprus."

"We'd still have to book new flights. And how can we be sure that the borders would not be completely closed by then? Both Syria and Cyprus are struggling to cope with the number of refugees landing on their territory."

"Then we'll just miss the concert."

Reem's pragmatism felt like heresy to Elyssar.

"Sorry, but I'm not going to miss it," she said.

"Sweetie, there's a war going on." Reem gestured to attract her sister's attention to the bombing noises coming over the mountains from Beirut. "It's called a *force majeure* and tends to disrupt people's plans."

"There's always one conflict or another in this country," Elyssar replied. "To hell with it, I'm not letting anything ruin this for me."

Reem shook her head. "You're such a drama queen," she said.

Their mother appeared in the balcony doorway. "Elyssar, we're blessed to be alive with food on our plate and a roof over our heads," she said. "Don't be ungrateful."

Elyssar had killed herself to get these tickets on the black market. "I will start looking for ways to leave," she said, "This way I can make sure I'll be in Paris on time."

Reem turned to her mother.

"Your daughter behaves like such a teenager sometimes," she said.

"Yes, especially where this Madonna is concerned," her mother concurred. "She just loses her ability to be reasonable."

Elyssar left the living room, fuming. She didn't want to accept the realities of Lebanon anymore, didn't want to hear herself and other people say "we'll get on with our lives when this or that conflict is over", didn't want to wait on dirty politicians' whims to seize the rare opportunity of a good quarter in business or to just plan a simple holiday. She looked out at the garden. In her teens she used to set up concerts on the patio where the parents paid a small fee to watch her and her cousins perform. Elyssar had acted as the producer, choreographer and lead singer of the show, copying Madonna's routines to the letter. The gigs invariably sold out and they used the money to buy ice cream and chocolate.

Right now, only one person would understand the way she felt. She called Rouba.

"I feel like a monster. We're at war and all I can think of is some pop concert." she said after relaying the conversation with her mother and sister.

"You have nothing to feel guilty about. It's our right to go on with our lives," Rouba replied. "Besides, this is not *some* pop concert, this is *the* pop concert you've been dreaming of your entire life. You used to watch recordings of Madonna's performances for hours on end."

Elyssar smiled. "I had dozens of pirated VHS tapes..."

"The one you watched the most was her tour in Italy. I'll never forget the look on your face when the cameras showed the crowd. You envied them *so much* for being there."

"That was seventeen years ago."

"Yes, but in your head you're still the Third World kid who never gets to attend the show."

"I hate it when you go all Psychology on me."

Rouba chuckled. "I hate it when I go all Psychology on me too, but I'm always right."

"OK," Elyssar said. "Let's both keep trying to find a way out of here and we'll leave together."

"Did you bring the concert tickets with you or will you have to rescue them from Beirut?"

"They were the first things I packed. They're now securely sitting in the safe."

"Why? Are the criminals of Rantour plotting to steal your Madonna tickets?"

"I'm not worried about anyone stealing them but I figured if the house was bombed, they would probably survive best in the safe."

Rouba's break came on the sixth day of the conflict, when one of the evacuation agencies finally picked up her call. A helpful man by the name of Ghassan explained that his organization, Assistance Worldwide, had global deals with government and corporate clients, whereby they evacuated nationals or company employees in cases of disasters or conflicts.

"So you don't evacuate individuals?" Rouba asked, very disappointed.

"No, ma'am, I'm sorry. We only work for our institutional clients. We were supposed to complete the evacuations yesterday, but we've had to extend for several days."

"So what if I told you that I am employed by one of your clients?"

Rouba knew this was a lame shot but she was trying to keep him on the phone to give herself the time to think of a way to grab a seat on that bus.

"Which one of my clients?"

"Tell me who your clients are and I will tell you which one I work for."

He didn't think her attempt was funny.

"Ma'am, I am sorry. Believe me, I would love to find a place for all those who call me." He sounded slightly irritated. "You can try with private taxis."

"Do you know any of these taxi drivers?"

"Unfortunately not, but you can ask around, someone will have a number."

"Ok, I will try," she agreed. "But can I reach you at this number again, in case I can get myself hired by one of your clients?"

"Sure, you can also call if you get a citizenship or residency in the Gulf."

Rouba's heart skipped a beat.

"Gulf residency?"

"As I mentioned, we have governments as clients, including all Gulf countries."

"So you mean you can evacuate the residents of these countries, not only their diplomats and citizens?"

"Yes."

"Well, Ghassan," Rouba gloated. "You just got yourself a customer. I'm a resident of Kuwait. When does my bus leave?"

Elyssar seethed as she sat with her family a few hours later to watch the news. Since she wasn't a citizen or resident of any foreign country, taxis represented her only way out. She'd called a few dozen to hear one answer from them all: "booked out". She had more numbers on her list and promised herself to harass them until someone agreed to take her.

On TV, the broadcast reported more misery than ever: death, displacement and destruction accompanied by the usual senseless political diatribe. The coverage moved on to describe the repatriation operations for Western nationals. Amongst others, the French, British and Americans had sent ships to pick up their citizens and take them to safety. People registered with their embassies and thousands of families, mainly Lebanese with foreign passports, overran the Port of Beirut waiting to flee to their adopted land.

The journalists interviewed a number of women and children, all Lebanese-Americans, who said that they had come to Lebanon for the summer break and found themselves stranded. Some cried as they told the camera about their fear and how they couldn't wait to get back to the US, but were worried about the loved ones they were leaving behind.

"They should count their blessings that they are citizens of a country that thinks they're worth the time and effort this repatriation is costing," Elyssar thought as she watched the report.

The camera then moved to a man in his late thirties who stood in a sea of suitcases carrying a sleeping toddler.

"How do you feel about your departure?" the reporter asked.

"I'm very grateful for this chance to get my family to safety," the man replied. "My employer has organized for us to leave on this boat."

"Are you a US citizen?"

"No. I only have Lebanese nationality, but I work for an American company who have organized this."

"So what would you like to tell your employers?" the reporter asked.

The man beamed into the camera. "I've never been prouder to work for this company. They've proved how much they value us and showed they do take our wellbeing to heart."

Elyssar listened very closely. Were American companies really able to get their employees evacuated alongside US citizens? If so, things were finally looking up for her. She took the time to think about this for a few minutes. The Beirut office had opened just two months ago with her as the only employee, so the corporate security team hadn't had the chance to fully work out their plans yet. She simply had to let them know this option existed and ask for it nicely. She decided to put her request in writing, instead of over the phone, to make sure she made the best pitch possible.

Back in her room, she stared at her laptop screen for a while. She suspected her manager couldn't take this kind of decision and would probably transfer it to more senior executives in the US. How do you sell an evacuation to your bosses? "I need to get the hell out of here to see my teenage idol live" would probably not cut it. She needed to rationalize her request and give it a 'business' perspective.

Basically, this was no different from any budget or headcount request she'd made before –all she had to do was create the killer slide deck that would take her to Madonna. She opened the presentation with the typical slides showing market size, projected growth, market share and most importantly her sales targets. Then she explained that she could still make the business figures if she were able to leave the country and operate from a temporary base where she would focus on the business in Jordan until the Lebanon market recovered. "This concert better be worth it," she thought.

In the house next door, Maya picked up her ringing mobile phone with a frown of surprise – the caller ID showed a series of zeroes in place of a name or number. She figured it was an international call, probably from her fiancé in Dubai. As soon as she answered, the chilling voice of a mechanical recording froze her for a few seconds.

"Israel means you no harm," it said in formal Arabic. "Your own people are causing this calamity on your country. Your government has to put an end to all acts of violence originating from Lebanon."

Maya clenched the phone, wondering whether to hang up. Could this be a joke? And who would want to play tricks at a time like this?

"Israel means you no harm," the voice repeated, sounding louder.

In a terrified reflex, Maya threw the phone away, crashing it onto the floor. This was a propaganda call from Israel! She'd heard about such psychological warfare tactics. But why would they choose her and how did they get her number? She sighed, maybe numbers were selected at random, or maybe all subscribers to Lebanese mobile lines were targeted. But weren't phone calls banned between Lebanon and Israel? Travel and communication between the two warring neighbours had been banned for as long as she could remember. As far as she knew, it was impossible to dial Israel's country code from Lebanon, but maybe it wasn't the case in the opposite direction.

She just hoped she wouldn't get in trouble with the Lebanese government for receiving a call from Israel.

"A good PowerPoint presentation never fails you," Elyssar thought an hour later as she picked up the call from her boss.

"I just received your email about business continuity," he said. "I really want to praise you for finding ways to deliver the business despite what's going on."

"Thanks for responding so quickly," she replied. "I wanted to make sure that we keep things running and make our numbers this quarter."

"Liar," a voice in her head admonished.

"Oh, please don't worry about that!" he replied. "The most important thing right now is your safety. I will take your request to the highest levels and we will do whatever we can to get you out of there. I will get back to you within a few hours."

After she hung up, Elyssar fought the urge to call everyone and announce the good news. She didn't want to jinx it, after all. Hadn't she been too sure of the future when she bought the concert tickets three months ago and sent jubilant texts to all her friends announcing the news? She decided to keep this development to herself until she had full confirmation. Madonna wasn't a done deal yet.

Her boss must have done a great job at "taking it to the highest levels": an hour later a man by the name of Chuck Gilroy called from the New York office, identifying himself as the head of security for the company. He spoke in the way only an ex-military officer would.

"We've contacted the US State Department to have you included in the evacuation from Lebanon," he said.

Elyssar knew that as a Fortune Five Hundred company and one of the largest employers in the technology sector, Integrated Systems had some pulling power with the US government, but she was still impressed to hear Chuck mention it so casually.

"This is wonderful," she said genuinely moved. "Please thank everyone for their concern; I am really touched."

"No need to thank us," Chuck replied. "We're sorry about what's happening in your country and the company is grateful to you for still trying to get work done despite the terrible events."

How could they be so kind when her motive was purely selfish? She fought the mounting guilt by telling herself that the arguments she made in her presentation held up: she stood a better chance of making the numbers if she worked from outside Lebanon.

"They've confirmed that you can be evacuated in forty-eight hours," Chuck continued. "They're looking into chartering a cruise ship that will be escorted by two US destroyers. You'll be taken by sea to Turkey and then we'll organize for you to fly to New York and work from the HQ here until the situation is resolved. Of course, all your expenses will be taken care of until the conflict is resolved."

It took Elyssar a second to internalize the information. Forty-eight hours! That was so soon, she wasn't prepared. It dawned on her that as focused as she had been on finding a way to leave she hadn't actually thought about the departure itself. How long would it take? Was it dangerous? Would she get seasick? And where would she live in New York? Was it safe to leave her family behind? When would she be able to come home?

This whole Madonna thing didn't feel like such a good idea anymore... "Chuck," she heard herself say. "Is it OK if I take some time to think about this?"

Had she been in Chuck's shoes she would have flipped if – after making such a dramatic request – an employee suddenly had a change of heart. But if he did get irritated Chuck didn't let it show.

"Certainly," he said in his baritone. "But I need you to let me know in four or five hours. I'm not sure how much longer these operations will last. We need to guarantee you a place on the vessel."

As soon as she hung up she went to see the cousinettes next door. The girls were lounging, each clutching a small cup of Turkish coffee. Reem was kneeling next to a side table trying to hook up her iPod to a battery operated set of speakers.

"Oh my God! New York!" Maya said enthusiastically when Elyssar told them about Chuck's call. "You're so lucky."

"Mmmm, I'm not so sure."

"Are you serious? You're getting the chance to live in New York."

"I know it's stupid," Elyssar said. "But I'm having second thoughts. This doesn't sound like such a good idea anymore."

"Don't be silly," Maya retorted. "You know very well that anyone who can be evacuated will do it. All those with foreign passports have already organized to go."

Elyssar still looked unsure. "I don't know anyone in the US. What would I do there?"

"Every time you go to America you come back raving about it and saying how you wish you could live there. Guess what? Your chance has come knocking."

"I was never really serious about that. And if I leave now, who knows when I will come back?"

Reem appeared to give up on her attempts to connect the speakers. She stood up and looked at Elyssar. "I can't believe you," she said. "You made such a fuss about attending the Madonna concert. How could you change your mind now?"

"Maybe the war will end before the Paris concert date."

"Then you know something that even Condoleezza Rice doesn't. I just saw an interview with her where she said this conflict should take as long as is necessary."

"I don't know about you, but *necessary* sounds long to me," Maya added.

Elyssar looked at her sister pour herself a cup of coffee. "Reem, if I leave with the Americans, how would you go to the concert?" she asked.

"I will meet you there if the war ends on time," Reem answered. "Otherwise give my ticket to one of your friends in Europe... Or you could sell it."

Elyssar remained hesitant.

"I know your main reason to make the request was the concert," Cousinette Lara intervened. "But let's face it you're not able to get much work done sitting here and the business has to run if you want to keep your job in the long run. Your company will have to close the office if your sales crash."

Elyssar sighed. They had a point. As she figured it, her choices were as follows: she could either spend her summer doing nothing except listen to depressing news and be terrified at the bombings; or she could get to safety, keep her job and enjoy her vacation. But the latter option meant leaving her family behind in dangerous conditions…

Having said that, it was unlikely the attacks would ever target Rantour and if she worked from the New York office she would definitely be more productive. Also, what if Madonna never toured again?

"OK, you've convinced me." She took a deep breath. "I will go to the US and then I'll make my way from there to Europe for the concert. Then, no matter what, I'll come straight back to Beirut."

Chapter 4

On D Day, Elyssar and her father kept silent on the empty road as the car made its way towards the port of Beirut (or *el Port*). Seemingly, the jets didn't come out at four in the morning and the skies were empty for a change. Despite recent strikes in the area, the air felt clean and fresh. Under any other circumstances, this day would have appeared full of promise.

Elyssar didn't know what to think. In a somewhat surreal scene the entire family had gathered by the car at dawn and they each had kissed her goodbye. No one cried and they all told her to take good care of herself and call often to let them know how her journey progressed.

As they moved further away from home, she yet again questioned her decision. What if things went terribly wrong? The raids had started targeting some telecommunication towers and there was a big one at the top of the mountain in Rantour. What if it got raided too? It would completely destroy their building. She would lose her entire family...

Elyssar sneaked a look at her father who pretended he hadn't noticed, as he tried to look focused on his driving. She wondered what went on in his mind. Did he ask how on earth he could have raised a daughter who abandoned her family in the middle of a war?

"Dad, are you sure I should be doing this?" she finally asked.

"Doing what?"

Denial was her father's usual tactic to avoid potentially emotional conversations. Normally, she found this behaviour endearing; today it saddened her.

"Do you think I should leave? What if they invaded the country, what if the phone lines break down and we can't communicate?"

"This is exactly why you should go. Your company will put you up in America and look after you."

It surprised her to see him so keen on her departure. It must feel terrible to drop your child at the port and let her go to foreign lands not knowing if and when she would come back – or if you would live to see her return. But in a way, she understood: he probably deemed himself luckier than most fathers because he could get one of his daughters to safety.

"Make sure you call your uncle Ali," he told her. "He's been there for a long time and will help you out."

Elyssar had heard about Uncle Ali but never met him because he'd emigrated to the United States before she was born. The idea of calling out of the blue and potentially spending time with him felt too awkward, but she didn't want to argue now with her father. "Yes, I'll call him," she said, not meaning a word of it.

They arrived fifty minutes later to a scene of chaos: hundreds of cars were dropping their passengers, the teary farewells and people hugging in the middle of the street making it impossible to circulate.

Grim-faced and silent, Elyssar's father found a spot for a quick halt and got out of the car to help her with her suitcase. Nearby, a Lebanese security officer watched them impatiently. He had the impossible task of keeping the cars moving.

As her father handed her the suitcase, Elyssar gave up the struggle against tears and threw herself in his arms. "I'll be back in a few weeks," she sobbed.

"Enjoy your vacation," he replied, his voice flat and mundane. His way of not crying.

He released himself from her grasp, gave her a quick peck on the cheek without really looking at her then got in the car and took off.

Elyssar looked around, overwhelmed by the thousands of people milling round, the prospect of the journey at sea and the thought of being a refugee all alone and continents away.

"To hell with it," she decided on impulse. "I'm staying."

Her father's car was still stuck in traffic some fifty meters away. Dragging her suitcase on the uneven asphalt Elyssar tried to run, struggling to make her way against the flow of people moving in the opposite direction. The car started to pull away. She sped as fast as she could, precariously balanced on her new platform shoes, but soon lost sight of it.

Breathless, she stopped and rummaged to find the phone in her purse. The damn thing was enormous and full of travel documents, cosmetics and other things that wouldn't fit into her suitcase.

"Ma'am, can I please ask you to move?"

She turned around to see a young man wearing a cap that read 'usher'.

"The boats are this way." He pointed in the opposite direction. "You need to go there and speak to the embassy staff. They will provide you with more details."

"I'm trying to call my father," she replied, still foraging in her bag. "I decided not to go."

"Those who can go, don't want to," he said, shaking his head in sadness, "while others only dream of the chance to leave this madness."

The misery in his voice brought her up short.

"This place has no future," he said. "You're very lucky to have a chance to get out. No one cares about the rest of us."

He looked about twenty years old. To hear a young person with so little hope startled her. But in a way he had a point: foreign governments pulled out all the stops for their nationals, while the world watched as millions of Lebanese remained under daily bombardment.

She wanted to find words of encouragement for him, but couldn't think of any.

"Did you study in America?" he asked. "Is this how you got citizenship?"

"I am not an American citizen," she replied. "I work for an American company. They made the arrangements."

"See?" he exclaimed. "If you merely work for an American company your life has more value than that of an ordinary Lebanese."

"I... had work to do," she lied. "They're sending me to finish it and then I'll come back."

"You must be very important if they're going through all this hassle for you," he said. "I bet that when you get to America, you won't want to come back".

His words still resonated in Elyssar's mind a few hours later. Although she sent reassuring messages and made an effort to sound in control every time one of her friends or family called, the anarchy all around made her nervous. People were still arriving in droves, pushing strollers, carrying luggage and circulating in all directions. The bigger the crowd grew, the more Elyssar felt like a drop in a human tide. She prayed evacuation organisers would be able to put order into this chaos.

People's frustration was increasing and complaints grew about the lack of organization. The would-be evacuees didn't know where to report their presence, what time they should embark or exactly how they would get to Turkey. After a while, a US Embassy official spoke through a megaphone, pleading for patience and reassuring the crowd that the team would assist all those registered.

After a few attempts to move through the crowd in order to find embassy staff to speak to, Elyssar gave up on the idea. All she was doing was adding to the commotion. She figured she'd help the situation best if she waited on the side. She found a small place in the shade and settled down on the ground to wait until the staff announced the next steps.

Rouba called her at around nine o'clock. "Tell me all about your adventure," she said. "Are you surrounded by Super Stallion helicopters and amphibious transport ships?"

"Sorry to disappoint you," Elyssar replied. "But I'm still at the

Port." She tried to look above the crowd to spot fancy military gear, but couldn't see anything beyond the people around her. "What's an amphibious transport ship anyway?"

"There's been a lot of coverage about them on TV. They're little boats that can travel by sea and land. Apparently the US navy has deployed them to take the evacuees from the beach to the ship." Rouba said.

"You know more about this than I do. It's been hard to find anyone to talk to here. I have no idea about what to do next."

Nearby, a toddler erupted in screams, soon followed by his older sister. Elyssar covered her ears, cradling the phone between her cheek and shoulder.

"And there I was imagining you wearing a navy striped shirt and singing sea shanties with hot marines!" Rouba said.

"Not a single one of those in sight. I'm surrounded by Lebanese-American families with cranky babies."

"I just saw on the news that several hundred marines have been deployed on the beach to help with the evacuation. This is the first time they've come back to Lebanon in twenty years. You go out there and find them. You never know, this could turn into an epic love story."

Elyssar smiled at Rouba's efforts to cheer her up.

"Yes, it has all the ingredients of a Hollywood blockbuster," she replied. "They'll call it *The Arab Woman and the Hot Marine*."

Rouba chuckled.

"How are things with you and your family?" Elyssar asked.

Sighing, Rouba told her that she was still hauled up in her room most of the time, trying to avoid difficult family conversation and waiting to get a confirmation on her departure.

After she hung up the phone, Elyssar decided to change her shoes. Back in Rantour, the decision to wear her new Louboutins had felt like a good idea but by now they'd turned into instruments of torture. To work within the one suitcase rule, she had only packed smart-casual clothes and worn the platforms to save luggage space, but she wouldn't survive the boarding in these. She needed something more 'refugee wear'. She found a pair of Sketchers and somehow forced the platforms into the suitcase and closed it.

An hour or so later, it looked like things were getting more organized and the staff started making boarding announcements through the megaphones. Families with young children or elderly would go first and the rest would follow in the afternoon. Long queues formed, facing the sea. Thankfully, at around the same time, a group of young people began to circulate, distributing cold water. Figuring she had at least a few hours more to wait, Elyssar stocked several bottles.

Only a few spots remained in the shade as the sun moved across the sky. Her little corner was one of them. After more than half an hour of trying to ignore the elderly lady opposite her sat in direct sunlight, Elyssar felt compelled to offer up her place. The old woman thanked her as she sank down into Elyssar's place with a sigh of relief.

The woman's daughter-in-law, a very tall, very blond and very American woman married to a Lebanese man, complained to Elyssar about the US government for their late organization of the evacuation when the Europeans had shown so much more concern for their citizens. "They even considered making us pay for this," she said. "Our government has spent billions and billions on the war in Iraq but can't spare funds to save American lives elsewhere. Luckily, the State Department backtracked. People were furious."

Elyssar, still considering herself a bit of an usurper on this trip, didn't find it appropriate to provide any opinions, so she kept quiet. But she couldn't help think that this woman should speak to Tante Bernadette. They could have a field day griping about their respective governments. It was remarkable to see Western citizens' sense of entitlement towards their government. In a country like Lebanon, all you really wanted was for your government to stay out of the way, because every time they did anything it seemed to hurt the country instead of benefiting it.

By the late afternoon, only a few dozen people, Elyssar amongst them, remained onshore waiting for their turn. Finally, one of the staff approached to inform them that all the families had boarded and they were now free to step onto the boat. Despite the long wait, Elyssar felt a tingle of panic when she realized the time had actually come to leave. She stood up and joined the queue, her heart pounding in her chest.

She couldn't see the boat yet because her view was blocked by the people in front, but the one thing she was very much aware of lay behind her: Beirut; the Charles Helou Boulevard which ran along the coastline and, a little further up, downtown Beirut with its recently rebuilt old souks. Then the hills that led to the neighbourhoods where she grew up, with their mix of charming turn-of-the -century mansions and dreary 1960s building blocks. Overlooking it all stood Mount Lebanon where she knew her family was now gathered, no doubt chatting around their kettle of afternoon coffee.

Elyssar wanted to turn around for a final look but her ears buzzed and her heart raced so fast, it felt like she didn't have the strength to move. Her whole body was stiff, as if frozen, and all she found herself able to do was keep her head down and stare at her own feet. Everyone else probably had the same thoughts. All were quiet, except for one woman who was only half attempting to hush her sobs.

As the queue started to move, she followed it automatically. Her head was still down when she stepped from the asphalt onto a sand beach. She could hear the sound of the waves and people splashing into the water.

"Can I help you, Ma'am?"

Elyssar looked up at the American marine who had appeared next to her.

"Can I help you, Ma'am?" he repeated as she stared at him blankly. "We need you to cross to the transport ship right there."

He pointed at a small boat anchored at a short distance, several meters from the shore. Ahead of her, people were paddling towards it, carrying their luggage above their heads to keep them dry.

Elyssar snapped out of her trance and peered around.

"I can't see the umm... the..." Her English failed her. "The wood structure that you walk on to get to a boat." She said.

"I'm afraid there isn't one, Ma'am," he replied. "You need to walk through the water to the boat. Don't worry, it's not deep and I can help with your luggage."

Elyssar gratefully handed him the suitcase, took her Sketchers off and rolled up her jeans. Then, holding purse and shoes high up, she stepped into the sea, the marine at her side. Very soon, she was chest deep in the water and her wet clothes slowed her down. Holding her suitcase above his head with one arm, the marine put his hand on her shoulder to help her move forwards. As they got close to the boat, a wave almost knocked her over. The marine grabbed her arm to stop her from falling.

"Thank you!" she gasped through the hair stuck on her face, still struggling to regain her balance as she held her arms up to keep her belongings dry. She could have sworn she saw a glimpse of a smile on the marine's stern features, but he recomposed his expression before she could be sure. With his crew cut, his bulging triceps and his very blue eyes, he was the quintessential US soldier. Rouba would love this, she thought.

When they reached the transport ship he took her purse and shoes so she could climb the ladder at the side of the boat. As she hauled herself up the steel rungs, through her sadness, she grasped the strangely exciting aspect of her situation: she'd just boarded an American military carrier!

The marine came up after her, carrying all her luggage in one hand while holding on to the ladder with the other.

"You must have evacuated thousands of people by now," she said, as he appeared beside her on the deck, trying to show her gratitude by making courteous conversation.

"Yes, Ma'am."

"Who would have guessed there are so many American citizens in Lebanon?" she continued.

"Yes, Ma'am."

Ok, so he wasn't the talkative type. She guessed his instructions were to get as many people boarded as he could, not make small talk with them.

The boat was about fifteen meters long, completely made of grey steel. Around twenty-five people sat on the deck awaiting the departure while two marines looked on. Her trousers dripping water, Elyssar found an empty spot on a steel bench and took a seat, her back to the railing. She tried to find a dry spot on the floor for her luggage, but puddles had formed everywhere. She put the suitcase on her lap, hoping the damp from her clothes wouldn't seep all the way through.

To Elyssar's surprise, the mood seemed quite light as people chatted about the upcoming trip and their eventual destination in the States. Still, they kept their voices down, obviously impressed by the number of uniforms surrounding them.

Once the boat moved, the mood became grim again. Everyone stared at the Lebanese coast as they moved away from it. The sad part, Elyssar thought, was that this moment was picture perfect. The waters of the Mediterranean sparkled in the last sunrays of the day, forming a shimmering base to the green silhouette of Mount Lebanon – which at this distance seemed to rise straight out of the sea. Elyssar had never seen her country from this angle before. It was beautiful.

The lady sitting next to her broke down in tears. Elyssar dug in her suitcase for dry tissues and handed her a few.

"May God never forgive them," the woman sobbed as she wiped her eyes. "All these politicians. I hope they all go to hell for what they make us go through. Because of them, we have to leave our homes, separate from our families..."

She continued to weep as Elyssar looked at the gloomy faces around her. Several people, including grown men, had tears running down their cheeks. How many people throughout history had lived through this same experience? How many sat on a boat and watched their country fade away in the distance? So many never made it back. Did they suspect as they left that this would be the last time they set eyes on their homeland? Was she cheating herself by thinking she would be back? What if...?

"Are you OK?"

She looked up and saw the man to her left peering at her with concern.

"You're shivering," he said. "Are you cold? Do you need a jacket?"

He was right. Her body was trembling.

"I'm fine, thanks," she smiled. "I think I just need to stand up." Trying to keep her balance on the moving ship, she stood and took a few steps to the railing on the opposite side. There, the sound of the boat cutting through the water stifled the woman's weeping, and Lebanon disappeared with the last rays of sunshine.

Chapter 5

A day after she'd left home, Elyssar's mood swings hadn't eased in any way. She went from being depressed one minute to excited the next, and in between found herself questioning yet again her decision to leave and what it said about her as a person.

Last night, the transport boat had carried her and her fellow passengers to a navy destroyer where they joined the hundreds of other evacuees. The sheer size of this ship overwhelmed her. When she'd first caught a glimpse of it she'd mistaken its lights for those of a coastal town and only realized her error when they got nearer and she saw the ship's distinctive flags, towers and revolving radars.

She'd been lucky to find a bed on the deck, but hadn't been able to sleep all night, and now, almost at midday, she desperately needed the rest but her eyes wouldn't shut. All around her people napped, either on the collapsible beds provided by the crew or on the floor using their luggage as pillows. She considered going for a little walk to offset the stress but decided against it. She needed to stay close to her bed so that no one else took it.

Uncapping her sun block, she refreshed the layer on her face. In the past two years her face had developed a tendency for pigmentation which she kept nearly invisible by undergoing a series of expensive treatments: glycolic peels, micro-dermabrasion and fotofacials. Her dermatologist pronounced her lucky at her age to have a wrinkle-free skin, but said she'd spent her "sunshine quota" by overexposing herself to harmful rays during her teens and twenties. Evacuation or not, she had to make sure she kept up her skin care regimen.

A crew member with brown hair and an especially jovial smile appeared by her bed, dropping a small parcel at her side and moving on to the next passenger without saying anything. She grabbed the plastic bag and examined its contents: a bottle of water and three peculiar looking sachets: one of them was marked "peanut butter", the other "picante sauce" while the third and largest read "Ready-to-eat-meal". None of them looked particularly appetising.

Elyssar wasn't hungry but knew that she ought to eat: she hadn't put anything solid in her system since her mother forced her to have eggs and *fool moudammas* before she left home. As she examined the sachets trying to convince herself to open them, a tall man in uniform approached her. The two stars on his shoulders indicated a higher level of seniority than the soldiers she'd seen on deck.

Like many of the others, his blue eyes sparkled so much they seemed to be lit from within. Did the US only enlist men with gorgeous eyes? If so, this army could definitely win *her* heart and mind!

"Hello, Ma'am."

She smiled back. "Hello."

"Are you Elyssar Awwad?" he asked.

"Yes."

"I require some information from you."

Elyssar's heart missed a beat. Why did the US military need information from her? Was he going to detain her for questioning?

She struggled to maintain her composure. "Sure."

"Are you travelling alone?"

So what if she travelled alone? Would that make her a terrorist?

"Yes, the company I work for organized it." She congratulated herself at sounding confident despite the anxiety gripping her insides.

He must have sensed her tension because he flashed a reassuring smile. "We have an unaccompanied minor aboard. Would you be so kind as to look after her until her parents collect her in New York?"

Phew! "Of course, I would love that."

"Thank you, Ma'am. I'll bring her over."

He walked back towards the inside of the ship and she almost laughed at herself. How stupid of her to panic. Just because an American in a uniform spoke to her she'd started having visions of herself in Guantanamo... Orange was *not* her colour.

The officer came back a few minutes later and introduced eleven year-old Jumana Koory.

Jumana wore a navy lined T-shirt with an imprinted kiss laid over the stripes. Multicoloured rubber bracelets covered both her wrists and she'd had the sense to wear shorts and flip-flops. Elyssar wished she'd done the same. Her linen trousers were sticking to her more by the minute and she'd taken off her Sketchers as last resort to stop her feet from catching fire.

Jumana told her she'd arrived in Lebanon the day before the war broke out to spend the summer with her grandparents but now was desperate to get back to her family in New York where her father worked as a dentist.

"It's much nicer out here than inside," she added, pointing to Elyssar's foldable bed. "You have a sea view."

She ventured a timid smile, standing with the demeanour that tweens get during the awkward phase when their limbs grow faster than the rest of their body. Her long brown hair sat in a messy bun on her neck, dripping with sweat, and the slight redness in her eyes told of her sleepiness. Elyssar thought she was sweet to put on such a brave face.

Seemingly pleased that the introduction went well, the officer excused himself, asking them to make themselves comfortable and let him know if they needed anything.

Elyssar gestured for Jumana to take the bed. "Let's take turns," she proposed. "You can nap for a few hours and I'll go next."

Jumana didn't hide her delight at the suggestion. "Is your family in the States too?" she asked as she lay down.

"No, they're in Lebanon," Elyssar replied.

"So why did you leave?"

"I have something important to do." Elyssar hoped the guilt didn't show in her voice. "But I'll be back soon."

Thankfully, Jumana didn't ask for more information, turning her attention to the enormous rifle attached to the railing nearby.

"Is that dangerous?" she asked.

"The crew assured me it's not loaded."

Jumana relaxed. "You can borrow my ipod or my PSP. I just recharged them." She handed the music player to Elyssar and closed her eyes, falling asleep almost immediately.

Jumana looked like she would be out for hours and she was in full sunlight. Careful not to wake her up, Elyssar took a seat at the corner of the bed so that her shadow protected Jumana's face from the rays. With nothing better to do, she checked the ipod, half expecting it to be full of lullabies. Surprisingly, some of her favourite songs were on there.

The eleven year old and I listen to the same music, she thought. Kids grow up fast these days and adults don't grow up at all.

Elyssar had decided a long time ago that she wouldn't stress about her age or the fact that she'd been without a relationship for over two years. The way she figured it, people in their thirties were young and healthy, but society forced them to think of themselves as having passed their prime. Instead of enjoying themselves, they spent what could have been the best decade of their life being depressed about the passage of time.

This thought normally cheered Elyssar up but right now she couldn't fight the gloom that descended on her. She wished Jumana had loaded some Disney feel-good songs.

Another woman in need of the feel good factor was Rouba. She was getting ready to head to the Assistance Worldwide gathering point when Teta appeared in the living room.

"Morning, Teta. Why are you up so early?" Rouba asked.

"You know I'm always up at this time. I thought I'd make you coffee."

Rouba remembered how as a child she pestered her grandmother to wake her up at the crack of dawn. She felt special spending time with Teta when everyone else was asleep.

"Someone called for you when you were in the shower," Teta said.

Rouba sucked in her breath. The worse thing during times like these was an early morning call. It could only be bad news.

"Is everyone OK?" She asked.

"Don't worry, everyone's fine," her grandmother answered. "It was the man from your bus company."

Rouba knew she meant Assistance Worldwide.

"What did he say?"

"He wanted to let you know that today's departure is cancelled. They've had word that the road won't be safe. They will call to give you a new date."

"Why did he not call me on my mobile?"

"He said he tried but couldn't reach you."

Rouba felt her eyes tear up and hid her face by going to the window. Teta followed her.

"I made coffee and your favourite hot cheese sandwich," she said, still carrying the tray.

"Why do things have to be so complicated?" Rouba asked herself out loud. "How come no one started a war seven years ago to stop me from getting married? I will sue for obstruction of divorce."

Teta darted her a disapproving look, shoving the tray under Rouba's nose. "Eat your sandwich, it will make you feel better."

As Rouba struggled to get over her disappointment, Maya was

hoping that a tan top-up would make her feel better. She found the perfect location, lying away from prying eyes at the far end of the garden. It was vital to keep a healthy complexion for the wedding.

Ziad called twenty-five minutes into the session. He started with the mandatory: "So what's the situation like today?"

"Rubbish. The helicopters are flying extremely low, I worry they're going to trim off the roofs of our houses."

"They're probably on reconnaissance to deter fighters from moving to the mountains," Ziad said.

Maya smiled. Although he worked in financial services, Ziad liked to think that he understood military manoeuvres.

He asked her about her day so she told him how she and her cousins had kept themselves busy by sorting through old clothes, looking at pictures and just making idle conversation all morning.

"Now I'm by myself, tanning in the garden," she concluded.

"Do you mean you're in your bikini?" he asked.

"Yes."

As Maya turned around to tan her back; she noticed patches of yellow grass under her lounge chair and throughout the lawn. With the expected water cuts, the family had decided to stop watering the grass, it wouldn't be long before it would die out completely.

"You know how conservative Rantour is," Ziad continued, "You shouldn't do this."

"I'm at the far end of the garden. No one ever comes here."

"You just said the helicopters are flying low."

Again, his obsession with military tactics. Maya smirked.

"You're talking as if they can see me," she said.

"Yes, they *can* see you. I hate the thought of Israeli soldiers peering over you in your bikini."

Maya laughed. This was a little too paranoid.

"Baby, I hope I'm a bombshell in your eyes, but believe me, their radars don't pick up my kind of weapons."

"I mean it. They take all kinds of photos during surveillance missions. You'd be surprised at how clear they can be."

Maya sat up, irritated. She wasn't sure whether he was serious or not, but she didn't like being told not to tan in her own garden. "My bikini's white, so they'll know I come in peace," she said.

At her abrasive tone, Ziad made the wise choice to drop the topic. "Have you heard from the wedding planner?" he asked. "I've been told that the hotels issued ultimatums for people to cancel wedding reservations immediately or run the risk of being charged in full whether they're able to hold the event or not."

"I haven't heard of any such thing."

"We should check anyway. I would hate to lose the money because of this mess."

"Will do. But it's probably for people whose weddings are in July and August. Ours is in September. We don't have to worry about it."

Half a world away, Elyssar's travel worries were coming to an end. She smiled at Jumana as the two of them walked through customs at JFK Airport. Jumana hopped as if her legs had been replaced by a set of springs; Elyssar grabbed her by the hand to stop her from running in all directions. They didn't have to go very far; a couple rushed towards them as soon as they stepped out into the arrivals meeting area. The man ran so fast he almost tripped on the baby stroller that he was pushing.

Elyssar guessed these were Jumana's parents even before the little girl had jumped into the woman's arms. They clung to each other, crying. Little sobs came out of the stroller, attracting Elyssar's attention to the toddler in the pram. With his mop of brown hair and black eyes that seemed to have barely left space on his face for his tiny nose and red lips, he was as adorable as babies could get; Elyssar now understood why Jumana hadn't stopped talking about her baby brother throughout the trip. He seemed mesmerised by the scene, his lips trembling as his eyes went from his sister and mother to Elyssar. He was probably wondering if this strange woman was the cause of the drama and whether he should join in the tears. His father bent over the stroller to appease him by rubbing his hair.

Jumana extracted herself from her mother's arm and ran to her father who lifted her up, showering kisses on her cheeks.

"My little girl, I'm so proud of you," he said. "I missed you."

Elyssar felt her eyes moistening and looked away to hide it. Jumana's mother turned towards her.

"We can never thank you enough," she said, tears still running down her face.

She was the thirty-something version of her daughter: luxurious brown hair and almond shaped eyes of the same colour.

Elyssar smiled. "I should thank *you*," she replied, giving Jumana a wink. "Your daughter took more care of me than I of *her* on this trip."

The little girl beamed.

"Can we invite you to lunch?" the father asked. "Or drop you somewhere?"

"Thank you, but I have a pre-organized pick up," Elyssar lied. "They're waiting for me at the transport counter."

Although Elyssar felt a little anxious at the thought of separating from Jumana who'd been such comforting company, she was desperate to get to her hotel, take the longest bath in history and put some order to her feelings.

Jumana turned to Elyssar.

"You'll visit me?" she asked.

Elyssar struggled to control her tears. Who would have thought she could bond so well with someone twenty years her junior by talking about clothes, boys and music? "I'll come as soon as I get the chance," she said as she hugged the little girl.

After a final kiss on the cheek, Jumana took her mother's hand and Elyssar waved goodbye as she watched the family head out in the direction of the parking lot. Soon, they were out of sight; she turned around and pushed her trolley in the direction of the arrows pointing to the taxi line.

There, standing alone in the queue and surrounded by chirpy European tourists and the damp heat of summertime New York, she could almost sense each of the thousands of miles that separated her from home.

Chapter 6

Two days had passed and as Rouba still hadn't heard back from the evacuation organizer, she called him. As usual, his line was busy one minute and closed the next. It took several attempts to get hold of him.

"Ghassan, my dear friend, where have you been? I thought you were going to get me out of this place," she said.

Silence at the other end of the line.

"Ghassan? Are you still there?"

"Yes. I'm just checking some of my documents."

Why did he want to check documents when the only thing he had to do was tell her which was her next bus? She hid her impatience as she heard him shift papers around, sporadically answering questions from someone next to him.

"Rouba," he sighed, having presumably found the correct piece of paper, "my documents show you cancelled."

"Pardon?"

"It says here that you called on the day of departure to say you no longer wished to leave."

"I never called," she replied. "*You* phoned to inform me the trip was called off that day."

"Are you sure you didn't speak to someone else? Maybe another agency? We didn't have such a cancellation. And I certainly didn't talk to you."

"You called my home line and my grandmother took the message."

"All the buses departed normally that day."

Just her luck. A stupid mistake happens and it had to be her who suffered. She decided to be constructive.

"Why don't you simply put me on the next bus?" she suggested.

"Because the evacuation programs are complete. Our operation has shut down."

Rouba felt like he'd just dropped a bucket of ice on her head. What did a girl have to do to get divorced in this country?

Across the mountain in Rantour, Maya was having as much trouble getting married as Rouba was having arranging her divorce. When her wedding planner, Carine, called her, Maya concluded that the world was conspiring to abolish positive thinking.

"I think we'll have to change the florrrrist," Carine said.

She had spent a few years in France and come back incapable of pronouncing her R's correctly; she now only used the French RRR, whether she spoke Arabic, English or French. For some reason, a lot of people found this specific speech impediment cute – and a whole generation of Lebanese, especially young women, had developed it as proof that they had lived in France and that they were more comfortable speaking French than Arabic.

"How come?" Maya asked. "I thought Jannaat were the best in town."

"Their chief creative director has gone. He has to work on a big Saudi wedding in London. He left last night and won't come back until after the war is over... Whenever that is."

Maya had taken an insane amount of time to decide on the flowers and finally selected these specific arrangements because Toni had the talent to make such amazing creations. She couldn't run the risk of entrusting the same design to anyone else. She would have to change the design to match the new florist's skills.

"I guess there is nothing we can do about it," she sighed. "Can't we just get another of Jannaat's florists to replace him?"

"The other one is called Eddy," Carine said. "He's not as good, but still acceptable. The problem with him is that he might also leave anytime. He holds a Canadian passport and has put himself on the embassy's list for evacuation."

"So do you have another florist in mind?" Maya asked, maintaining her calm with an effort.

"Yes, Florrreka," Carine answered. "Remember them? They were second on our list. We could visit them and have a look at their work. Or I could send you pictures by email since it's difficult to move around right now."

"Please email me, it's easier. And for heaven's sake, double check that all their employees carry only Lebanese passports and are as stuck in this God forsaken country as the rest of us."

In New York that afternoon, a certain Lebanese passport holder was feeling special for a change. Elyssar could barely hide her excitement as she walked up to the entrance of the Cole Haan shop on Fifth Avenue and introduced herself to one of the women standing by the door. The group of onlookers gathered outside the velvet rope granted her a quick scan then turned their eyes away in anticipation of the next arrival. They were here to spot celebrities and she sure didn't look like one.

The black clad girl checked her list and flashed a well aligned smile.

"Please come in, Ms. Awwad," she said, unhooking the velvet rope as if it were the gate to heaven.

Elyssar returned the smile and stepped into the store. She congratulated herself on finally getting out of her hotel. She'd given herself two full days to cry and watch the news in her room but as everyone in Lebanon had reassured her of their safety, she'd decided to make the best of her stay in New York and called *Bespoke*, her personal concierge service, asking for a list of things to do in New York.

This event was the first one on the calendar and couldn't have been more serendipitous: it featured a discussion with Cynthia

Nixon, the actress who played Miranda in *Sex And The City*. Elyssar had begged and pleaded with Bespoke to get her name on the list. They obliged, but not without highlighting how difficult a task they'd been able to complete, since her request came in at the last minute.

Once inside, she found herself in the midst of the ultimate New York crowd as she'd imagined it: well groomed women in designer clothes that highlighted their emaciated bodies; and handsome gay men in tight shirts chatting away, while a herd of photographers recorded every detail. The shop had been modified to fit a small stage in the back, with three bar stools ready to seat the speakers.

Elyssar glanced at herself in a mirror, making a quick comparison with those around her. There was no matching the women's super thin frames, shiny hair and toned legs; but her Chloe top-skirt combination and brown Jimmy Choo sandals screamed "on trend" and looked presentable enough. Thank God she'd had the sense to pack decent clothes; otherwise she would have never had the guts to go out in New York.

It took her a few seconds to realize that the person standing next to her looking in the mirror was none other than Cynthia Nixon herself. The actress was shorter and slimmer than she appeared on TV and had changed her hair color to blond, from the famous "Irish" redhead look she sported in the series.

Elyssar wanted to act blasé, but she was too star-struck to hide it. She stared without saying a word.

Nixon smiled.

"I like your bag," she said, looking prettier than her character did on the TV show. Elyssar looked down at her purse. A twenty-five dollar beaded number she'd bought at a charity event in Rantour.

"It's from Lebanon," she replied, "handmade by the women in my village."

"It's beautiful."

A skinny girl in a black suit and black nail polish placed a bony hand on Nixon's arm as a signal that the discussion was about to start. The actress nodded politely and moved away. Elyssar immediately took to her phone, texting frenetically.

"*Guess who I just chatted wt? Miranda fm SATC!*"

She sent it to all of her cousins, as well as Reem and Rouba.

Rouba's reply came back on the spot.

"*U kidding! Wher did u meet her?*"

"*@ an event Bespoke put me on guest list*"

Elyssar looked around; a lot of other people appeared to be texting or emailing from their phones so she didn't feel too awkward.

"*What did u tell her?*" Rouba replied.

"*Invited her 2 visit us in Lebanon. She said she heard it's this summer's hottest destination*".

"*LOL! U been n NYC 2 days and ur rubbing elbows wt A-List!*"

"*Ya*" Elyssar replied "*I'm an It! refugee.*"

Back in Lebanon, it was night time. Rouba texted back a smile to Elyssar and opened the door to sneak a look into the living room. Everyone had gone to bed – giving her the opportunity to fix herself a drink.

Padding across the dark living room barefoot, arms stretched in front of her, she managed to get to the kitchen without bumping into the furniture or breaking anything. There, the moonlight filtered through the window and helped her find a pack of candles, a box of matches and a glass. She couldn't locate a stand for the candle, so she lit it and held it in her hand as she made her way towards the dining room.

The flame flickered, cutting a tiny glow in the pitch dark. Rouba felt the way forward with her foot before every step. She remembered many an excruciating incident where she'd hit her toe while trying to move around during a power cut. In the years of peace since 1991, she'd forgotten about the good habit of stocking candles in her room. Well, this war sure refreshed her memory.

Feeling her way to the dining room dresser, she leaned to peer inside the display cupboard where her mother stored the alcohol. She recognised the shape of a wine bottle at the very end of the shelf, behind several rows of plates and glasses. Holding the candle with one hand, she manoeuvred with the other to clear her way towards the bottle. She'd almost reached it when a lump of burning wax dripped on her fingers.

Biting back the cry of pain, she dropped the candle. It rolled on the floor, still alight, heading straight to the rug. Rouba jumped towards it, but her other hand was still behind the glasses and in a roaring crash, her mother's collection of fine tableware smashed on the floor in a kaleidoscope of thousands of pieces of broken Austrian crystal.

Rouba froze, standing immobile between the scorched dresser and the burning carpet. Within seconds, the entire family swarmed through the door in their night clothes, shrieking in horror at the sight of Rouba standing barefoot in her baby doll as the fire spread on the rug. Someone was carrying a flashlight and aimed the beam straight at her face, startling her even more.

Her father reacted first, running to the kitchen and coming back with a gallon of water that he emptied out on the ravaged rug. The flames were replaced by thick black smoke. Everyone tutted, covering their noses with their hands. Half of their remaining stock of drinking water had just disappeared.

"Rouba, don't move," Teta said. "There's broken glass all around you. I'll get a broom."

"How did this happen?" her father asked.

Rouba blushed in shame, grateful that no one could see her in the dark.

"I was trying to make myself a drink and the candle fell from my hand..."

Her uncle, who'd recently professed to a more conservative life-style, tutted.

"May God help us all," he said in a tone of voice that meant, "That's what you get for being a drunk".

Her mother just stood there, contemplating the singed hole in her precious Persian carpet and the broken crystal that made the ground shimmer under the flashlight.

Rouba broke down in tears. "I am so sorry, Mama, I will replace everything."

Her mother carefully made her way through the shattered glass to hug her. "It doesn't matter, *habibti*. It's just glass," she said, crying as well.

But Rouba knew it was a lot more than glass. Her mother was weeping for the daughter whose life had derailed and brought everything crashing down with it.

Teta and Eva, the Ethiopian housekeeper, reappeared in the room, each carrying a broom. Teta ignored Rouba's request to let her do the cleaning.

"You're barefoot. Don't move until we've cleared it up."

When the two women had swept up as much of the shards as they could see, Teta sighed. "This is the best we can do for now," she said. "We'll clean properly tomorrow in the daylight."

The others left the room without even looking at Rouba or speaking to her.

"Thank you, Teta," she said as her grandmother headed back to her room.

Teta nodded. "You'll be OK," she said. But the way in which she put her head down as she walked out of the room denied every one of those words.

Chapter 7

For the fourth time Elyssar picked up *Happenings* magazine on the desk in her hotel room and stared at the ad titled 'Of Serendipitous Things". She read it again:

What are you looking for? This must be the question I most get asked. But I know exactly what I want, and I also know whom I want, and that's you.

We've crossed paths, you and I. A few times on the streets of Manhattan, once in London when I saw your tall slender silhouette disappear in a black cab, twice in Paris where I caught a glimpse of your smile lighting up a café on Boulevard Saint-Germain, and then in Rome as you walked by, surrounded by friends on a sunny afternoon.

You're stunning and bright with that confidence one only gets from the upbringing of a loving family. You're happy to be out and about, you enjoy good films and fine dining as much as you love spending lazy weekends à Deux, sometimes not getting out of bed all day.

You want your lover to be as honest and successful as you are, but you demand that he wear this success well. No bragging, logo flashing or name-dropping for you, you've always been above that. You understand that life's true treasures lie in the embrace of the one you love.

So is it serendipitous that we yet have to meet, have yet to exchange a word or lock gazes? Absolutely, and it is very much worth the wait; I will be right here when you come along.

It was signed PB.

Below it was another note:

A successful financier, PB owns a private equity firm but has not limited himself to the gray universe of business. He is also an accomplished photographer and painter in his spare time, and his travels often take him to Europe for work or leisure.

So if you are stunning in a natural way (no enhancements please), of fair complexion, between the ages of 25 and 35, and sizes 2 to 6; if his movie star dark hair and green eyes would send your heart racing, if his words touched you, email your reply to michelle@michellepriers. com.

About the matchmaker:

Michelle Priers is one of New York society's most renowned match-makers with two graduate degrees in psychology and many appear-ances in national and international media. Michelle only works with carefully selected clients and has successfully matched many of New York's elite. Client confidentiality is her paramount concern. For more information visit www.michellepriers.com.

Elyssar rubbed her temple. The lack of sleep was playing tricks on her mind, otherwise how could she explain the fixation with this silly ad? It was probably designed to target gullible jetlagged tour-ists and lure them to some cheesy escort service.

But what if a man in New York really had taken up a full ad to find his soul mate?

She'd never seen personals before because Lebanese don't use them; in a small country, friends and family looked around until they found you someone.

Too bad in her case the "someones" never worked out, but she wasn't giving up hope. The blurb about the matchmaker also grabbed her imagination. She'd seen TV reports about them but had never met one. OK well, she had, but in Lebanon they're called mothers and get extra active when they have a boy of marriageable age, or a daughter who needs a push to be noticed by mothers whose boys are of marriageable age.

She opened her laptop and went online to Michelle Priers' web-site. Instead of the pink coloured portal that she half expected, she got an elegant page that pledged "exclusive" matchmaking services as well as "life consultancy and coaching". The site featured a login page for clients as well as a press section with links to articles writ-ten about the agency in publications like *Vogue* and *Vanity Fair.*

She closed her laptop and went back to bed. She needed the

sleep for her first day in the head office tomorrow.

Two hours later and not a second of sleep to show for herself, she was still obsessed by the ad. As if driven by an unconscious force, she found herself getting out of bed, returning to the laptop and typing away:

Was it you? Those beautiful eyes that met mine in a lounge in Heathrow, or the deep American voice that made me turn my head just in time to catch a glimpse of you greeting someone as you boarded a flight in Charles De Gaulle?

I always thought that I've been in sales and marketing far too long to let an advertisement catch my thoughts, yet 'Of Serendipitous Thoughts' resonated with me.

Born in Lebanon, I've spent a lot of time abroad, survived a war or two, and been around enough unimaginable wealth to know that money does get you many beautiful things but that at the end, we only take with us what we've acquired for our soul.

I've seen real loss and I understand that time is the single thing we can never buy. Shared laughter and the days we spend with our loved ones are the most valuable gifts one can ever get.

I am a country manager for an American corporation, which allows me to be independent and do all the things I love: fine dining, nights out clubbing, hosting dinners and parties, frequent travel on business or holiday and lazy weekends with my family in our mountain house.

I've been lucky to meet many interesting personalities, from presidents and CEOs to selfless aid workers and the innocent victims of conflict, all of whom helped me gain confidence, a key asset in life. I am fluent in three languages.

It feels a little surreal to be sitting up in my bed at 5 a.m. writing a lengthy answer to an ad! It could be my jetlag or maybe I truly believe that you're somewhere out there. So even if I never meet you, at least you've carried me through this sleepless night.

Here's to imaginary soul mates.

Elyssar.

She read the text a few times, then started a new email, added her letter as a file attachment and typed:

Hi Michelle,

I came across your advertisement titled 'Of Serendipitous Thoughts' in this week's Happenings magazine. I've written the attached in response.

I am not sure if your ad is open to people who live outside New York, yet this gentleman's words were special and I wish him the best of luck in his search. I often visit New York on business and am currently in the city for an extended stay.

The attached letter includes part of the information that you requested in your ad. Please find below some additional details that may be helpful. I trust that all information will be treated in confidence.

Age: 33

Height: 5'3"

Dress size: 6

OK, after all the food in Rantour she had turned into an American size eight but a girl is expected to cheat on her dress size, weight, and age. Anyway, she was intent on losing the extra inches in no time.

Professional Experience: Country Manager for Integrated Systems in Beirut, Lebanon.

Single, no children.

She took a deep breath, and hit send.

Relieved, she went back to bed and drifted into a solid sleep as soon as she closed her eyes. But less than an hour later, she woke up in a panic. Had she really sent an email from her work account in response to a personal? What if this Michelle woman belonged to a sex slavery operation? Or porn? This could get her in all kinds of trouble with HR.

She ran to her computer hoping it would all turn out to be a dream. But sure enough the message sat proudly in her "sent" email folder. Lord, she'd even attached three pictures of herself. The first one showed her in a business suit, in the second she was attending a wedding sporting a chignon, professional make up, a long black dress and her most expensive jewellery, and in the third, taken in New York last year, she was at the Tribeca film festival wearing jeans and a black jacket.

She must be more desperate for a man than she'd imagined. "I did check the website and it appeared legit," she comforted herself out loud. "Anyway I'm too old to be abducted as a sex slave."

She closed the laptop and went back to bed.

"No one will bother reading it," she told the pillow. "Anyway, the word Lebanon alone will freak them out. If I do get a reply, it will say terrorists need not apply."

Chapter 8

Due to the time difference, Elyssar was reading her email at the same time as Maya was waking up in Rantour, bright and early, excited about her dress fitting. The designer's studio had called the day before to confirm the appointment and inform her that they'd be working full hours despite the war to ensure delivery of all orders on time.

No planes in sight this morning and she prayed they kept it that way until she came back from the fitting.

The cousinettes met her in the driveway as she and her mother prepared to leave.

Her mother tied a white shirt around the car door handle. "We'll be passing roads that overlook Dahyeh," she explained. The cousinettes gave her bemused looks on hearing mention of the notoriously targeted southern Beirut suburb leading to the airport. "It gets bombed everyday so there's no harm in flying a white flag. This is the closest thing I have to one."

Maya got behind the wheel and the drive progressed nicely until they neared Beirut. Under normal circumstances, Maya enjoyed driving on this road with its spectacular views across the coast line. But now it felt steep and winding. The number of jets increased, their vapour trails drawing a canvas of threatening white lines in the pure blue sky.

Maya started to feel uneasy and a glance towards the passenger seat showed that her mother felt the same. No other cars around.

"Do you think we should go back?" Maya asked.

Her mother hesitated.

"They're unlikely to bomb this side of the mountain," she finally said. "Let's keep going."

Ominous words. The helicopter gunship came out of nowhere, stirring the earth beneath them and causing a racket that seemed inside their very minds.

Maya instinctively hit the brakes. The car screeched.

"Get out!" she yelled over the noise.

The two women tumbled out and sprinted away from the car.

"Stay on the road!" her mother shouted, clinging to Maya's elbow.

They ran as fast as they could, too scared to figure out the best direction. They just knew they had to be as far away from the car as they could get, while remaining in the open so they wouldn't be mistaken for fighters. They struggled to maintain their pace as the road curved uphill.

The commotion went on for an eternity: an ear-splitting mixture of bombings, the screeching blast of warplanes and the roar of helicopters.

Then everything went dead quiet. Maya and her mother stood still for a few minutes, hearts still racing and arms above their heads, apprehensive that the mayhem would return.

They finally turned towards each other, struggling to regain their breath. Maya looked around; the narrow asphalt road appeared intact. So did the trees on both sides. Only the heavy smell of gunpowder testified that hell had opened its gates a few seconds ago. "They bombed the other side of the mountain," she said. "Nothing here."

They stumbled back towards the car, realizing the doors were still open and the engine running. Maya gave thanks that she'd had the reflex to put the car in park; otherwise it would have ended up in the ravine.

Still trembling with shock, she sat behind the wheel; her mother reclaimed the passenger seat.

Maya attempted to reverse and realized that her body was shaking so much she didn't have the strength to move the gearshift nor push the pedal.

Her mother burst out crying. "Look at us. I thought we were going to die out here. Why do we have to live like this? What's wrong with us? What's wrong with this country?"

Maya broke down in tears too. "I'm so sorry, Mama," she sobbed. "This is my fault. I put your life at risk for my silly fitting."

Her mother hugged her and they both cried out their fright.

Moments later, her mother looked up, her lips set in a thin line of determination. "You still have to get the dress made," she said, undeterred. "Let's go home and call to reschedule."

Elyssar also had clothing on her mind a few hours later as she stood in her office's ladies' room, giving herself a critical appraisal in the mirror. Integrated Systems prided itself on its jean culture but wearing a pair of denims to her first day in the New York office and, more importantly, her first ever meeting with the CEO hadn't crossed her mind. She'd chosen black trousers and a grey shirt for the occasion. Her efforts to straighten her own naturally wavy hair had proved disastrous, so she'd pulled it back into a ponytail. Under different circumstances, she would have booked a hairdresser appointment to get a proper blow-dry, but she'd only been informed about this meeting late last night.

She didn't look great, but then again, turning up in salon-styled hair and a killer outfit would shatter her refugee image forever. A glance at the clock told her it was nearly time.

Leaving the restroom, she took the staircase to the second floor where she made her way through the bustling workspace. Integrated Systems had an open plan office policy, everyone operated from cubicles, including the CEO. But meritocracy worked in mysterious ways, and in the New York HQ, being on this floor meant you'd made it in the corporation.

Elyssar recognised many faces around her because she'd seen them on the company intranet and press releases: VPs, Senior VPs or the ones everyone knew were on their way to becoming VPs.

She followed the directions given to her by the receptionist earlier and reached the far left corner of the floor. She knocked on one of the partitions.

"Come in!" a happy female voice sounded from behind the panel.

Elyssar walked to the desk.

"Hi, I'm Elyssar Awwad, here for my appointment with Craig," she said, trying not to look shy. She liked to think of herself as a strong worldly woman but her blushing habit didn't help. Well, better blush in front of the CEO's assistant than the CEO himself.

The lady behind the desk looked up from her screen. "He's waiting for you."

Elyssar followed her to the bigger cubicle next door.

The CEO rose to his feet, his six-foot frame blocking a part of the amazing view of Manhattan behind him. He extended a big hand and she shook it firmly, his bonhomie putting her at ease straight away. "Please sit down," he said. "I'm happy to meet you. We were worried about you out there."

She knew from his corporate bio that Craig Briggs was pushing sixty-four, but he looked younger and seemed quite fit.

"I can never thank you enough. Integrated Systems has been wonderful throughout this situation."

He shrugged. "It's our duty."

Again the lingering remorse about her Madonna lie. Elyssar ignored it. "This is for you," she said, digging a box out from her bag and placing it on his desk. "Sweets from Lebanon. My mother insisted that I bring them with me as a thank you."

Her mother had forced her to carry three boxes. The other two were for her colleagues on the third floor.

He opened it and took a piece of *baqlawa*.

"It's very syrupy," she cautioned.

He nodded as he chewed. "It's excellent. I know I will eat too much of it and get in trouble with my wife."

Elyssar appreciated that she couldn't waste the CEO's time talking about dessert. He'd been kind to ask to see her and she wanted him to know the company had a worthwhile employee in her.

"Sir, I know my region is small, but now that I have some time with you I thought I should tell you about the business there."

He shot her a big smile, looking pleased with her for talking business. "All markets are important and yours is a growth area. I plan on visiting some day."

Elyssar provided facts and figures and the CEO asked a few questions, which luckily she had the answers to. She'd heard about meetings with him going terribly wrong and thought he might be going easy on her because of her situation.

She made sure she wrapped up the meeting within her allocated twenty minutes. After she left his cubicle, she dropped by the assistant to thank her and headed to the temporary desk she'd been allocated on the third floor to call her line manager. He'd asked her to update him immediately after the meeting. Country managers never met Craig one on one, and she guessed her manager worried that she'd do or say something stupid that would make him look bad.

She related the conversation with Craig and he sounded relieved. "Well done, Elyssar. You've been exemplary throughout these events."

And all of it is inspired by Madonna, she thought, grinning to herself.

"I was thinking I should work from the Dubai office," she said on an impulse. "It will be easier to handle the Jordan deal from there." She wasn't sure where this idea had come from or why she'd blurted it out to her manager without giving it proper thought. In many ways she was happy to be in New York. She'd always loved the city and this was her chance to spend more time here than the usual three or four day business trips. Then again, she was getting lonely, having no friends here, not even acquaintances whom she could spend time with. Walking the streets of Manhattan was exhilarating but doing it on your own for days on end got a little tiring. Also, the thought of being in Dubai with Rouba at this difficult time was tempting.

"I'd rather you stay in New York. It's a good opportunity to network with key people in the HQ." Her manager replied.

"Dubai is the nearest office we have to Jordan, it's also in the same time zone. It will be easier for me to communicate with our Jordanian distributors from there. It will only be for a week or so before my holiday starts and I want to make sure things are set correctly." A voice told her she shouldn't push. In all fairness her boss had already been kind enough to support her evacuation request. Also, it did make more sense to work from Dubai than New York.

There was a short silence while he considered the proposal, then conceded.

"OK, send me a travel request and I'll approve it."

They hung up and Elyssar powered up her laptop, excited about the move to Dubai. Many of her friends had moved there in the past years and although the city sizzled at this time of year, having them around would make her situation easier. She opened her email and, from the multitude of new messages in her inbox, one immediately jumped to her eye; titled 'Hello Elyssar', it was sent by a Paul Bayes.

She clicked on it.

Dear Elyssar,

Michelle Priers from the matchmaking agency forwarded your email and I told her I would answer this one myself. You intrigued me; I feel there's a lot more I should learn about you.

Also, please allow me to say that I'm so sorry about what's happening to your country and its people.

Hope to hear back from you,

Paul.

Elyssar sat, gazing at her screen. She'd completely forgotten about her crazy email from three nights ago and now that the response stared her in the face, she still didn't know what to make of the whole thing.

Only one way to find out. She typed her reply:

Hi Paul,

Thank you for the message and kind words about Lebanon, we're praying that it will be over soon.

I am in New York as my employer organized to have me evacuated from Lebanon along with US citizens. I've been here for a few days but am planning to move to Dubai the day after tomorrow.

Best regards,

Elyssar.

The response came back almost immediately.

Elyssar,

Since you're here, shouldn't we try to see each other? I would love to meet you. Let me know if you're free tomorrow pm. I have to attend a play at 8, but we can meet before that for drinks.

P.S. You look wonderful in your pictures. If you want, you can have a look at my company website, my picture is in the corporate section. www.BayesandAssociates.com

The link took her to an impressive page that listed the financial services offered by the firm, as well as quotes from the press and links to download case studies. She found Paul Bayes under Corporate Info. He held the title Chairman and CEO and the picture showed him standing in an office lobby, dressed in a black suit. Probably in his mid forties, with black hair and cool round glasses, the picture was distant but he didn't seem bad looking. Quite attractive, actually.

She examined his biography.

Holds a master's degree in finance. Started his professional life in California then relocated to New York where Bayes and Associates soon became a recognized name in finance...

No mention of a wife or a criminal record but then corporate websites tend to leave that information out.

She replied: "*Yes, it would be good to meet you. Shall we make it 5pm at the bar in Bryant Park hotel?*"

She'd visited that bar a few times and never found it empty. One of the trendiest places in town, and therefore a safe venue to meet someone you suspected might be plotting to sell you to the fetish trade.

"*See you tomorrow,*" he wrote, adding his mobile number.

Wow, that was fast...

She browsed his company's website a little more and couldn't find anything to fault him by. Then she Googled his name and found several online articles that quoted him on news releases issued by his firm.

People, this refugee had a hot date!

Chapter 9

The next day in Beirut, Maya heard nothing but the sound of her own heels on the pavement as she crossed Hamra Street towards Cousinette Dana's office where Uncle Najeeb would pick them up to drive back to Rantour. Around her, the usually effervescent and chaotic commercial district looked almost empty – and quieter than she imagined it could ever be. The bombings hadn't reached this part of the city, yet she sensed the desolation through the impact of halted commercial activity. The stores remained open despite the lack of customers, most shopkeepers pulling a chair onto the sidewalk to keep busy by observing the rare passersby.

Following her botched attempt to make her dress fitting, Maya had been reluctant to go on the road again but she needed to meet with her shoe designer , and the opportunity had come up to take the trip today with Dana who'd been summoned by her company to a meeting in Beirut. Uncle Najeeb had offered to drive the two of them, citing some errands he needed to run in the city. Maya suspected he wanted to play bodyguard.

She was happy with the day's results. Most brides bought ready-to-wear shoes but she wanted hers custom made, so she'd hired Simon Yarfi, an up and coming graduate in shoe design from Paris, to create her dream stilettos. The shoes would only be seen beneath her long dress for the removal of the garter, but that was enough to motivate her. In addition to the night itself, she and her family would watch the wedding video a hundred times and she wanted to guarantee she had no shoe regrets. Simon had done a great job with the sample he showed her today: perfectly shaped sandals that incorporated delicate reminders of the dress. Maya also loved the heels he'd selected: high enough to boost her taller than average frame, but without making her tower over her fiancé.

Maya walked past her favourite *manakish* bakery. Usually full of people queuing for a delightful piece of hot cheese or thyme on dough, it was deserted today. On an impulse, Maya turned to go in.

The store clerk jumped behind his counter.

"How long would it take for three cheese manakish?" she asked.

"We haven't had any customers today, but I've kept the oven hot. It will only take a few minutes. Would you like them with vegetables?"

"No, thank you. Just cheese, but I really need them quickly; I'm heading to the mountains in a few minutes."

She checked her watch and realized that she was starting to push late. As if prompted, Dana called.

"I can't believe you stopped for manakish," she exclaimed when Maya told her of her whereabouts. "You know my father's temper. If you're not here when he comes to collect us, he'll go without you and you'll have to spend the night in Beirut."

"It just feels wrong that Hamra is so empty, especially the bakery."

"So you're saving the Lebanese economy one manakish order at a time?" her cousin mocked. "Hurry up. I would really hate to face my father's wrath, I've had a depressing enough time at the office."

As the shopkeeper promised, her manakish came out of the oven in no time. Maya grabbed the bag, which smelled of heavenly dough and warm cheese, and sprinted towards her cousin's office. She arrived out of breath; Dana was waiting for her on the sidewalk.

"Right on time," she said. "Dad just called, he's two blocks away."

A few seconds later, Uncle Najeeb pulled up and the girls got into the car. Maya unwrapped the manakish and offered one to each of them. Her uncle declined. Maya guessed he wanted to focus on the risky drive ahead.

"How was your meeting?" Uncle Najeeb asked Dana.

"Not good," she replied. "The business is dead for the summer. They said they will pay us half salaries until the war ends and things pick up."

A reflective silence followed.

"Your shipment is right outside Lebanese waters, right?" Maya said, trying to comfort her cousin. "The moment things get better, you'll be able to bring it in."

"Yeah, let's hope there are people left in the country to buy products," Dana replied, sounding glum.

The car whizzed through deserted streets. After a while, Maya realized they weren't moving in the direction she would have expected. Dana seemed to have the same thought.

"Which road are you taking?" she asked her father.

"The airport road," he replied.

Maya's heart tingled. The airport road? The one that passed right along the most bombed part of Lebanon?

"Why don't we go through Aley?" she asked.

"This is faster," her uncle replied, "and shorter. We need to save fuel."

The fuel shortage didn't warrant putting their lives at risk, yet Maya remained quiet. Uncle Najeeb had a heart of gold, but his short temper was legendary and you never wanted to piss him off, especially when he was driving.

"What if they attack?" Dana asked cautiously.

"They won't," he replied, sounding sure of himself. "They're busy in the South and The Bekaa today."

Uncle Najeeb's knuckles whitened on the wheel and Maya told herself that continuing the argument wouldn't help. Anyway, they had already started on the highway with no possibility of a u-turn.

Dana put down the passenger shade and Maya caught her gaze in the mirror, giving her what she intended to be a reassuring wink.

The car travelled fast, with the sea to their right and Beirut's southern suburb to their left. A column of smoke appeared in the distance.

"Look," Dana pointed out. "What do you think that is?"

"Someone must be burning garbage," her father said in a calm voice.

He accelerated and the car sped on the empty highway.

Burning garbage! Uncle Najeeb had a way of ignoring truths he didn't like, but this time he had outdone himself.

Maya could have sworn she heard Dana gulping in the front seat. Looking at her reflection in the mirror, she saw her cousin's petrified face and for some reason found herself on the verge of breaking out in uncontrollable laughter. It must have been the adrenalin rush. Barely able to control herself, Maya winked again at her cousin.

While Maya was praying to make it home safely, Elyssar's trip to the hairdresser was turning out to be a bit of a culture shock. *Bespoke* had booked her into a renowned salon in midtown and, the moment she walked in, she realized the coiffeur-going etiquette was quite different from that in Lebanon. No jovial hairdresser aides welcomed her with lots of comments on how great she looked while ordering her Turkish coffee. Generally, the more compliments they gave you, the clearer it became that your roots needed colour, your highlights had faded and the bags under your eyes were big enough to fit your weekly groceries.

No over made-up, silicone-enhanced, bleached blond receptionist either; instead, a middle aged woman with short grey hair greeted her by barking "Go reception!" in a strong Russian accent.

Embarrassed, Elyssar realised she was heading for the cloakroom instead of the reception. She followed the general direction of the woman's threateningly pointed finger and saw a fancy counter decorated with coloured lights and a plasma screen behind. She headed there, relieved to see the young receptionist smile at her. Perfect eyebrows and glossy hair; Elyssar made a mental note to come back another time for a similar colour.

Elyssar introduced herself.

In Lebanon, the only productivity tools on the receptionist's desk, no matter how fancy the place, would have been a nail file, a packet of cigarettes, an empty cup of coffee and a cell phone glued to her ear; but here the receptionist examined her computer screen and then looked up.

"Who is your appointment with?" she asked in her perky, super-well-trained, American retail staff voice. The look in her eyes indicated she was in fact terribly bored and would have preferred to chat with her friends all day long.

Elyssar panicked for a split second. How could she know this information? Remembering that the concierge had provided some details, she pulled the list from her purse.

"Kirsten for manicure, Sue for pedicure, Laurie for blow-dry and Allison for make-up," she read out.

The girl fiddled again with her PC. "You start with Sue," she carefully read from her screen as if revealing some kind of universal truth. "Then it's Kirsten, then Laurie and your last appointment is wiiiiith... Allison for make-up!"

Elyssar didn't like the arrangement. It meant that she would be having her pedicure first, then her manicure, then the hair. Couldn't she do her hair, manicure and pedicure at the same time? She made the mistake of voicing her thoughts. From the look on the receptionist's face, it was obviously a corny suggestion to make in New York.

"I can't change your appointments. Everyone is busy," the girl said, her contempt clear from her clipped tones.

So much for New York efficiency, Elyssar thought; Beirut beauty salons scored higher on productivity. She checked her watch. Thank God she had planned an extra hour and a half, otherwise this could have been trouble. She still needed to go back to her hotel to get changed and then make her way in New York traffic to meet Paul at five.

"OK. Where do I start?"

The girl gave her a few paper slips and pointed towards the opposite wall. Darn, she had to go back to the cloakroom.

Unsure of what she was meant to do there and worried about being yelled at again, she held out the papers she'd just been given at reception.

The gray-haired woman gave her a dirty look and, without saying a word, almost threw back the papers and what looked like a folded robe.

"I don't need this," Elyssar said. "I'm not getting a colour."

The Russian woman didn't answer, she just stared. Elyssar found it hard not to snap. What kind of manners were these? She reflected on the comfortable relationship Lebanese women developed with beauty parlour staff. Because services and beauty rituals were so affordable, visiting the hair salon in Beirut was routine and no one regarded it as luxury, which meant the ambiance was more cheerful than snobbish.

Another customer came out of a dressing room, sporting a robe over her jeans. She handed her top to the Russian. Good. Now Elyssar knew what to do. Anyway, she was excited about this date with Paul and wanted to look her best, so she gritted her teeth and ignored the rudeness.

A few hours later, Elyssar gave herself a final look in a glass door before walking past the Bryant Park's reception desk and taking the steps that led down to the Cellar Bar. The hairdresser had done a good job, blow-drying her hair in a way that gave it a thick texture and brought out the colour of her highlights. Her black and gold blouse worked well with the dark blue jeans to hide the recently added extra pounds, and her black stilettos completed the look by giving her a ten centimetre lift. She definitely looked more size six than size eight today.

The highlight of the trip to the beauty salon was definitely the make-up artist's work; she'd given Elyssar a wonderful looking complexion and made her eyes appear huge, without creating that over done professional made-up feel.

Elyssar held on to the railing as she made her way down the opulent staircase leading to the bar. A multitude of small lamps highlighted the vaulted ceiling. Depending on one's mood, she could see that this setting could be slightly dark or highly sophisticated.

She recognized Paul right away, sitting on the banquette opposite the entrance. He spotted her immediately as well and stood up to meet her half way. Taking the hand she held out, he surprised her by pulling her forward for a kiss on the cheek.

"We finally meet," he said.

He looked better in real life than on his website: black hair, green eyes, and full lips. He was about five-foot-seven. Elyssar had expected him to be taller, but his dark suit and T-shirt brought out a lean silhouette.

"I appreciate you taking the time before the play," she said.

"I wanted to meet you," he replied as they sat next to each other on the banquette.

From there on, the conversation flowed with the drinks: Martinis for him and champagne cocktails for her. Finding him easy to talk to, Elyssar let her guard down, telling him about her dream to see Madonna in concert, her journey to New York and her three days so far in the city.

Further on, he ordered Cosmopolitans for both of them.

"I wanted one earlier," she laughed, "but after the publicity on *Sex and The City*, I imagined it's now a groupies' drink, and was too embarrassed to order one."

"It *is* a groupie drink," he replied, "but it's still good."

He touched his glass to hers.

"I don't know a lot about Lebanon," he said. "Which part of the country are you from?"

She told him about her village in Mount Lebanon and how her family stayed the winters in Beirut, spending the summers in their mountain houses.

"Are you Moslem?" he asked.

In her inebriation, she didn't mind the question, but took her time before replying. "I believe in one God but not in religions," she said. "They're man-made."

"But you come from a place where people have been warring for centuries over religion."

"Exactly. Religions are just brands, and their loyalty program is to tell you that you will burn in hell if you buy from their competition."

Paul reclined against the leather banquette, gazing at her. "I've never heard it said so well."

Elyssar smirked and sipped her drink, telling herself she should take it easy on the alcohol. This upscale lounge's crystal chandeliers, sultry red undertones and seductive music could be dangerous in the company of a man like Paul. He owned the room.

Even the bar staff seemed gorgeous and the fashionable crowd had started moving in for after work drinks, occupying the banquettes around them.

They continued to chat until he asked her about her dinner plans.

"I don't have any plans," she confessed, a little embarrassed. "I don't really know anyone here, so..."

"I know a great place uptown I can take you to. Do you like Asian food?"

"I thought you had a play to attend."

"I'll catch it another time. I'm not ready to let you go yet."

Elyssar wondered if the play was just an excuse he had made up so he could leave if he wasn't enjoying the date. Her heart beat faster at the thought that he'd liked their time together as much as she had.

Outside the bar, Elyssar loved the *so* New York way in which Paul hailed the taxi. On her first trip to the city a few years ago, she'd noticed the way people raised their arm while calling out an authoritative "Taaaxi!" but, despite her best attempts, she hadn't been able to replicate it and sometimes taxis didn't stop for her. Laughing, she shared this thought with Paul.

"Stick with me and you'll learn a lot," he said.

How did he manage such sexy smiles?

He caught her eye for a second, maybe guessing her thoughts, and she blushed.

"We're going to Philippe," he said. "It's an uptown/downtown kind of place."

"An uptown/downtown kind of place," she repeated, laughing. "What does that mean? I thought New Yorkers only used such expressions on TV."

"Hollywood got it right. We do speak like this. It means that it has the feel of a downtown restaurant but it's located uptown; better crowd."

Elyssar smiled. Where else would she hear a grown man talking about the "better" crowd?

The sight of the beautiful uptown people congregating around the bar, drinks in hand, greeted them as they arrived; quite a cosmopolitan pack, mainly women in their twenties, each more glamorous than the other. Stick thin, glossy hair, perfect nails and dressed in the latest fashions.

"Stay here," Paul said, leaving her by the entrance.

He flitted between the patrons towards the reception counter. Elyssar saw him exchange a few words with the hostess; a tall, blue eyed, brunette beauty who'd probably come to New York in the hope of landing a modelling contract and moonlighted at upper class restaurants to get herself noticed.

"Our table's at the back," he said, placing his arm lightly behind her shoulders to guide her through the crowd.

"Don't we have to wait for a table? I heard some of the people..."

"You don't have to wait when you ask nicely," he replied.

Again, the tantalizing smile. Elyssar's heart skipped a beat.

Although the name Philippe would have led naïve patrons to think they'd be eating French cuisine, the restaurant served excellent "modern" Asian food. Elyssar tried to go only for steamed dishes. The prospect of deep-fried cooking going straight to her buttocks felt less appealing than ever in such handsome company.

"What colour are your eyes?" Paul said, leaning towards her. "Hazel? Sometimes they look almost yellow."

She smiled, unsure how to answer. The dim lights played up the colour of Paul's eyes and the contour of his lips. Her tongue loosened by the alcohol, Elyssar blurted out the question that had been burning on her mind all evening.

"Why would a man like you resort to a matchmaker? You must be able to meet beautiful and sophisticated women any time."

Paul grimaced. "You don't know this city," he replied. "On a first date, you can tell that the woman is only interested in how much money you have in the bank and how much stock you own. It's disgusting."

"But there are plenty of successful women here who have their own money."

If anything, he looked even more disgusted. "Oh yes, those! In reality, they're just men in disguise. A bunch of aggressive bitches."

Elyssar found the use of strong language a little shocking but she didn't let it bother her. She looked around; beautiful, successful-looking women everywhere. "It's hard to believe all the women here are like that," she said.

"I'm sure the city's got its gems but they're hard to find amongst the rest of them," Paul replied.

She didn't insist.

They chatted over dinner and many more drinks, talking about everything from global money markets to travel and music.

At the end of the meal, Paul took her face between his hands and brought his eyes very close to hers. "I've found a real lady from half way across the world," he said. "Tonight's been wonderful."

Again, Elyssar blushed hoping it wouldn't show in the soft lighting.

Letting go of her face, he sat back. "You're going to Dubai tomorrow, right?"

"That's the plan."

"Why don't you postpone your trip?" he asked.

The suggestion took her by surprise. "The tickets are booked ..."

"How about this," he interrupted. "You postpone your trip to Dubai and I take the day off tomorrow. Elyssar, I can't let you go just yet," he insisted. "There are so many places I want to show you in New York."

She had to admit Dubai was a lot less appealing when his face was so close to hers; and those gorgeous eyes of his had asked nicely.

She pulled back from him and forced herself to think. Her boss didn't like the thought of her leaving the New York office after the drama she'd created to get there. He'd only approved her trip to Dubai because she made a strong case for it. Maybe she could come up with a way to tell him something had changed and she could now stay in New York... That would make three major lies in as many weeks.

Brushing off the thought, she decided she would deal with her conscience tomorrow. "OK," she said. "I'll reorganize."

Paul settled the bill and held her by the hand as they left the restaurant. Elyssar tried to hide her excitement, feeling like a giddy teenager about to hit the town with her latest crush. What a surreal couple of weeks – the war in Lebanon, her long trip to the US, and now this handsome New Yorker wanting to tour her around the greatest city on Earth.

The next morning in Rantour, Maya was sitting in the living room, still reeling from a fight with her mother over the need to change the wedding plans when the ringing phone pulled her out of her thoughts. She just stared at it, unable to bring herself to pick it up. It was Ziad calling, and she knew that if she picked up, she would likely end up in a fight with him too. It would be better to ignore the call and give herself more time to think.

Still equally fuming from their argument, her mother walked into the room, and held the phone up. "It's Ziad," she said, reading the screen. "Aren't you going to answer him?"

"What's the point? I know what he wants to talk about and I don't want to get into it again."

Her mother glanced at her. "Remember the country is at war. He will imagine the worst if you don't pick up."

"We just texted each other ten minutes ago, he knows I'm alive," Maya snapped.

Her mother shook her head and answered the phone. "Ziad, hiiii, it's Hala," she said, her voice giving no hint of the stress in the room. "Maya is next door with her cousins. She forgot to take her phone with her. I will take it to her if you want to try her in fifteen minutes. I will let her know you called." She hung up and placed the phone back on the table, giving Maya an angry look before leaving the room.

Maya wanted to scream. It seemed like everyone wanted a piece of her and she didn't know what to do. She grabbed the remote control to turn the TV on but realized the power was down.

She decided she had to go next-door and vent to her cousins if she didn't want to drive herself crazy. As she walked between villas, she heard a jet flying overhead.

"Thank you for ruining it for me," she said out loud, both her middle fingers pointed at the sky.

Reem, Dana and Nadia were in the room; thankfully no parents around.

"I just had a fight with my mother," Maya announced as she let herself fall on the couch. "Why is everyone asking me to make decisions about the wedding like I know if and when this rubbish war will end?"

The cousinettes stared at her. They'd rarely seen her this angry and she knew they would be worried about saying anything that would aggravate her even more.

"The hotel just called asking us to cancel or confirm within seventy-two hours, she explained. "If they don't hear back from us they will take the full payment whether the wedding takes place on the third of September or not."

The cousinettes held their silence.

"What am I supposed to do?" Maya wailed.

She saw the expression on Reem's face change, and her cousin burst out laughing; Dana and Nadia followed suit.

"What's so funny?"

"Look at you," Reem giggled. "You're Bridezilla, Lebanese Edition. Instead of getting into fights with your parents and your fiancé about the colour of the floral arrangements, you're being difficult over the details of war and peace: you think the bombings should be timed around your nuptials."

Realizing what she must have sounded like, Maya relaxed and joined the laughter. "Yes," she agreed. "I should have my own reality show."

They laughed uncontrollably for a few minutes, until Maya found herself depressed again.

"What does a girl have to do to get married in this country?"

Chapter 10

While Maya's mother was fielding calls from her fiancé, Teta had taken it upon herself to answer her granddaughter's telephone. When Rouba's mobile rang that afternoon, Teta hurried to fetch it.

"It's Majed," she said, darting a meaningful look at Rouba before leaving the room. Teta really had to stop with the melodrama, Rouba thought as she answered the call.

"Roobs!" The caller wasn't Majed, but his youngest daughter, Noora. Rouba smiled. The eleven-year-old had recently taken to calling her "Roobs"; a turn of speech she must have picked up from the cool kids in school. "I'm worried about you," Noora continued.

Noora had been four years old when she met Rouba and they'd bonded instantly. Rouba imagined that parents couldn't love their biological kids any more than she did Noora. The little girl's round cheeks, olive skin and huge hazel eyes made her difficult to resist, but, most importantly, she had the kindest soul and Rouba spent sleepless nights worrying about the way in which the divorce would affect her.

"I'm fine, sweetheart," Rouba said. "I'm with my family and we're safe in Kafarneem. The bombings are elsewhere."

"I watched the news and they said that the war has spread to all parts of Lebanon."

"They're exaggerating," Rouba replied, trying to sound assuring. "It's fine here. We just have to be careful."

"Do you know you can come back here? I saw reports about people returning from Lebanon."

"I'm working on it. God willing, I'll be back in Kuwait very soon. Now, tell me about yourself. How are you spending the holidays?"

Noora told Rouba about the busy summer schedule with her friends, which seemed to consist of spending a lot of time at the pool and in the mall. Of course, they also visited the nail bar at least once a week.

"My nails are blue this week," she announced proudly.

"Sounds wonderful. Send me a picture. But be careful not to spend all your money there."

"I know. Dad said he won't raise my allowance, so I've learnt how to put the colour on by myself."

"I'm proud of you, sweetie," Rouba replied.

"I will pass you on to Dad now." Noora sounded satisfied with the conversation.

"I hope you're not bothered that she called," Majed said when he came on the line.

"Don't say that, Majed," Rouba replied. "You know what the kids mean to me."

Majed grunted in agreement.

"How is she doing?" Rouba asked.

"She's fine."

Majed loved his children dearly, but he wasn't the most expressive man in the world and didn't know how to communicate with them. His way of dealing with the divorce was by not talking about it. He had even refused to tell the children about the separation and Rouba had found herself compelled to talk to them about it on her own.

"She can't be fine," Rouba said, unable to hide her exasperation, "She's just a child and there's a divorce happening in her family."

"Kids bounce back. She'll be OK."

Rouba hated him when he dismissed his children's feelings in this way.

"They don't bounce back on their own, Majed. You have to help them through it. And the first step is to stop being in denial about it."

Majed mumbled something and said he needed to go. Rouba sighed as she put the phone down, trying to focus on the book in her hand, but her phone rang again. This time it was Reem, Elyssar's sister.

"My cousin Nadia found a taxi to take her to Damascus the day after tomorrow," she said. "From there, she will fly to Dubai. We know you're trying to leave as well, so we thought you could go together. You know Nadia so you could look out for each other."

Having grown up with Elyssar, Rouba had become close to the entire Awwad clan. Their love and support for each other never ceased to amaze her, especially when it extended to family members' friends. When you needed something, you could go to one of them, knowing they would ask each other for help until they sorted you out. Rouba had come to rely on them more than on her own family at times.

"Is it safe for Nadia to take this trip? Isn't she pregnant?"

Nadia was married to an Englishman and they lived in Dubai. She had come to Lebanon to spend the summer with her toddler son and deliver her second baby. Her husband had been planning to join her in Lebanon close to the delivery date but, with the war, they'd found themselves stranded in different countries.

"She's seven months pregnant so it's not ideal," Reem replied. "But her husband is very worried."

"Poor Englishman, he must be panicking about his family being in the middle of all of this."

"Actually, he's relatively cool about it. He said he has relatives in Ireland and they faced similar situations in the eighties," Reem replied.

"Well, that settles it. Thank you all so much. When all this is over your entire family is invited to my divorce party."

Maya was wrapped up in the preparations for her wedding. This is *The Reveal* she told herself, as she sat in the designer's studio, waiting for her dress to be brought out.

She could barely hide her excitement. The sales assistants had done nothing but tell her about the beauty of the dress since she'd arrived. The anticipation made her extra chatty, and she talked about everything and nothing with her mother and Carine, the wedding planner.

As they sipped the last drops of their Turkish coffee, a woman who introduced herself as Joyce appeared, cradling a mountain of ivory-coloured fabric and frills.

Maya shrieked, jumping to her feet to inspect the dress.

"Are you the bride?" Joyce asked.

Maya gave her a wide smile.

"Yes."

"May God's name protect you," Joyce replied. "You're beautiful. The dress will shine on you."

Maya knew that the wedding industry dictated that anyone working in the field, that is to say, designers, hairdressers, wedding planners, event managers etc., profusely complimented brides-to-be; but the flattery still tickled a chord. She giggled.

Joyce made a show of dressing the mannequin at the centre of the room and turned towards Maya. "What do you think?" she asked. "Please have a look here before we try it on you."

"It's gorgeous," Maya replied, her voice submerged by the ecstatic shrieks coming from her mother and Carine. "I'm glad we selected this shade of white."

The dress looked even better than she'd imagined; the rich fabric came down from the shoulders in a flattering wide V that overlapped on the chest, curved nicely at the waist then widened in a mixture of textile and gauze over the hips and legs, ending in a five-foot train.

Maya congratulated herself for selecting Zahy Rammini as her dress designer. He had great taste and enough edginess to create something special but not over the top.

Her mother and Carine raved about each detail as they went around the mannequin, examining it from every angle. Glowing with pleasure at the reactions, Joyce invited Maya to go behind the curtain.

"We'll call Zahy when you're dressed," she added. "It's his best work. He told me after your initial fitting that you look like a model, but better because you're the real thing."

The never ending compliments didn't bother Maya at all. She undressed in a hurry and stood with her arms spread out as Joyce and an assistant dressed her up. The women busied themselves around her, ignoring the questions from the other side of the curtain:

"So! How does it look?"

"Does it fit you well?"

Joyce kneeled to work on the bottom of the dress for a few more minutes then spread the train behind Maya and fluffed it. Taking out the pins she held between her lips she declared:

"We're ready for Zahy."

Maya hid her smirk at Joyce's solemn expression. She looked like a Maitre D' announcing the imminent arrival of an emperor.

The assistant left the room to fetch Zahy, and Joyce gestured at Maya to stay in place. Maya grunted, eager to get to a mirror but Joyce's glare kept her in check. They clearly didn't want anyone to see the dress before the big man arrived.

The assistant reappeared, holding the door open for Zahy, who came in flanked by two of his "directors". All three men wore black satin shirts and equally shiny black skinny jeans. They looked like they had reinforced their tans with a substantial dose of foundation; but while the other two sported spiky, highlighted hair and follicle free faces, Zahy had a shaved head and goatee. Quite an attractive man, if you were into super sophisticated gay types.

"Maayaaaa, darling, it's so good to see you," Zahy exclaimed as he hugged her. "I am sooo happy you could make it today."

"Thank you for doing a fitting under the circumstances," she replied.

From what Maya had read in fashion magazines lately, Zahy seemed set for the big time both in the Arab world and the international scene. Several Arab pop singers had worn his dresses in recent months and he had been granted a spot in the next Paris fashion week.

"We can't let the crazy people ruin our lives," Zahy said as he appraised her from head to toe with a critical eye. "We have to keep going. At least we cheer people up by making them beautiful."

The directors stood a few meters away observing her with the same critical look.

Maya's mother couldn't wait any longer on the other side of the curtain and she materialized in front of her daughter, looking emotional.

"Mrs Awwad, how are youuu?" Zahy gave her the same squeeze he'd just bestowed on Maya. "You look fabulous as usual. I forget you're Maya's mother, not her sister."

"Zahy, you're too kind," her mother replied, eyes set on her daughter. "So how do you find the dress?"

"It's beautiful of course," Zahy answered. "How can it not be, on such a gorgeous bride?"

But somehow, his tone contradicted his words. His eyes were glued to Maya's stomach.

"Jooooooyce!" he commanded. "Pins, please."

Joyce jumped, holding out a silver box containing a red velvet cushion carrying pins of all sizes and shapes. Zahy kneeled beside Maya. "Please can you turn around?" he asked.

She obeyed and felt him pulling and flattening the fabric around her waist. "Joooooyce," he said again. "I need the measuring tape and the bride's chart."

The extraordinarily efficient Joyce produced both items. The two directors moved from their observation post and kneeled next to Zahy. Maya felt the three of them poking at the same point at the bottom of her back, and heard them exchange hushed comments.

"Is everything OK?" she asked.

Zahy ignored her and measured her waist, then hips. He stood up, checking the chart he had in hand.

"Jooooyce," he asked, "did someone make a mistake in Miss Awwad's measurements last time?"

Maya's heart raced. How could anyone take bad measurements? And what did that mean for her dress?

Joyce turned red as a tomato. "Ummm... I... think you noted them," she ventured.

If Joyce's answer embarrassed Zahy he didn't show it. He checked his chart again and gave Maya a nasty look.

"Is there a problem?" she asked.

"Yes, there is a problem!" he replied. "I don't know how you let it happen, but there's been a change in your measurements. The dress doesn't fit any more."

Of all the bombs that Maya had heard in the past few weeks, this must have been the loudest.

"W... what do you mean?" she asked.

"Have you gained weight?" Zahy accused.

"Err, maybe... I mean... Yes, it's possible. We're sitting around doing nothing all day, so... I've been munching. I haven't weighed myself."

"You've put on two dress sizes around the waist," Zahy said, livid.

Her mother stepped in to the rescue. "It can't be that terrible," she said. "Can't we adapt the design?"

"Look at this, Mrs Awwad," Zahy replied. "The back was supposed to be bare, until here."

Pulling Maya by the shoulder, he made her pivot and poked at her lower back, almost hurting her. "But now several centimetres have been added on her stomach and her back. There's no way we can bring it smoothly down her back now, not with this cut and fabric."

Maya leaned against the wall to recover from the shock as the implications of Zahy's words dawned on her. Lifting the gown, she rushed to the corner of the room where opposing mirrors allowed her to see a 360 degree reflection of herself. The problem area jumped at her the moment she saw her reflection. The fabric didn't wrap correctly around her waist, and the back looked awkward, cheap and badly tailored. Clearly, the result of a two-size difference as Zahy said.

"What do you suggest we do?" she begged.

"I suggest for the bride not to be packing up the kilos before her wedding," Zahy snapped. "Normally, brides *lose* weight."

Maya fought back the tears. How could this be happening? Her dream gown looked terrible and the designer didn't know how to fix it.

Zahy turned to her mother, completely ignoring her. "I need to think about this, Mrs Awwad," he said. "I'd have to redesign from scratch."

"She can lose the weight," Maya's mother said.

"That would mean more fittings. My staff and I have other clients. I'm not sure we have the time."

Without giving anyone the chance to react, he left the room, his two directors at his heels, in a swirl of shimmering black satin.

Chapter 11

Maya and her mother drove back to Rantour in complete silence. As soon as she parked the car, Maya headed to the villa next door. She couldn't face spending another minute with her mother, knowing they'd both be obsessing over her expanding waistline. The cousinettes were watching TV, but they immediately switched it off when she entered.

"What?" she asked, as she saw the odd look on their faces. "You're acting like I just caught you watching porn."

"Don't be silly." Reem replied. But they all went silent again, squirming in their seats.

Maya grabbed the remote control and pressed "play". The DVD restarted, playing *Sex and the City*: the episode where everything goes wrong in Charlotte's wedding.

The irony made her laugh. "Were you really watching this, or are you doing this to me on purpose?" she asked, letting herself fall (and now, aware of her two extra dress sizes, she realized she fell heavily) on the couch. She didn't really expect an answer, but something in the looks that her cousins exchanged made her cringe.

Oh God, they knew already. Who could have told them? Could it have been Carine, the wedding planner? The only other possibility would be her mother, but she hadn't left her side since they'd been at the studio.

"OK," she said. "Who told you? It can't be the wedding planner. I would hope she has some sense of client-planner confidentiality. Is it my mom?"

"Yes, it's your mother. She texted us from the car so that we wouldn't harass you with questions when you arrived," Reem replied.

Once again, Maya found herself in awe of her family network: everyone knew everything in the blink of an eye.

"Don't worry about it," Reem said, "You can lose the weight quickly. We'll cut out the junk food and you can work out in the garden. We'll exercise with you."

Knowing her cousins, Maya knew they would be finding the situation hilarious but didn't dare say it for fear of upsetting her even more.

"Who said I want to lose weight?" she replied. "Actually, I'm going to get myself a big bowl of popcorn and a drink right now. Who wants to join me?"

"We'll all join you," Cousinette Dana said. "After we got your mother's message, we tried our dresses on, and guess what? Nothing fits any more. We're all too fat."

Unaware of the dress drama in Lebanon, Elyssar stood outside Paul's door a few hours later, twisting the straps of her purse around her fingers. How unwise of her to go to a near stranger's apartment in a foreign country without telling anyone. If Paul did turn out to be a serial killer, he'd just gotten lucky. He could murder her in the most horrible way and no one would ever link them. The police barely had any records that she existed; they'd never identify the body...

Pushing the idea away, she rang the bell. A dog barked from behind the door. Elyssar took a step back, resisting the urge to get into the elevator and run out of the building as fast as her Manolos allowed.

Paul opened the door wearing a dark grey T-shirt and blue jeans. His hair was still wet and the scent of aftershave filled the hallway. Not the overstated musky stuff, something more subtle and sophisticated. The kind of smell women want to wrap themselves in and never come out of for air.

The amused flicker in his eye brought her back to earth; he'd caught her staring again. She looked away over his shoulder. "Is the dog as big as its voice?" she asked. "I'm worried a monster is about to emerge from behind you."

Paul laughed. "He wishes!" He motioned for her to come in. "We won't be long here. I've booked us for lunch nearby."

As soon as she'd taken a step into the doorway, a seven pound ball of black and tan hair shot towards her, yapping louder and louder as it circled around her feet, almost making her lose her balance. Elyssar laughed and leaned against the wall.

"Meet my roommate, Vix," Paul said, picking up the Yorkshire Terrier. "He likes to embarrass me in front of company."

The little dog's eyes sparkled with excitement as he fidgeted in Paul's arms.

Paul led Elyssar inside the hallway; she stopped to admire the green stone structure that occupied most of the space.

"It's an abstract cubic sculpture," he said. "I bought it in a gallery here in New York; it's by an artist from Zimbabwe..."

"It's beautiful."

"I like to collect art from around the world," he replied.

The intricate green sculpture comprised interlaced columns. The tallest ended in a pointed shape, almost touching the ceiling. Elyssar couldn't resist running her finger on the stone.

"It's Malacite," Paul explained. "The stone is very hard to carve. That's why I love it. The amount of work that went into creating the lines amazes me."

"It looks like it's been glazed," Elyssar said.

"It's the natural colour of the stone."

Paul put the now calmer Vix on the floor. "Would you like me to show you the rest of the apartment?"

"Sure."

She felt something brush her hand. Instinctively, she jumped backwards, knocking the sculpture which would have tilted over had Paul not leapt to hold it in place.

"I was just trying to hold your hand, Elyssar."

"I'm so sorry. I don't know what got into me. Maybe it's the way we met. I mean, how do I know you're not a dangerous criminal or that you don't have a wife or girlfriend somewhere?"

The dejection on that handsome face of his sent her guilt-ometer through the roof.

"You mentioned something like this last night and I thought we'd clarified it. What do I need to do to prove to you that all I really want is to meet someone?"

"You don't have to do anything." She held out her hand. "I'd like nothing more than a tour around your apartment."

He gave her a full on Paul smile: generous lips, white teeth and eyes that sparkled like green marbles, linking her back to the green glow of the hallway.

"Let's start with the living room."

He led her from one room to the next, explaining his decision to ensure he had nothing but white all around his home: walls, furniture, bathroom tiles, kitchen counters. Even the china, the sound system and the frame of the plasma screen had all been carefully selected to suit the limited colour scheme. The only touch of colour beyond the green sculpture came from the dark wooden floors, the abstract paintings in the lounge and the bright orange dining table.

"This is my favourite piece," he said sliding a sensuous hand on the table top. "Thirties Art Deco. I had to battle a dozen serious bidders for this one in Saint-Germain-des-Prés."

From the sound of it, St-Germain-des-Prés referred to a global Mecca for furniture collectors. Elyssar had a faint idea that a district in Paris carried this name, but played it safe by saying nothing. She nodded in silence, pretending to grasp the importance of the piece of wood in front of her.

"Come, I'll show you the bedrooms."

Bedrooms? The word alone sent every drop of blood in her system rushing up to her cheeks.

Paul grinned. "Elyssar, God knows I would like to take you to bed. But not just yet."

Blushing even more, she grinned and followed as he showed her the white guestroom and then led her to the master bedroom. She gasped at the sheer size of it and the faultless décor. A brown wooden desk stood beneath the window, carrying an open laptop which was surrounded by abstract statuettes, made of thin metal. She decided not to ask about them, in case they turned out to be another famous art form that she knew nothing about. She made a mental note to scour the internet for a crash course on modern art.

"See?" he said. "No wife or girlfriend in sight." He went to a door at the other end of the room and opened it. "And in case you still have any suspicions, here's my closet. Nothing but a lonely man's clothes in there."

Laughing, she went to the closet and looked. It turned out to be a fully fledged dressing room. Shirts and jackets hung on the main wall, organized by colour, starting with the dark ones to the left all the way to white at the far right. The trousers had their own section. One wall was dedicated to shoes and another to the biggest mirror she'd ever seen outside of a fashion store.

"No sign of a woman living here," she said. "But your closet would make any female green with envy."

As she turned, she noticed a fireplace opposite the bed. "I love fireplaces," she said. "It must feel great to light one in the New York winter."

"There's nothing like being warm by the fire while the city lies outside your window, covered with snow." He smiled at her. "I remember reading that Lebanon is quite the ski destination in the winter."

"It's not France or Switzerland, but we have some decent slopes."

"Can you ski near your mountain house?"

"Not really. But we get a bit of snow every winter and when we do, I make it a point to spend the weekend there just so I can see my father light the fire. He's like a child playing with his favourite toy." As she spoke, she felt tears rushing to her eyes. Being at Paul's house must have made her all emotional and stupid. She turned her face away, hoping he wouldn't notice, but he put a hand on her shoulder.

"We haven't spoken about this," he said, "and I'm not sure whether you like to talk about it at all, but every politician in the world seems to be working to resolve the situation in Lebanon right now. It's bound to get better."

"I know." She smiled, but kept her face turned because she could tell her nose had turned red and felt a sniffle or two coming her way. She rushed back towards the living room to get a tissue. Paul followed her.

"So how about we grab that lunch?" he asked.

They left the apartment and Paul led her to Central Park, which was only a block away.

"I thought you'd enjoy lunch here," he said. "We'll have a little walk on our way to the restaurant."

Despite the heat, Elyssar loved wondering through the park by Paul's side. She'd never been to this part of Central Park before.

"This is where real New Yorkers come." Paul explained. "The other parts are for tourists. You should see it in the winter. Residents of the Upper East Side come here to get some fresh air. The lake freezes and there are almost no tourists at all."

Elyssar laughed. "Now I can claim to hang out with real New Yorkers. This will impress everyone back home."

They followed the side of the lake and she stopped herself from commenting any further on the beauty of the place, for fear of sounding 'touristy'. People were walking their dogs or sat on benches enjoying the surroundings. Boats floated in the water, their passengers taking time in-between rows to enjoy the moment.

Elyssar's phone rang, sending her heart racing when she saw her father's name on the screen.

"Is everything OK?" she asked.

"Yes, all is well," her dad's voice replied. "I'm calling to check on you."

Elyssar said a silent prayer of gratitude. The fear of getting a call from Lebanon with bad news haunted her day and night.

"I'm great," she replied, smiling at Paul to let him know that all was fine.

Although he hadn't understood what she said in Arabic, he'd seen how worried she was when she picked up the call and was looking at her with concern.

"You have to be careful in New York," her father said. "Stay close to your hotel and don't go out at night."

They exchanged a few more words, Elyssar trying to convince her father that she wouldn't be mugged at the next street corner.

"It was my dad checking on me," she explained to Paul when she hung up the phone.

"Is everyone back home safe?"

"Yes," She replied. "They're worried about me. They think New York is dangerous."

Paul laughed. "They live in a war zone and they think New York is dangerous?"

"Yes, isn't it hilarious? I used to be scared of New York too, until I travelled here for the first time a few years ago. I guess we've watched too many thrillers set in this city."

"How did your eyes get so green?" Paul asked, taking her by surprise.

"Excuse me?"

"Where did you get these changing eyes? It's like they change colors. Last night, I thought they were hazel, but now they're almost the color of jade."

"I inherited them from my mother." she said, realizing the compliment got her batting her lashes like one of those female cartoon characters in Tom and Jerry. "If you think mine change colors, you should see hers. When we were kids we could tell how angry she was by her eye colour."

"Well, she did a good job passing them on to you."

They'd just arrived outside the restaurant. "This is the Boathouse," Paul explained. "The terrace will be full of tourists so we'll eat by the bar."

Elyssar looked at the wooden building. It had a nice outside deck right on the water and the rest of the building boasted floor to ceiling windows. Paul led her through a little walkway to the entrance where a host invited them to have a few drinks until their table became available. As they stood by the bar, Elyssar's phone beeped with a message from Rouba.

"*U in Dubai yet?*"

"*No*" Elyssar keyed back, "*Decided 2 stay in NYC.*"

"*How come?*" Rouba asked in return.

"*Enjoying the weather.*"

Rouba would probably not buy this excuse. But if Elyssar mentioned anything about meeting a man in New York, her friend would call and want to know all about it immediately.

"*What about u,*" Elyssar texted. "*Ready 2 leave?*"

"*My taxi comes in a few hours.*"

"*Take care & text me when you arrive 2 Syria. Luv, xx.*"

As she put the phone back in her purse, Elyssar realized that several patrons were staring at them. She glanced down at herself; no open zipper, no broken heels and her pedicure was still in place; Paul looked flawless as usual. One man in particular wouldn't take his eyes off them. She looked back at him, hoping he would turn away, but he kept checking them both out from head to toe. Oblivious to the little drama, Paul gazed at the tables near by.

Another couple walked in and all eyes, including Paul's, moved onto them.

Oh, Elyssar thought, finally getting it. This is people-watching, just like we do back home. Glad to know we have such a fine tradition in common with the citizens of New York.

Chapter 12

It was three in the morning Lebanon time when Rouba kissed her mother goodbye in Kafarneem and got into the taxi. As the old Mercedes took off, she turned and gave her mom a thumbs up and a smile. She meant it as a reassuring gesture, but somehow it came out looking defiant. Her mother's eyes teared up as she waved goodbye.

No one else from the family had come out to bid her farewell, but Rouba tried not to think about it.

"We need an hour to get to Rantour," the taxi driver said.

"Great, thank you," Rouba replied absent mindedly.

"I will take a few detours," he continued. "They will make the road longer but safer."

Rouba was relieved. She didn't want to take any unnecessary risk.

"It was quite bad yesterday," the driver continued. "A civilian convoy was attacked on its way to the border. I had passengers and we had to take a diversion. They missed their flight out of Damascus airport."

Rouba took a closer look at him. Early fifties, probably the father of a large family, maybe even a grandfather.

"Are you on the road every day? It must be incredibly dangerous."

The man shrugged. "It is," he answered. "But I'm making per day more than I would normally make per month. Today, I will drop you at noon and I have another load of passengers in the evening." He sighed, peering through the windscreen at the road ahead. "My wife and kids don't want me doing this, they say my life is worth more than all the money in the world, but my son will start university this year and I have two other children in high school. I've borrowed a lot to pay for their education."

Funny how wars bring to the surface all the drama in people's lives. If Rouba had been a passenger in this same taxi under normal circumstances, she would have never had this conversation or known that this family provider put his life at risk every day to pay for his children's education.

"I'm sure your children appreciate what you're doing for them," she said, humbled.

His face lit up in pride.

"My eldest has already been accepted to study computers at university, and my second son is first in his class in math. My daughter loves science and wants to be a pharmacist."

Rouba smiled. Difficult to find a parent in Lebanon who didn't tell you their kids were extraordinarily intelligent and the top of their class. She just hoped this man's children deserved the sacrifices he was making.

The old Mercedes whizzed up the road. "This car is twenty-eight years old," the driver explained. "But I just installed a brand new engine on it."

They reached Rantour in less than an hour and pulled up in the Awwad property before dawn. Rouba did her best to come out of the car without making any noise but as soon as she set foot on the ground, the doors to all four villas opened, and people came out one by one. She recognized Elyssar's parents, aunts and uncles, as well as the cousinettes.

All were in their sleeping attire except for Nadia and her son, Ryan. Nadia had always struck Rouba as a bit of a stress bunny but today she looked positively terrified... and about to pop her second child. Rouba gave her a hug that she hoped would be encouraging.

"Hey there! How is my travel partner?"

Nadia smiled, or to be precise, she twisted her face in an attempt to smile but looked on the verge of tears. Everyone around them remained grave and quiet. Nadia's mother held a tissue against her nose. A major cry-athon must have just taken place.

Rouba went over to kiss Nadia's mother hello. "You seem worried, Aunt Elham," she said. "But I just drove from Kafarneem and things are quiet this morning. We'll be at the border in no time."

The words she hoped would appease Aunt Elham had the opposite effect. She burst out crying. "We're glad that you're with them, Rouba," Aunt Elham said when she regained control. "You're a dear friend of the family and we trust you'll help them on the journey."

The "you're a dear friend of the family" speeches were usually reserved for weddings and funerals. A jolt of panic ran through Rouba as the size of the responsibility crystallised in her mind: she was about to embark on a dangerous road with a pregnant woman and a baby to look after. "I wouldn't worry about us," she lied. Pointing at baby Ryan who was asleep in his mother's arms, she continued, "We have an angel in the car."

Again, she'd said the wrong thing. Aunt Elham's sobs doubled in intensity and this time Nadia joined in. Everyone else seemed very close to tears as well. The Awwads cried at everything that involved a family member, even happy events.

Rouba stood fidgeting, terribly uncomfortable and wishing she'd never opened her mouth, but Reem came to her rescue. "Don't mind us," she said. "You know we cry at everything."

Rouba smiled. "I know, I've attended some of your weddings, remember?"

Nadia's brother finished installing a car seat with the help of the taxi driver and loaded the luggage into the trunk. They were ready to go. Rouba waved everyone a quick goodbye and, expecting a new eruption of weeping, got in the car with no further ado. She watched Nadia install her baby in the car seat and then go for a final round of hugs. As predicted, not a pair of eyes remained dry.

The driver seemed relieved when Nadia finally got into her seat and he was able to drive off at last. Rouba reckoned the long goodbyes had delayed them more than anticipated. He was calm, yet Rouba could tell from his whitened knuckles and his sudden gear changes that he was pushing the old Mercedes as hard as he could to make up for the lost time.

Nadia snuffled, patting her eyes with a tissue. Rouba reached across the baby seat to give her hand a reassuring squeeze. There was silence in the car until they came to a sharp turn that seemed to take them down the valley.

"We'll take the Ghaboun road," the driver said. "It's snaky, but beautiful."

Rouba repressed a smile. He obviously wanted to use this road because it was relatively secure, but didn't want to say it in front of the distraught Nadia.

The road turned out to be in fact more of an un-kept pathway. It couldn't have seen more than one coat of asphalt in the past thirty years, making the old Mercedes wiggle like a tractor. The brakes screamed as they manoeuvred the steep declines. Rouba remembered visiting this area on a school trip. After they arrived at the bottom of the valley, they'd have to climb up the Shouf mountains to the other side. She hoped the allegedly new engine would hold up.

"This area has some excellent fig orchards," the driver said, "and a lot of water. I've brought my family here many times for a weekend picnic. No matter how hot a day it is, the springs are fresh and the trees so big that it's cool in the shade."

Rouba and Nadia politely acknowledged his words as they looked around. The area was indeed beautiful and unspoiled; worth exploring someday.

"The sun is rising!" The driver pointed to the top of the mountain in front of them. "Look at those colors."

He was right; the rainbow of colors emerging from behind the peaks was breathtaking, making the mountains look like curved shadows.

"This road was built in the eighties...."

The driver seemed intent on delivering his geography lesson. Every now and then, Nadia regarded her son with apprehension, worried that the monologue would wake him up, but he remained sound asleep.

Rouba poked her, whispering "I think we get a free guided tour with the evacuation."

Nadia sneered. "If we die today we'll be that much more educated," she said.

"We're not going to die today," Rouba said, holding Nadia's hand. "We've survived worse. The only thing I'm worried about is you going into labour in this car. I know how to escape bombs but I sure as hell don't know how to deliver babies."

"Oh, I know how to deliver babies," the driver interjected. "My first son was born during the civil war and we had to deliver him at home."

"See?" Rouba said. "We get a free tour guide *and* an experienced midwife! This taxi ride is excellent value for money!"

Both Rouba and the driver laughed but Nadia didn't find it amusing. She just stared out the window, hands clasped on her lap.

They followed the sinuous road all the way down the mountain and then upwards again on the opposite slope. The way was so narrow, it looked barely wide enough for one car. But somehow, when they crossed other cars, and on one or two occasions even a pickup truck, the road accomodated both vehicles.

Little Ryan woke up, crying.

"Look at him," Nadia said. "There's something wrong. He looks so pale."

Rouba looked closely at the little face. If anything, it was red because he was crying so hard.

"He doesn't look pale to me." she said, "He must be ..."

The vomit stopped her in the middle of the sentence, hitting her in full force on the face. Nadia shrieked, and the driver stopped the car to see what had happened. His first concern was to check that nothing had splashed on his car seat. The moment he made sure that all of it had hit Rouba, he seemed barely able to stop himself from laughing.

Rouba didn't move. The warm substance trickled down her hair and face as it dripped onto her blouse. She held her mouth as tightly closed as possible to keep it from going past her lips. It smelled deadly.

Ryan had stopped crying and stared at her, vomit trickling from his chin.

Nadia finally recovered her senses and took out a pack of baby wipes. She handed a few to Rouba. "This should help you clean up as much as possible," she said apologetically.

Rouba wiped as much as she could as fast as she could, then she stepped out of the car and looked at herself in the window to assess the damage. Not only did she now smell like vomit *and* a baby's bum, but the beige substance was still well and truly entangled in her hair, gluing it to her scalp.

The stench made her stomach turn. "I feel like throwing up too," she groaned.

Nadia followed her out of the car. "I'm so sorry," she said. "What can I do?"

"Find me a shower?"

Rouba forced a little smile, she didn't want Nadia to feel guilty about the incident.

"I... have water and soap in Ryan's baby bag. Would that help?"

"I didn't seriously mean a shower," Rouba replied, trying to find a solution before she fainted of asphyxiation.

"With a baby, I've learned you can clean up anything anywhere if you have a couple of wipes and a little water and soap," Nadia said. "We just need to wash your hair and your chest. And then you can change into another shirt from your suitcase."

Rouba looked around her. With no other cars in sight, Nadia's offer made sense. She could step off the road to get cleaned up and changed in the woods. "Fine," she said. "I've never had an alfresco bath, might as well start today."

Nadia got the baby bag out of the car and somehow managed also to carry a howling Ryan in his car seat. She explained to the driver that they had to go for a few minutes. He checked his watch.

"We're running very late," he said. "I have another pick up in the afternoon, so please make it very quick otherwise I won't be able to get you there. I would have to turn back to Beirut to pick up the second load of passengers on time."

Rouba took the bag from Nadia and they walked into the woods with Ryan, who was screaming again, until they reached a safe distance where the pine trees would hide them from view.

"Take your shirt off," Nadia said. "And hold your head down, I will pour water and you can wash your hair with the soap."

"Thank God it's summer," Rouba said as she got out of her T-shirt. "They timed the war well. Imagine having to go through this in the winter."

Nadia didn't reply, she put Ryan on the ground, kicking and yelling but well secured in his seat, and opened a big bottle of water. "This is the only one I have," she said. "So we can't use all of it. We need to be smart about how we do this."

Now wearing only her bra, Rouba bent over while Nadia let water dribble from the bottle onto her hair.

"I can hear Emm Kemel," Rouba said. "Do you think they're filming us right now?"

Nadia didn't reply.

"The guy watching the tapes will think that girl-on-girl action happens in the woods of Lebanon." Rouba added.

Nadia groaned, clearly not enjoying the jokes. Elyssar would have laughed, Rouba thought.

Rouba did her best to wash her hair with a bar of soap, before Nadia helped her rinse it.

Maybe they didn't notice the sound getting closer, or maybe the helicopter gunship materialized from nowhere, but within a split second, they could hear nothing other than the maddening rumble of a helicopter. Before they even realized it, they were both sprinting through the trees towards the road. Rouba clutched Ryan in his chair, while Nadia did her best to keep up.

The driver came running towards them, out of breath. "You have to get out of the woods," he shouted. "They've seen movement under the trees and they think you're military. They'll shoot any time. Run faster!"

Rouba handed Ryan to him. "Take him and go to the car. I will stay with her."

The driver grabbed the baby seat and dashed, Rouba ran back towards Nadia.

"Where is he taking Ryan?" Nadia screamed.

"To the road, it's safer there," Rouba answered. "We need to get out from under the trees. Can you run faster?"

Nadia shook her head, she could barely breathe. "I'm running as fast as I can," she said.

Her belly was blocking her from seeing the ground properly and Rouba was scared she might trip. She grabbed Nadia by the arm to help her keep her balance and move faster. The gunship seemed to be directly over them, the noise of its propellers making the ground shake. Rouba pulled Nadia until they arrived at the road. Nadia came to a standstill as soon as they stepped in the open on the asphalt.

"I can't...I can't..." she repeated, leaning over to catch her breath, hands on her abdomen. Rouba observed her, heart thudding. This run couldn't have been good for the unborn baby.

She half expected Nadia's waters to break and a baby to come out screaming any moment.

She didn't dare raise her head to see where the helicopter had gone, but the noise had faded and the ground wasn't shaking any more. "Are you OK?" she asked, her hand on Nadia's back. "The helicopter has gone. We're safe now. Do you want to sit down?"

Nadia shook her head, tears now streaming down her face. "Where's my son?" she sobbed.

Rouba's mind was filled with images of a premature labour right here on the side of the road.

"He's safe. We're all going to be fine, Nadia," she said. She looked around, trying to get a sense of where they were in relation to where they'd left the car a few moments earlier. She couldn't see it anywhere, but since only one road went through this area, the driver and Ryan couldn't be far. "Let's go this way," she said, pointing downwards to the left. "We need to find Ryan and the driver. Do you think you can walk?"

Nadia nodded and Rouba held her by the elbow, walking down the steep incline with care. Nadia shrieked in relief when they took a turn and saw the old Mercedes parked a dozen meters away. The driver was leaning against it, carrying an agitated Ryan.

"Keep your arms away from your body," Rouba said. "In case they're still watching us. To show we're not carrying any weapons."

"OK." Nadia had regained a bit of her breath and stopped crying.

"I know why they didn't shoot at us," Rouba continued, somehow finding solace in her own words as they reached the car. "They must have seen we're with a pregnant woman and a little boy."

"Errrr... I don't think that's what did it," Nadia replied, giving Rouba's chest a pointed look. "It's your wet bra."

Oh God! In her panic, Rouba had completely forgotten she'd taken off her T-shirt. She looked down at her chest and barely suppressed a scream: soaked in the water that Nadia had poured on her and the sweat caused by their run, her white bra had turned transparent; her nipples couldn't have been more visible if she'd attached laser beams onto each one of them. Mortified, she realized the driver's face had gone crimson as he kept his eyes firmly on the ground.

Elyssar was facing a sartorial crisis of a different nature. Had her feet not hurt so much from walking around New York in her stilettos, she would have been convinced that she'd been floating on cloud happiness all day as they returned to Paul's apartment that evening.

After they finished lunch, he'd taken her for a long walk around town, acting the consummate host, explaining the city's history and development.

Elyssar couldn't remember a time where she'd been this infatuated with anyone. It felt like a galaxy of stars shining on her soul.

They sat next to each other on the sofa. Elyssar was tempted to take her shoes off and massage her feet, but she didn't feel comfortable enough to do it. Instead, she slid her feet out the back of the shoes to relieve some of the pain.

Her heart skipped a beat when Paul leaned over to hug her.

"I'm having an amazing time," he said, "Today was fabulous."

"Me too. Thank you for showing me around."

"Did you think yesterday before we met that we would end up doing so much together?"

"Definitely not," Elyssar replied. "I still can't believe all of this has really happened. I know I'm repeating myself when I say it, but it's all surreal: the ad, the blind date, spending the entire evening together and today..."

Paul got up and kneeled by the fireplace.

"What are you doing?" she asked.

"Lighting the fire."

"Are you serious?"

"Yap."

"But it must be over thirty degrees centigrade. I don't know how much that is in Fahrenheit, but it's *hot*."

"I want to light it while you're here so that you'll remember a certain fireplace in New York when you light your own in Lebanon in a few months' time," He turned towards her and his face creased into the most irresistible smile. "Also, I figured this could be one way to get you to take your clothes off."

Elyssar felt herself blush.

Once the fire was on, Paul came back to sit by her side, sweat forming on his forehead. Elyssar wiped it off and looked back towards the fireplace. "This is so mesmerising," she said. "I don't think I could ever be bored of watching fireplaces. Even in the middle of the summer when the room is boiling hot," she added, winking.

Paul seemed absorbed in his thoughts. "I've been thinking," he said after a few minutes of silence while they both watched the flames. "You said your vacation starts soon. Why don't you stay in New York instead of going to Europe?"

"I have to be in Paris for Madonna's concert."

"There's a couple of weeks left until the concert. Why don't you stay here until then?"

Paul paused, then turned to her. "Ellie, I can't imagine letting you go," he looked intensely into her eyes. "These two days with you have been wonderful; you can't just take off like that."

The room sweltered. With his pleading green eyes turned to her, and the little drops of sweat on his forehead Paul was so magnetic, he couldn't be real. Maybe she was still on that military ship and hallucinating from sea sickness.

Before she realized it, she'd leaned forward and kissed him. She'd never initiated a first kiss before, but his lips were so full and soft it felt like fireworks going off all over her body.

"I've been dying to do that all day," Paul whispered when she pulled her face away, "But I worried it might offend you."

Offend! The man didn't know his own talents. She could think of a lot of ways to describe his kiss but "offensive" didn't figure anywhere on the list. Wiping his forehead again with her hand, she came to a decision. "Maybe I can stay in New York for my two week vacation and go from here directly to Paris for the Madonna concert."

Paul grinned at her and, turning her hand in his, lowered his head to give her a long kiss on the palm. She shivered. "That's wonderful," he said, "I need to go to LA for three days but when I'm back I'll work short hours so we can spend time together every day."

"Are you sure you want to put up with me for that long?" she asked, smiling.

"Right now, it feels like I never want to let you go."

Elyssar thought her heart would stop from too much happiness.

Chapter 13

Elyssar didn't even notice the time passing.

"It's five a.m. Time for me to get ready for the airport." Paul said

Without realising it, they'd been up chatting all night, unable to stop talking. Paul had asked her a lot of questions about Lebanon and her family. He'd also told her about his own life, talking about his twenty year-old daughter, Ashley. She was only two years old when her parents divorced, so Paul hadn't been able to be as involved with her during her childhood as he would have liked. She'd recently moved to New York for her studies and the two of them were spending more time together.

Paul walked her downstairs and they headed towards Fifth Avenue, accompanied by a leashed Vix. The tiny dog ran in all directions, ecstatic to go out at this unusual time.

A taxi stopped almost as soon as they arrived to the corner.

"Thank you for everything," Elyssar said as she opened the car door. "I had the most amazing time."

Paul pulled her towards him and gave her a long kiss. "I can't wait to be back with you," he said in her ear. "These three days in LA will feel like a month."

Elyssar got into the taxi and he closed the door. As the car moved, she looked back at him through the window.

"Three days," he mimed, gesturing with three fingers open.

"Three days," she mimed back.

He turned to walk back towards his apartment. Twisting in her seat, Elyssar kept looking until she couldn't see him anymore. She knew she would always remember the sight of his silhouette walking with Vix in the early morning light. Most importantly, she would never forget the way he made her feel.

In Rantour, the slow dial-up connection wasn't helping Maya's mood, neither were the emails in her inbox. All the well-wishers wanted an update on the wedding: Was it still happening? Had the date changed? What about the venue? One friend, a girl she'd known since college, even asked about plans for her bachelorette party.

Maya stared at the TV. The news report showed footage of Condoleeza Rice arriving at Beirut's airport onboard a US army helicopter.

"American Secretary of State, Condolezza Rice, has just arrived in Beirut as part of her regional tour to discuss the current situation..." the announcer read.

The TV showed Rice coming out, all smiles, from the helicopter and giving a huge hug and two kisses on the cheek to the waiting Lebanese prime minister. Maya couldn't take it any more.

Adding all her Hotmail contacts to the recipient list of a new email message, she typed:

"Hi everyone,

Since you've all been so kindly asking, here is the update about our wedding: Our event planner, Condoleeza Rice, is currently holding different meetings to finalize the date and the venue. She will announce the plans in her next interview with CNN."

The news bulletin had moved to show more devastation in southern Lebanon. Today had been especially violent in the town of Bint Jbeil.

Maya resumed her typing.

"And we found THE hottest location for the bachelorette party: it's Bint Jbeil, South Lebanon. That place is ON FIRE! Men, women and children are welcome. See you there!

Love,

Maya and Ziad."

Liberated by her public outburst, she hit the send button. She sat at her desk, still staring at the PC. A moment later, Ziad called, pulling her back to reality.

"I see Condie is our new wedding planner," he said. "Do you think she'll be any good?"

"She'd better. She's probably behind this entire mess anyway."

Ziad went into a diatribe to tell her how he understood the stress that she was under and wished he could be in Lebanon to help. Must have been his way of calling her a bridezilla just like her cousins did.

"You know you don't have to go through all of this, right?" Ziad asked.

"I wish," Maya replied. "But I need to continue planning at best I can. Everyone is saying that the war will be over before September."

She heard a deep sigh on the other end of the phone line.

"I'm not so sure. I was just listening to a news report on the BBC and things don't look good. This whole thing could go on forever. Maybe we should seriously think about plan B."

Maya held her breath. "I didn't know we had a plan B."

"I mean that we can revisit the whole idea of having a wedding." Ziad said, his voice indicating that he knew he was treading dangerous territory. "We can organize for you to leave Lebanon. We can get married in any other country. We don't need to have a reception and ..."

He didn't get the chance to finish his sentence. Maya hung up the phone. She had nothing more to say or hear from him right now. Actually, she had nothing to say to anyone. She was going to close her phone and barricade herself in her room. Maybe she'd re-emerge when the world became a better place.

In Damascus, Rouba was unloading her suitcase and helping Nadia get her luggage out of the trunk. The airport's tiny parking lot seemed on the verge of sinking under the invasion of evacuees.

Their driver, who had disappeared a few minutes earlier, came back, accompanied by a porter. "Meet my friend Abou Imad," he said. "He and I have an agreement whereby he assists my passengers with their luggage."

Abou Imad, a very short, middle aged man with the thickest black hair Rouba had ever seen on a man, gave them a nod and started loading the luggage onto his trolley.

"We can never thank you enough," Rouba said, as she handed the driver his fare. She didn't have an envelope, so put the small stack of American dollar bills directly in his palm. The two women had decided that he deserved a lot more than the going rate, so they'd each put in an extra two hundred dollars. They couldn't show enough gratitude after he'd not only put up with their delays, but also risked his own life when he came after them in the woods.

The driver seemed to guess from the size of the stack that they'd left more than he asked for. "Thank you, madam Rouba and madam Nadia, " he said. "May God protect you on the rest of your journey."

"You too," a tearful Nadia replied. "And please say hello to your family. You told us so much about them that we feel like we know them."

The driver waved and got into the car with a last look towards them. As soon as the Mercedes was out of sight, Rouba hugged Nadia."See? I told you we'd make it."

Nadia smiled, her eyes tearing up even more. "Thank you so much. Having you around was the best support I could have had on this trip."

Rouba smiled. "Let's get in the line to check in," she said.

"Let's text everyone first to let them know we've arrived," Nadia reminded her, "And I have to call my husband."

"Good thought. Let me call my dear, soon to be ex-husband."

Nadia rolled her eyes to show she didn't appreciate divorce humor. Rouba winked at her and dialled Majed's number.

"We're here!" she said, hearing the triumphant relief in her own voice, "At Damascus airport."

"God be thanked for your safe arrival." Rouba noticed he sounded genuinely relieved. "How was the road?"

"Hmm, let me just say it was scenic," Rouba replied.

"Were you ever in any danger?"

She hesitated, but then decided to tell him about the episode in the woods - minus the part about her wet bra.

"You should have known better than to go under the trees," he said. "It's been made clear to civilians that they should stay out in the open at all times."

"So what was I supposed to do? Take my top off in the middle of the road?"

"You were supposed to stay home and wait this thing out." He spoke very softly. Rouba knew this tone of voice; he used it rarely and only when extremely furious.

"Just think about it this way," she replied. "You would have come out a winner either way: either I died and you became a free man, or I made it out and gave you your divorce."

"Don't forget that you're the one who wants this divorce by hook or by crook. Now if you excuse me I have work to do."

Majed knew Rouba hated nothing more than for someone to hang up the phone on her, and that's exactly what he did.

Rouba had forgotten all about her anger with Majed by the time she landed in Kuwait, a few hours later. The goodbyes with Nadia and Ryan as they boarded separate flights at Damascus airport had been a little teary, but now she was so relieved to be back that she had to hold herself from planting a kiss on the immigration officer's cheek.

"Rouba?" he asked, reading from her passport and shooting her an inquisitive glance.

"Yes, it's me."

She never understood why they had to do this at airports. She appreciated that the idea was to double check that the person carrying the passport was its real owner, but if you'd stolen someone's identity, surely you would have planned enough to answer to their first name...

The immigration officer stared at her a bit more and then started pushing buttons on his keyboard.

Rouba didn't remember passport control being so lengthy, but then again, she'd never been so eager to get into the country, so maybe it just felt longer.

"Your residency is cancelled," the officer said after a few minutes.

Rouba frowned at him, confused. "It's a permanent spouse residency. It doesn't expire."

"It's not expired," he corrected. "It's terminated. Did you have it cancelled before you left on your last trip?"

"No, I didn't."

"Well, that's what the system says."

"Please can you try again? The system may be slow or something."

"Wait here." He left his booth and headed into a backroom marked private.

Rouba gave the people behind her in the waiting line an apologetic smile and checked her watch. She'd organized for a hotel pickup and they wouldn't wait too long. This had better get resolved quickly.

It took the officer a good ten minutes to come back, during which time Rouba did her best to avoid the frustrated looks from those behind her.

"We called the Ministry of Interior to double check," he said. "They retrieved your file and confirmed that your residency has been cancelled by your sponsor. This isn't a system error."

He couldn't have sent worse chills through Rouba's body had he shot a bullet in her heart.

"My ... sponsor?" she repeated.

"Yes."

She caught a hint of compassion on the officer's stern features, maybe even a little embarrassment on her behalf. Since she was on a spouse permit, he must have known that the sponsor who cancelled her visa without even informing her was no other than her own husband.

Taking a deep breath, Rouba tried to stay calm. "So what do I do now?" she said.

"I'm afraid I can't allow you into Kuwait. You need to go to the transit desk to book a return flight."

"How could I do that?" She felt the tears rushing to her eyes, "I'm Lebanese, I can't go home."

"I know," he replied.

Kuwaiti passport control officers didn't exactly have a reputation for kindness, but he seemed to feel sorry for her and took a moment to think of a solution. "Why don't you try Dubai?" he asked. "They are taking in Lebanese refugees without a visa. There are flights every two or three hours from here."

Refugee? Rouba thought of Kuwait as her home. She'd moved here seven years ago to be with Majed, and had relocated her business from Beirut. Her small PR agency now employed twenty people and had branched into corporate consultancy. She also had dear friends here and a life that didn't depend on the association with Majed.

She thanked him and collected her passport, realizing she really had to let the other passengers go through and that pleading her case to him wouldn't get her anywhere.

Picking up her hand luggage, Rouba kept her head down as she walked back through the queue. She prayed to God not to let her run into anyone she knew. Not only was she too embarrassed to handle small talk or inquisitive questions, but she also looked terrible. Her hair had frizzed in the most horrible way following her impromptu shower in the woods of Ghaboun and the white t-shirt she'd hastily pulled out of her suitcase to replace the one Ryan vomited on was as wrinkled as an old raisin and not all that white anymore.

She walked back in shock towards the transit desk. Surely the ministry had made a mistake; Majed couldn't have possibly cancelled her residency. She just had to get him to call his friend, the Minister, to have her residency reinstated immediately.

She dialled his number but it went directly to voice mail. He must be in an elevator or the underground parking lot in his office building, she thought and waited for a few minutes to call back. Same thing, the line remained closed.

After a few attempts, she called his office number. His assistant picked up.

"Hi, Atheel, is my husband there please?" It felt a little awkward to be calling Majed "her husband", but the other option would have been to call him "my soon to be ex-husband" which was even more awkward.

"Mr. Majed is out of the country," Atheel replied. "He left this afternoon."

Rouba reeled in shock at the information. Why had he not mentioned anything when she spoke to him a few hours ago? "Do you know where he went?" she asked, trying to conceal her growing anger.

Atheel was obviously not happy to find herself stuck between a man and his wife who didn't even know he was travelling. "He didn't tell me."

"But you book his flights, you should know," Rouba said, frowning. She heard the sound of footsteps behind her and turned to see a group of passengers coming out of a gate nearby. From the mix of Westerners and Kuwaitis, she guessed they had just arrived from Europe. Two middle aged Kuwaiti women wearing traditional black robes walked past her. The scent of their Arabian oud perfume, with its combination of rose water, sandalwood, musk and amber lingered in the air long after they'd gone.

"Mr Majed took the jet," Atheel said.

Why would Majed suddenly decide to use the private jet that he shared with his brothers? He found it easier and more environmentally friendly to fly commercial, and hated having to coordinate schedules with his siblings and their travel-crazed families.

"Are you sure he didn't say why he took the sudden trip?"

"No, Missus Rouba. He called from the airport after he'd boarded."

"Do you have the number of the satellite phone on the jet?"

"Unfortunately, I don't have it. Mr. Majed never uses the jet and he doesn't like to be disturbed when he's flying so...." The poor woman clearly wanted out of this conversation and there was no point in pushing.

Rouba thanked her and hung up, dropping the phone back in her handbag. The urge to cry was almost irresistible. She hid her face in her hands. For a split second, she let a horrible thought creep in. What if he'd really cancelled her residency? That would explain why he'd taken off without a warning. She shook her head. No, not even Majed would do something like that when he knew she had nowhere else to go. He had more heart than to humiliate her in this way.

Rouba walked aimlessly around the terminal, trying Majed's number every few minutes, but the line stayed adamantly closed. She thought about calling her family or friends to vent, but she couldn't handle telling people she'd been denied entry to Kuwait. The ensuing analysis of her personal life would be too much to handle.

An hour later, Majed was still MIA and Rouba was starting to get funny looks from the duty free staff and other airport personnel. She decided to abandon hope of her dear husband rescuing her and went up to the transit desk. Thankfully, she found herself alone there – a long line would have obliterated her already frazzled nerves.

"Can I get a ticket to Dubai please?" she asked. "On the first available flight."

"Do you have a visa?" the ticket desk officer, a young Kuwaiti woman, asked.

"No, I don't... I..."

The woman cut her mid way through her sentence.

"Oh, you're Lebanese!" she said, having guessed from her accent. "No problem. You can get a visit visa at Dubai airport. They have opened it to refugees."

Could everyone please stop calling her a refugee?

Rouba decided not to say anything and just smiled at the woman as the latter fiddled with her PC.

"I hope everyone in your family is safe," the woman said, keeping her eyes on her monitor. She was around twenty five years old, and was dressed in typical fashion for a Kuwaiti woman of her, age in a white shirt, a fitted black jacket and a pair of loose jeans. Her hair was covered with a monogrammed designer scarf.

"Yes everyone is fine. Thank you for asking." Rouba replied.

"I heard that Nancy Ajram refused to leave and vowed to stay in Lebanon until the war is over," the woman continued.

Rouba didn't have much interest in pop stars, but she knew that Nancy Ajram, the Britney Spears of the Arab world, had a huge following in Gulf countries. "Oh really? That's good of her," she replied.

"She has a big heart," the woman said, her facing lighting up. "And she's brave, like all the Lebanese."

Thankfully, the woman seemed able to multitask and she managed to find a flight as they continued to chat.

"Please can I see some identification before I issue the ticket?"

Rouba handed her passport over the desk.

The woman flipped through it then looked up at Rouba. "Oh! You're Majed Al Riyyad's wife? My brother works in one of his companies." She looked even more interested in Rouba now, staring at her from head to toe.

Rouba hoped her face didn't reveal her irritation. Majed and his siblings held quite the celebrity status in Kuwait because of their wealth and the size of their businesses. In a small society that loved gossip, she often found herself the object of curiosity for being his young Lebanese wife. She thought she'd get used to the assumption that she was a gold digger, but it proved to be harder than she'd imagined and she'd spent the last seven years demonstrating to people that she could work hard and make her own money, thank you very much.

She'd also tried to control his kids' spending and once took them shopping during the sales. Her behaviour had scandalized Kuwaiti society so much that the owner of the country's largest designer boutique called Majed to ask if they were in any financial trouble.

As Rouba struggled to hide her impatience, the clerk flipped a few pages in the passport, probably to check Rouba's date of birth. But she suddenly looked back up at Rouba and stared, as if she'd just seen a revelation in the passport.

Rouba glanced at the document in her hand and saw it was open on the Kuwait residency page. "Can I have my passport back please?" she asked.

The woman obliged and there, on top of the Kuwait residency the newly added stamp jumped to Rouba's eyes: CANCELLED BY THE SPONSOR it said in bright red ink. The passport officer must have added this stamp when he'd taken her passport into the side room. No wonder the woman's sudden interest. The smell of solid gold gossip was reeking out of this page.

Majed and she had decided to keep the news of their divorce confidential until the paperwork came through. It would make it easier to break the news to their friends and business associates, but most importantly it would ensure that the children had time to adjust before everyone in Kuwaiti society quizzed them about the reasons behind their father's divorce.

A multitude of questions succeeded each other on the woman's face, but Rouba held her eye firmly, indicating that she expected the ticket to be issued with no further delays. She bet the woman would have a field day this evening with her family and friends, debating why Majed Al Riyyad had cancelled his wife's residency. Actually, she knew for a fact that the moment she turned her back, the news would be flying by SMS all over the country. In a day or two, juicy rumours would be circulating about the state of her marriage. Kuwait loved scandals, especially in the scorching summer heat when nothing else happened to keep people busy.

The woman handed her a boarding pass. "Your flight is in eight hours," she said.

"Eight hours! I thought there's a flight to Dubai every hour."

"There are normally more flights, but they get reduced during the low business season in the summer." The woman tried to look sympathetic.

Rouba thanked her and moved away from the desk to find a place where she could think straight. First thing's first, she had to get the logistics out of the way: get her luggage re-routed to Dubai, find a hotel there and inform everyone about her little change of plans without giving away what had happened...Then she had to find her ex-husband and cut off his balls....

She looked round for the correct place to resolve the luggage issue. Unfortunately, in a small airport like this, only one desk handled passenger transactions inside the terminal. She found herself a few seconds later standing in front of the same lady. "I came here on a flight from Damascus," she said, bracing herself for the tsunami of inquisitiveness that she knew would sweep over the other woman. "I need to have my suitcase re-routed onto the flight I just booked to Dubai."

The woman seemed on the verge of a curiosity-induced stroke. Her heavily kohled eyes doubled in size. Rouba could have sworn they turned into perfect three-sixty degree circles.

"So you were meant to come to Kuwait, but then had to divert?"

Rouba ignored the question. "Here's the luggage receipt," she said, handing over the slip. "It will help you track my suitcase."

The woman readjusted her veil, making sure a few strands from her jet black fringe peeked from underneath it, then picked up the phone to follow up on the luggage. Rouba listened. It sounded as though her luggage had been located and about to be redirected.

"It's nearly done," the woman said as she hung up. "If you come back in an hour, I should be able to print out the new baggage receipt."

With the luggage sorted, Rouba could now concentrate on her hotel stay in Dubai. Since she didn't want her assistant in the office to know about any of this, she called her private concierge service.

"Will you be using the credit card we have on file for this reservation?" the member assistant asked her.

Rouba paused. The card on file was her spouse card from Majed's account, and she'd stopped using it a while ago. Since then, she'd charged everything on her own card instead.

"I'll give you another..." she started, then on the impulse of a vicious thought, continued, "Yes. Please use the card on record."

"Do you have any preference for a hotel?"

"The Burj Al Arab. I need a suite for five nights."

During their marriage, Rouba had been opposed to staying at the famous seven star hotel because she found it to be an unjustifiable expense. She'd convinced Majed to stay in "regular" five star resorts instead when they'd visited Dubai. But right now, short of killing Majed for his disappearing act, spending his money felt like sweet revenge.

"I will call you back you within a few minutes, Mrs Al Riyyad," the assistant said. "But I'm confident we can get the suite at short notice. It's low season in Dubai."

OK, time to set up camp somewhere in the terminal for the next eight hours, but first she had to get a few things done. She bought herself a cup of coffee then dropped by the duty free bookstore where she bought a novel, a few magazines and two packs of baby wipes.

She then went into the ladies room. Only one other woman was there, applying her make up in front of the mirror. Rouba locked herself in the stall at the very end. She closed the lid of the toilet seat, put her luggage on it, and removed her T-shirt and bra. She used the wipes to freshen up, running them over her torso. She repeated the exercise for her lower body, taking off her trousers and underwear to clean up as much as possible. Then she put her clothes back on. Funny, this reminded her of an episode of Oprah where a well presented homeless woman had explained how she did the exact same thing, using public toilets to stay clean despite her living conditions. She opened the door and looked around, thankfully no one was there. She went to the water taps to wash her face and did her best to smooth her hair. The result wasn't great, but it was the best she could do.

Once outside the ladies room, she looked round for a free bench. The best one she could find was right opposite the first class lounge. Not the most private of locations, but she didn't have many options in the small terminal.

Rouba tried everything to distract herself, but neither the hot gossip magazines nor the best selling thriller could keep the memories from pouring back into her mind. So many family vacations had started here in this very building. She still remembered each one of them and the chaos they'd have to put up with as they tried to contain the start of the holiday excitement with three teenagers and a preteen. Despite their best attempts, Majed, the nanny and herself always had to chase at least one child around the duty free zone right before boarding.

These had been happy times. But now she found herself dishevelled and in need of a shower, sitting alone on a bench as a refugee, shut out of the kids' lives and no longer Majed's wife.

She picked up the phone and dialled Elyssar. "Your friend is an international outcast," she said.

"My friend has always been a global troublemaker. What have you done this time?"

Rouba told her all about the situation. "Elyssar, do you think Majed could have done it?" she added, "Cancelled my residency?"

Elyssar considered it for a few seconds. "Of course not," she replied, "He would never do something like this."

Rouba could have sworn she heard hesitation in her friend's voice.

"Why are you defending him?" she said. "He's perfectly capable of doing it."

"Roobs, you know I've always liked Majed," Elyssar replied. "I'm sure there's a perfectly good explanation for all of this."

"Then let's hope he resurfaces!" Rouba replied. "It's so typical of him. He disappears when you need him the most."

"Don't be unfair," Elyssar said.

"You wouldn't have been saying that if you'd been the one stuck at an airport," Rouba replied.

Elyssar laughed.

"Don't be mad at me, Roobs, but I find your situation hilarious. You remind me of Tom Hanks in the movie Terminal. He was stuck at an airport forever because he couldn't go back to his own country and no other state would have him."

Rouba chuckled; Elyssar could bring out the fun in any situation. But the reality of her circumstances hit her as soon as they hung up the phone. Where had Majed disappeared and how long was this going to last?

Chapter 14

In Lebanon, the focus was on the other end of the marriage relationship. Maya was hoping for a relaxing afternoon but the sound of angry voices pulled her away from the book she'd been reading. She was in no mood to talk to anyone, but this sounded like a heated argument. She left her room and followed the noise to the garden. As she stepped towards the lawn, Reem called out from behind her.

"Pssst! I don't suggest you go out there."

"What's going on?" Maya asked. "Who's shouting?"

"Your mom and Uncle Najeeb are having a fight," Reem replied.

"What happened now?"

"Your mother watered the roses," Reem said, a smirk on her face.

Since the beginning of the conflict, the usual restrictions on water provision had increased to a full-on rationing policy where each village only received a few hours' worth of water supply every several weeks. The Awwad villas shared a common water tank, but its contents had dwindled, very much to the dislike of Uncle Najeeb who obsessed over ensuring an ample reserve of water at all times.

"God," Maya said. "Knowing his temper, it's better we keep out of it and let them resolve it amongst themselves."

"Yap," Reem replied. "And if the war continues, we'd better brace ourselves for a lot more family drama."

Maya turned to head back towards her room. Reem put a hand on her shoulder.

"Are you OK?" she asked, "You've disappeared."

Maya nodded and went back to her room; she wasn't ready to talk about it, not even to the cousinettes.

Reem watched Maya walk back into the house then went next door where the cousinettes were gathered. "Our Bridezilla is on the verge of turning into Frankenstein," she said.

"Did you see her?" Lara asked.

"I ran into her just now and tried to have a talk, but she just won't hear it, she went back to her room," Reem said.

The cousinettes sighed. They were worried about Maya but despite several discussions about how to help her, they hadn't figured anything out yet.

"She's having a hard time adjusting to the fact that she has no control over anything," Lara said. "She's too young to remember what life was like in the civil war, so she hasn't learnt to take things in her stride."

"True," Reem replied. "But it's not fair that everyone is pushing her to still have the perfect wedding. And it didn't help that Ziad went from wanting no less than a grand wedding to no wedding at all."

"So what do we do?" Dana asked. "We have to help her calm down."

"I'll call Ziad to see how he's doing since she's still not taking his calls," Reem said. "And then I suggest a wedding embargo of three days where no one talks about anything related to marriage or weddings."

A few hours later in New York, Elyssar left the meeting room hoping that no one noticed how distracted she'd been, or that she'd sat in a dark corner so she could stare at Paul's picture on her laptop. How embarrassing, especially as she'd always thought of herself as a level-headed, strong woman. Guess all you need is for a man with a killer pair of eyes to show up in your life and the hard-built façade crumbles.

As she walked back to her temporary desk, she reminded herself that losing focus now could cost her; she needed to get things done at work. She'd heard good news about her deal in Jordan today. The offer she'd sent had been shortlisted with that of two other companies. Now the prices would determine the winner and she'd just gotten approval from her management to reduce by a further seven and a half percent. She knew the competition's pricing structure and hoped they wouldn't be able to meet her new price. This deal represented her only chance to make her numbers this quarter. I really have to nail this, she told herself. Cooing over a man's pictures like a loved-up teenager is not helping.

Paul had made every effort to maintain contact in the two days he'd been in Los Angeles. He kept her informed of his whereabouts and stayed in touch throughout the day by SMS. Despite the three-hour time difference between the East and West coasts, he emailed first thing each morning and called in the evening before she went to sleep. He'd even surprised her today by giving her an early morning call. Elyssar had never been a morning person, but waking up to the sound of his voice made her day. She'd always found the American accent sexy, but now, coming out of Paul's sexy lips it mesmerized her. She'd even let the answering machine pick up a few of his calls so she could play the recording over and over.

Talk about the handsome devil: an email from him popped up as soon as she arrived at her desk.

"I've been thinking about your stay when your vacation starts. New York is not the right place this time of year. It's hot and no one's around. I'm worried you'll be bored when I am at work and you have to be alone all day.

My lease in the Hamptons doesn't start for another 3 weeks, so how about you spend a couple of days here and then we go to Miami? It's not the best time of year in Florida, but it's still better than New York, and I really want you to enjoy the US. I know a great hotel there, you will love it."

He'd pasted a link to the hotel's website. Called "The Delano", the hotel positioned itself as a staple with the rich and famous. Elyssar went through page after page of pictures of fancy rooms and restaurants on their website, but she wasn't convinced.

Somehow, this didn't come as good news. She'd never felt comfortable with beach holidays, mainly because she didn't revel in the thought of spending days on end in the pouring sunlight, where everyone had all the time in the world to check out the cellulite on her behind. Not to mention that, since she'd turned thirty, she had drastically reduced the time she spent in the sun and now only went a few times a year to the beach, either by herself or with her girlfriends and cousins, never in big groups or on dates.

To add insult to ego injury, a Google search on The Delano landed her on blogs that described the hotel as a "landmark for jet setters" and "hot bed for models and actresses on a break." She could already imagine size double zero goddesses lying by the pool, while she strolled her well-nourished size-six butt around...

Anyway, didn't Paul have his big important deal to prepare for? She had to persuade him that they would have a much better time staying in New York. Maybe she would plead cultural discovery and suggest a weekend trip to Washington, Boston, Chicago, or any other city where she could keep her cellulite under wraps.

Time to write a convincing reply.

"Hi Paul,

I checked out the website and the hotel seems amazing. I can't believe I've never heard of it before.

But you really don't need to worry about me. I'm from Beirut so how could I possibly be bored in The Big Apple? I have a long list of places to visit and it will keep me busy for my entire stay. Also, you've already told me that you have to work and I would feel bad if you took time off just for my benefit.

Why don't we do a weekend break in a nearby city? Maybe DC? I've always dreamt of visiting there. Maybe I'll even stage a one woman demonstration outside the White House to protest against the war in Lebanon ;-)."

Paul called her mobile a few seconds after she sent the email. "Don't worry about me not being able to work from Miami," he said. "All I need to do is stay in the same time zone as New York to attend conference calls and communicate with the office, but I don't need to physically be there."

"But it will be a hassle for you to work remotely. You know I love New York. I really don't mind spending my entire vacation here."

"You won't like it for long. It will get hotter by the minute. We'll suffocate. At least in Miami we'll have the beach. Did you read about the hotel? Did you see who co-owns it?"

"I read about the architect, but nothing on the owner. Who are they?"

"Madonna is rumoured to be one of the owners."

"Oh." Elyssar said, unable to think of more arguments.

A man went past her desk, carrying an open laptop and reading the screen as he walked between cubicles; a case of corporate email addiction if she'd ever seen one.

"You have no more excuses," Paul said. "I can't wait to show you Miami."

The Madonna argument killed any more objections she could have raised, short of her telling him the truth: her big fat ass had more orange peel on it than a truckload of organic produce. Now all Elyssar needed to do was lose three dress sizes and grow new skin in less than a week.

Elyssar's decision to go to Miami coincided with Rouba's landing in Dubai. She was painfully aware of the fact that she didn't look the part of the Burj Al Arab guest when she got into the white Rolls Royce that the hotel had sent to pick her up at the airport. But the suited hostess and the driver who met her in the arrivals hall pretended not to notice.

"It's a pleasure to have you stay at the Burj Al Arab, Mrs. Al Riyyad."

The Indian driver held the car door open for her with much ceremony. She thanked him and slid onto the amazingly comfortable back seat. Having been on the road for over thirty-six hours and after the ride in the old taxi in Lebanon, the hours spent on flights and on the bench at Kuwait airport, being in this car felt like paradise. She dozed off as soon as they were on the road to the hotel. A call from Elyssar woke her up and she smiled as she answered it.

"Hey terminal tenant," Elyssar said. "Did Dubai let you in?"

"Yes, the world community has taken me back into its fold. But all is not won yet. I'm on my way to the hotel and worried that the Burj Al Arab will turn me down when they see what I look like. I haven't slept or showered in centuries and believe me, it's visible... and probably fragrant too."

"Just give them some attitude, they'll think you're neo-grunge," Elyssar said.

Rouba groaned.

"I don't think I could survive the humiliation of being turned down at the hotel reception like I was at Kuwait airport."

"If they turn you down, will they send you back in a Rolls Royce, or do they provide a different type of transportation for their rejects?"

Running her finger through her lumpy hair, Rouba laughed. "I hope I never find out. And they better not call me a refugee either. It makes me feel terribly sorry for myself."

"Staying at Burj Al Arab makes you a *caviar* refugee." Elyssar laughed, adding on a more serious note, "You'll be fine, sweetie. Just make sure you get all the sleep you need, you must be exhausted."

They hung up and Rouba lay back against her seat, watching skyscrapers succeed each other through the window. Their tall glass and steel silhouettes gleamed against the dusty sky. She'd always had a lot of respect for Dubai, a tiny Emirate that took its fate into his own hands and went from sleepy desert town to world class city in little over a decade. In a region so encumbered by history and geography, the Dubai success story gave her hope. She wished more countries in the region would follow the same path.

The Rolls Royce left the highway and made its way towards the bridge that linked the Burj Al Arab's manmade island to the mainland coast. Two security guards nodded as they saw the car approaching. One of them pushed a button to lift the traffic barrier and let them in.

Rouba leaned back against her seat as they drove across the bridge and towards the massive sail-shaped structure. Jets of fire shot up towards the sky, rising from both sides of the road. "Aren't those the flames you launch when a VIP comes to the hotel?" Rouba remembered reading about this in a travel brochure. "Are you expecting someone important today?"

She knew that celebrities and royals often stayed here, and the thought of running into one of them excited her, despite her exhaustion.

"The flames are for you, Mrs. Al Riyyad," the driver replied.

Rouba couldn't help but smile. Elyssar had a point; she was blessed for having the opportunity to take refuge in such a place. She closed her eyes and silently recited the prayer of gratitude. Over the last few years, it had become difficult for Rouba to appreciate the small blessings of her everyday life. She'd come to resent Majed's wealth because it taught her the hard way that having lots of money masked life's problems until they became too profound to resolve.

Chapter 15

Rouba prepared herself for rejection as the Rolls Royce pulled up in front of the Burj Al Arab's entrance. She'd never heard of anyone being turned down here, but in her current state nothing would surprise her. As soon as the car stopped, a man in a white tunic and black trousers rushed to open the door for her. Two others materialised behind the car to take the luggage out of the trunk. Rouba stepped out, smoothing her hair with her hand and attempting to readjust her T-shirt.

A woman in a traditional *abaya* dress held the glass door open, while another offered Rouba a spray from the bottle of *oud* perfume that she was carrying in a wooden box. Rouba accepted with a smile, maybe the scent would help cover up the body odour she'd undoubtedly developed despite her mini clean up at Kuwait airport.

Like everything else in the Burj Al Arab, the lobby was designed to impress, and in spite of her exhaustion Rouba looked up to take in the surroundings. Stretched opposite the entrance, a flame coloured divan was set against a fountain which threw multiple water streams into the air. Two gigantic aquariums occupied each side of the lobby. Rouba walked towards the reception counter with its gold-covered wall.

As the driver before her, the receptionist didn't seem to notice Rouba's haggard looks and processed the check-in without any complications. Soon, Rouba found herself following another hostess who led her up the escalators to the lift and then on to her suite. The woman listed the services available at the hotel and left after pointing out that the luggage had already been taken up to the bedroom.

Rouba inspected the lower level of the suite. It featured a dining table for four people, a bar counter and a guest washroom. A flat screen TV was set against a gilded frame, dominating the living room. Rouba took the spiral staircase which led her to the bedroom, with its four-poster bed and dressing area. She opened another door and shrieked at the sight of the luxurious bathroom. Without further ado, she undressed and went into the Jacuzzi, starting it up with the push of a button. She lay there, focusing on her breathing to relax her muscles and tune out the frustration.

Half an hour later, she extricated herself from the warm water and collapsed on the bed, barely taking the time to dry up with a towel. But the solid sleep she'd hoped for didn't materialise. She napped for no more than two or three hours before finding herself wide awake with a multitude of questions running through her mind. Majed had still not opened his mobile phone and she felt herself on the brink of a nervous breakdown. She swallowed her pride and called his assistant again.

"Hi, Atheel." She tried to sound as confident as possible. "I wanted to know if you've heard from Majed yet."

"I got a fax from him a few minutes ago. He's still on the jet but said that they're about to land. I've asked him to call you as soon as he can."

Still feeling sorry for the poor woman who'd found herself in the uneasy role of mediating her boss's marriage, Rouba tried to make things a little less awkward by chatting for another five minutes with her, asking about her family and the weather in Kuwait.

After they hung up, she realized that she could have asked for the fax number on the jet. Should she call Atheel again? She weighed her options then decided to wait for Majed's call. He was bound to get in touch with her - *eventually*.

Two more hours had to pass before he had the decency to call. "Please tell me you're dead, otherwise there's no way to justify your disappearing act." Not the best way to pick up a call when you're hoping to keep a civilized relationship with your ex, but Rouba couldn't contain her anger.

As always, Majed either didn't notice her frustration or decided to ignore it.

"Where are you?" he asked.

"In Dubai. I'm staying at Burj Al Arab."

"Good."

"Good? I'm paying for this with your credit card. Do you know how much it's costing you?"

"That doesn't matter," he dismissed. "You're the one who finds that hotel too expensive. I like the place."

Typical Majed, she couldn't do anything to break his armour. The man didn't care enough about anything to be upset.

"At the very least, don't you want to know why I am in Dubai and not Kuwait?"

Majed didn't reply.

"Don't you want to know why I am in Dubai?" she repeated.

Again, he didn't answer, his silence confirming Rouba's suspicions.

"You *did* cancel my Kuwaiti residency, didn't you?" she said, livid.

Majed took his time to reply, but he finally confessed. "Yes, I got your residency cancelled."

Rouba felt as if she'd just taken a bullet.

"Rouba, I ..." Majed started.

"You what?" Rouba yelled. "You got me dumped at the airport like a dog! Do you have any idea of what it felt like? And you didn't even have the guts to tell me about it beforehand. Is that some kind of a Kuwaiti macho thing? Does it make you feel good about yourself to humiliate your wife?"

"Rouba, I ... I'm sorry that I did that."

"No you're not sorry." Tears of rage flowed down her face. "You always know exactly what you're doing, Majed. You had this planned all along."

"Rouba..." Majed interjected.

"Stop repeating my name like a parrot. And I don't care what you have to do but you better get my permit reinstated very quickly. If not, then, by God, I will make your life hit levels of misery you never imagined possible."

"Rouba, calm down." Majed spoke firmly. "Listen to me ..."

His ability to remain collected when she was angry had always driven Rouba up the wall; and right now it made her hate him with a passion.

"I don't want to listen to you. You make me sick. All I want is for my life to be clean of you. Just give me my divorce." She broke down in sobs. "For Heaven's sake, please give me my divorce."

Early the following morning, Maya woke up to the sound of voices and the TV. At this time of day, it could only mean bad news. She walked into the living room to a group of stern faces staring at the TV set. Family members occupied all the seats in the room, so she moved to the side and leaned against the wall to watch the newscast.

"...The repeated missile attacks, launched in the dead of night against the shelter while its innocent occupants slept, reduced the four-story building and surrounding houses to rubble, killing at least 57 residents, including 37 children..."

The footage showed the bloodied bodies of women and children being pulled from the rubble, still wearing their nightclothes.

"When emergency workers reached Qana, it was only to discover the full scale of the horror. Whole families have been wiped out; their smashed bodies buried beneath tons of rubble. Amidst the destruction, parents have to confront their worst nightmare: that of recovering the bodies of their children. A source tells us that half of the children housed in the shelter were disabled..."

Maya, like most of her cousins and aunts, couldn't take more of the scene without breaking down in tears. Her father, as well as uncles Najeeb and Saeed, left the room, like they always did when they found themselves on the verge of tears. Cousinette Lara covered her mouth with her hand and rushed to the toilet. The others continued to watch in horror as the footage showed more scenes of charred bodies, images of parents painfully digging through the rubble with their bare hands to find their children, a mother shouting at the top of her lungs that her three children had died.

They all knew this day would forever remain one of the darkest in their country's history.

Chapter 16

Elyssar dug into her couscous, laughing at the jokes Paul exchanged with his daughter. He had invited Ashley to join them at his favourite Moroccan restaurant so he could introduce her to Elyssar. Ashley was a younger female version of her father. "Tell Elyssar about Brian," Paul said.

Ashley's smile turned sour. "Brian was my boyfriend, but we broke up because he slept with my best friend, Sarah," she explained.

"But you forgot to mention an important point. Didn't you sleep with Sarah's boyfriend a few weeks prior to that?"

Elyssar did a double take. For a split second, she thought she misheard him, but Paul was looking at his daughter with a grin.

"Well... yeah," a vaguely guilty Ashley replied.

Elyssar posted a benevolent smile on her face. She didn't find Ashley's sexcapades as endearing as Paul seemed to think they were.

"Something weird also happened," Ashley continued. "I got a text the other day from this guy I didn't recognize. He said his name is Jordan."

"And?" Paul asked.

"He said we met at a club and hooked up afterwards. But I can't remember anything about it."

"Incredible," Paul laughed. "You know you should be thinking about studying instead of going after all these boys. Ellie, what do you think?"

Ellie thinks your daughter needs to keep her trousers on, Elyssar thought, but instead she said, "Since Ashley's studying psychology, I guess it could all qualify as research. It's about human behaviour, right?" She didn't find her own joke funny, but Paul and Ashley laughed.

"So what did you think of Ashley?" Paul asked a little over an hour later as the two of them walked to Elyssar's hotel.

Elyssar took the time to select her words. "She's very pretty and quite a character." She'd always thought of herself as non judgmental, but Ashley's talk about her sex encounters and Paul's casual reaction to it had pushed an easy-to-scandalize button that Elyssar didn't know she had in her.

"I wish she'd focus more on her studies," Paul grumbled. "But what can I do? Boys find her cute, and she happens to like them, too."

Again, Elyssar did her best not to show her disapproval. "You two seem to have a very good relationship," she said, preferring to divert the conversation away from Ashley's dating habits. "You behave more like friends than a father and daughter."

Paul shrugged. "I'm more liberal than her mother, so she confides in me."

Liberal is surely the term, Elyssar thought, but she shut off the idea, feeling guilty about passing judgment on him. "Let me tell you something," she said, "You'll never hear a Lebanese girl have a conversation like this with her father. I'm thirty-three years old and I can't even tell my parents that I'm dating."

"Yeah, I guess things are different for you." Paul pulled her close and squeezed her bottom. "So when I meet your father, I can't tell him that his daughter has the hottest ass on the planet?"

Elyssar felt the blood rushing out to her face.

Paul laughed. "You must be the only woman in New York city who still blushes."

He took her hand and they started walking again.

"New York is fabulous," Elyssar said, looking at the passersby and the buildings towering above them. "Even if I lived here permanently, I think I would be excited every single time I walked on the street."

"It wears off quickly," Paul replied. "I felt like this when I first moved from California eighteen years ago, but I was over it in about five minutes."

"I think I would never be bored with it."

He looked sideways at her.

"Do you think you could ever live here?"

"My boss and I have discussed the possibility of my working in the US for a year or so to get some international experience, but it was never serious."

"Maybe you can reopen that topic."

Elyssar considered the possibility for a few seconds, then shrugged.

"I don't think that's an option anymore. Also, I would feel terrible leaving Lebanon when the war is on."

"The war won't go on for ever, sweetheart. Work experience in New York would be great for you. If your company doesn't have any vacancies here, I could speak to some people to help you find a job elsewhere. You're smart, talented and multilingual; any company would love to have you."

Elyssar felt her heart pumping. She'd been avoiding thinking about the fact that she was in New York on a temporary basis and would soon be leaving the city - and Paul - behind. Now that he had opened the topic, she realised that maybe their relationship did have potential. But she didn't want to jump into anything yet. Despite her infatuation with Paul, somewhere in her mind a little voice called her to caution: she was too smitten right now to take long term decisions.

"Let's think about this after I get my country back." She said.

In Rantour, Maya had re-emerged from her room and was reconnecting with her family. She had just joined the cousinettes for the morning ritual of Turkish coffee and a newscast when Aunt Bernadette came in, all excited.

"*Girls*," she said. "Come out, you have to see this."

The girls, most of them still in their nightwear, wrapped their robes around them as they followed her outside. Aunt Bernadette preceded them up the driveway that led outside the Awwad property and onto Rantour's main road. She pointed to the right. "Look," she said.

There, a few hundred meters away, lay one of the most striking spectacles anyone had ever seen in these parts. A long procession was making its way through the village, made up of buses, cars and trucks. Maya and the cousinettes watched in awe as the convoy moved in their direction. They couldn't see the end of it.

"They're displaced because of the war," Aunt Bernadette said, stating the obvious. "They've just arrived from the South to take shelter here in the village."

Gray with dust, mattresses and luggage strapped to their roofs, the vehicles looked about to burst from the weight of their loads. A car led the convoy and came to a halt when it reached the village's community center, only a dozen meters away from where the girls stood. The rest of the motorcade came to a halt behind.

The handful of men who were standing outside the hall moved towards the car. Maya had been so taken by the sight of the long fleet moving through the road that she hadn't noticed the men at first. They greeted the car's occupants with big hand gestures of welcome.

"Is that the Mayor?" she asked, pointing with her chin to the man who seemed in charge of the welcome delegation.

"I think so," Lara replied.

The handshaking continued. Maya couldn't hear the conversation but the body language indicated that a warm meet and greet was taking place. At one point, two of the men, one from each side, appeared to give each other a short speech. Finally, the little welcome ceremony ended. The local team pulled up in front of the convoy and the procession started moving again. They moved in the direction leading to the other side of Rantour. Maya assumed they were headed to the only school in the village, since that's where other displaced groups had taken up refuge elsewhere in the country. The local school building was large and surrounded by a wooded area which could come in handy if they needed extra space.

By now, the two thousand inhabitants of Rantour seemed to have all come out and were lining the road. As the procession of buses and cars went past, Maya examined the sequence of faces that stared back at her with equal curiosity. All the women, including some that did not look older than eleven or twelve, wore head veils. Unconsciously, Maya and the cousinettes readjusted their robes around them.

In Dubai, Rouba was trying to take her mind off her woes. Thankfully the Burj Al Arab provided a guest laptop in the suite, and Rouba had made intensive use of it to communicate with Elyssar, who was clearly smitten with her New Yorker. She had just emailed Rouba several pictures of him, as well as a link to his company's website.

Rouba picked up the phone and dialled Elyssar's number. "I have one word for you," she said when her friend picked up. "Wow."

"Yeah, I know," Elyssar cooed. "He's even more handsome in person."

Rouba examined the photos.

"He looks so good for his age. Do you think he dyes his hair?"

She zoomed in on his hairline. Jet-black, with no gray at all.

"I didn't think about that," Elyssar replied.

Rouba heard clicking sounds on the other end of the line that told her Elyssar was zooming in on the picture as well.

"You're probably right, this can't be his natural hair color." Elyssar added.

"And Botox?"

"What? Don't be silly."

"You said he's fifty years old, right?" Rouba insisted. "Do a close up on his forehead: no lines. No one can be this smooth without Botox, especially at his age. You know New Yorkers obsess more about their looks than anyone else in the world. I'm sure he's getting a little help to look this good."

It was clear that Elyssar remained unconvinced. "I don't think so. His skin looks perfectly natural to me."

Rouba couldn't remember when she'd last seen Elyssar this besotted with a man. If anything, in recent years her friend had developed a reputation for being hard to impress. One of their other single female friends once said, "If a guy wants to break someone's heart he should date me, if he wants to get his heart broken, he should date Elyssar".

Rouba hoped with all her heart that things would work out for Elyssar and the New Yorker. "You know what, it doesn't matter," she said. "Botox or not, he sounds like an amazing guy. I haven't seen you this happy in a long time."

Chapter 17

Maya watched the children as they left class and headed back towards the school building, running and chatting. She stood up and dusted the sand off her jeans.

Maya had been anxious when Reem asked her to help with activities for the displaced children. But the French lesson that Maya had just delivered had gone well, and she found no better way of putting things in perspective for herself, rather than obsessing over her wedding plans.

Reem and the Mayor had organized a summer school to keep the children busy for a few hours a day. She provided lessons to students in their early teens and had asked Maya for help with classes for the six to nine year-olds.

Since the school building was acting as living quarters for the displaced families, they delivered open-air classes in the woods nearby. With no chairs or any other furniture, both students and teachers sat on the ground beneath the tall pine trees. Each session hosted around twenty five children. Quite a bit to manage, especially in an out-door environment where the teacher had to speak loud enough for the kids to stay put and listen. Yet, they seemed to appreciate the opportunity and behaved better than one would expect under the circumstances.

Maya had borrowed books from Reem and read stories to her students, keeping them involved by asking for guesses about the plot at each turning point. At the end of each session, she would stay behind to ensure that none of them strayed in the woods.

A little girl, the last one to get up and leave, made a turn and sprinted back towards her. "Miss?" she called, using the common term that pupils used with their teachers.

Maya smiled, enjoying the novelty of finding herself in a teacher role.

"Will you finish the story for us tomorrow?" the girl asked.

A missing front tooth told Maya she couldn't be older than six or seven. With her long brown hair, freckles and large glasses, she looked like the studious type. She'd participated well in class, answering questions and gobbling up every word.

"Yes, we'll finish the story tomorrow," Maya replied. "But you have to be here on time."

The thought of another session brightened up the little girl's face.

"Can you remind me of your name?" Maya asked. She had asked the pupils to introduce themselves at the start of the session, but hadn't been able to memorize all the names.

"I'm called Zainab," the girl replied. "My father is Haidar Hamad, we're from Bint Jbeil."

"Glad to meet you," Maya said, extending her arm to shake Zeinab's hand. "My name is Maya and I'm from Rantour."

"Do you live in that house?" Zainab asked, pointing through the trees to a tiled roof in the distance.

"That's my uncle's house, but I live right next door," Maya replied. "You can't see my house from here because of the big oaks around it."

"An oak tree is called *un chêne* in French," the little girl said proudly.

Maya smiled.

"Bravo, Zainab," she said. "I see you're a good student."

The child beamed at the compliment.

"My mom and I went for a walk yesterday and we passed that house," she said. "Mother told me that the teachers live there."

Funny. In a small village, such as Rantour, a newcomer needed less than twenty-four hours to place the inhabitants.

"We have a house too," Zainab continued, her little lips pursed. "It's in Bint Jbeil. We also own a garden where we grow fruits and vegetables."

Although she didn't know much about child psychology, Maya guessed little Zainab was worried about losing her home and felt the need to tell people about it.

"I'm sure your house is beautiful," Maya replied. "And everyone knows that fruits from Bint Jbeil are the best in the world."

Zainab's smile came back. "I will send you some when I go back home," she said.

"Thank you, Zainab." Maya replied, then remembering her educational role added. "I want you to pick them yourself and include a list that names them all in French."

While Maya was making her first incursion into a child's mind, Rouba was getting plenty more experience in that field. In her suite in Dubai, she switched off the gilded TV screen, sighing. She'd watched nothing but bad news about Lebanon for hours and couldn't take any more of it. She logged into her email and instant messaging. As soon as she was in, a chat window popped up on her screen. It was Noora, her step daughter sending her a bunch of animated emoticons: bouncing hearts, juicy smiles and colored stars.

"*Hi, sweetie,*" Rouba typed. "*I miss you.*"

"*I miss you too,*" the little girl replied. "*Come home.*"

I can't go home because your daddy has banned me from the country, Rouba thought, but instead, she typed: "*Soon.*"

She knew that children came with a built in lie detector, and that Noora would see right through it, but she couldn't think of anything else to say.

"*I know you're not coming back,*" Noora typed.

"*Noora, no one will keep me from going back to see you,*" Rouba replied with tears in her eyes. "*It's a little difficult now, but I will keep trying until I get there, OK?*"

"*Hiba has left too.*"

Hiba was Majed's eldest daughter and, at eighteen, she was about to start university.

"*Where did she go?*" Rouba asked. She was sure Hiba didn't have any trips scheduled this summer.

"*We don't know. She ran away from home.*"

Rouba's heart skipped a beat. She picked up the phone and dialled the home number in Kuwait. Mary, the children's Filipina nanny, answered.

"Madame Roubaaaaaaaaa, it's so good of you to caaaaall," she said in her sing-song Tagalog accent.

"It's good to talk to you too," Rouba said. "How are you?"

Mary had looked after the kids since their mother's death. After all these years, they all saw her as an intrinsic part of the family. She had cried a lot on the day Rouba left.

"Is everything OK?" Rouba continued. "I'm online with Noora and she mentioned something about Hiba running away. Is that true?"

"Yes, Madame Roubaaaa, it's true," Mary sighed. "Hiba asked the driver to drop her at her cousin's house, but a few hours later we realized she had disappeared. Mr. Majed checked everywhere, the police, the hospitals and the airport. He found out that she stole her passport from his desk drawer and left to America. He travelled there to find her."

Rouba gasped in shock. How could Hiba do such a thing? Where was she? America was so big! How would Majed find her? "Do you know where she went in America?" she asked Mary.

"Her ticket said Boston."

Rouba felt herself panic even more. Why would Hiba fly to Boston? She'd never been to Boston before. "Has Majed found her yet?" she asked.

"We don't know. He hasn't called us since he left."

"Mary, please call me immediately if you hear anything." Rouba said. "And please try not to talk about it in front of the younger children."

"I will, Madame Rouba," Mary replied. "God bless you."

"And please stay in the same room as Noora. She's using the computer," Rouba said. She worried about the kids going online without supervision.

"I know, Madame Rouba," Mary replied. "I never leave the room when they're using the computer, just like you told me to."

"Thank you, Mary," Rouba replied as she hung up.

She looked at the open chat window with Noora. She wasn't sure what to tell the little girl. "Hiba has done a very foolish thing," she typed. "But your Dad will bring her back home quickly."

"She won't come back with Dad. She's mad at him," Noora replied. "Because he made you leave."

Groaning, Rouba called the Kuwait home line again.

"Mary, can I please talk to Noora?" she asked when the nanny picked up.

Noora came on the line.

"Baby, I want you to listen to me very carefully," Rouba said, wiping the tears that were pouring down her cheeks. "I did not leave you, I will never leave you. I love you and we will always be a part of each other's lives. It doesn't matter if your father and I are married or not, OK?"

"You sound like you're crying," Noora said.

"I *am* crying. Because you think I left you. That means you don't know how much I love you."

"Don't cry." Noora seemed to be on the verge of tears as well. "I know that you love me. I love you too. All of us do... even Dad."

Rouba smiled through her tears at the child's naïveté.

"Good," she said. "I won't cry any more. Do you know where

Hiba went?"

"She doesn't want me to know because I would tell Dad. I just checked her Facebook page but there's nothing there."

For once Rouba didn't reprimand Noora for going on Facebook.

"Why don't you go to the playroom?" Rouba said, "You shouldn't spend so much time on the PC. I will try to contact Hiba."

"Maybe Hiba will answer you." Noora sounded more worried than a child her age ever should be.

"I will, and if she contacts you, you will tell me, OK?"

"OK."

Rouba hung up and went to Hiba's Facebook page. The news of her escape must have gone around the country: fresh posts from her friends filled her wall, asking her to "call or BBM". Despite her addiction to Facebook and BBM, or BlackBerry Messenger, Hiba hadn't replied to any one. How could she vanish like this when technology was supposed to keep her connected at all times?

Rouba clicked on "send a message", but the system prompted her to sign in. Damn that. She didn't have an account and it would take her forever to sign up. She decided to send a message to Hiba's email account instead.

Despite the millions of questions in her mind, she didn't know what to write. After careful consideration, she went with a simple:

"I'm worried. Call or email me. Rouba."

Rouba now understood Majed's disappearance. He must have jumped on the jet as soon as he realized his daughter had gone missing. Of course, that still didn't explain why he'd banned her from the country, but she felt terribly guilty for her outburst against him.

She decided to check the wall of each of Hiba's Facebook friends. There were 189 of them, but not a single post from Hiba in the past 48 hours; and nothing from her prior to her departure that could have indicated she planned on running away from home.

Rouba decided to stay by the PC. If Hiba was safe, the first place she would re-emerge would be online.

But what if she wasn't safe? What if a man had tricked her into running away with him? She was bound to get herself in danger in a big city like Boston. And what about Majed? Rouba imagined his devastation. The safety of his kids was sacred to him. She wanted to talk to him, but it didn't feel like the right thing for her to do right now. She'd probably stress him even more.

Rouba stayed by her desk all night, checking her email and Hiba's Facebook page every few minutes, but her step-daughter gave no sign of life.

At five a.m. she asked her suite's dedicated butler for a strong coffee and decided to send another email.

"*Hiba, please tell me you're OK. I love you,*" she wrote.

To her surprise, a reply came back almost immediately. She jumped on her seat.

"*I'm OK,*" Hiba wrote.

"Thank you, God, thank you..." Rouba repeated out loud as she typed a reply.

"*Please log in to chat or give me your phone number.*"

"*No need 4 the dramz,*" Hiba responded. "*I know Dad's looking 4 me, he won't have probz finding me.*"

Rouba hesitated, then wrote.

"*Please tell me where you are.*"

She stared at the screen for several minutes, but Hiba didn't reply.

Well, at least she'd given sign of life. Rouba feverishly dialled Majed; the phone rang several times but he didn't pick up. He probably thought she wanted to give him more grief and didn't want to pick up. She texted him instead.

"*Heard from Hiba. She's OK, please call me.*"

He called back on the spot.

"You spoke to her?" he asked without preamble.

"We exchanged emails," Rouba replied. "She won't tell me where she is, but she said she's fine."

"I've sent her dozens of emails, she didn't reply to any of them."

For the first time since she'd known him, Majed seemed truly distraught.

"You know what teenagers are like, she'll come round…"

"Yes, I'm learning the hard way," Majed acknowledged.

"She also said that she knows you're looking for her and that you can easily find her," Rouba told him.

"What is that supposed to mean?" Majed exclaimed. "Is this a game of some sort? Is she throwing out clues and making us take after guesses?"

Rouba sighed.

"I think she wants to be found. Let's hope she does something that reveals her location."

"I've hired a private investigator. I will let him know she's contacted you. Can you give me the password to your email account? Maybe he can trace her location from the messages she sent you."

"OK, but if she sends me any new messages, don't respond. I want to be the one to reply."

Chapter 18

Paul poured two glasses of white wine and handed one to Elyssar. She'd managed to find a Lebanese channel on his TV and they'd just tuned in, waiting for a program to start. Elyssar explained that it would be the live coverage of a speech by the Lebanese Prime Minister.

An anchor did the introduction and the broadcast moved to a live feed in Arabic from a large boardroom. Elyssar put the volume up. "Are you sure you're OK with me watching this?" she asked.

"Of course."

Despite her efforts to look relaxed, she was having a difficult time hiding the stress. The news from her country had only worsened in the past twenty-four hours. The broadcast showed the Lebanese Prime Minister addressing a group of politicians. Elyssar recognized several Lebanese ministers as well as western and Arab ambassadors to Lebanon.

"He has called all foreign ambassadors in Lebanon to a meeting," she explained to Paul.

The Prime Minister started delivering his speech, and Elyssar felt Paul stare at her as she listened. He seemed quite worried about her and to show it, he topped up her glass although she'd barely had a sip; she thanked him with a smile and turned her attention back to the TV screen.

The Lebanese Prime Minister was delivering a situation report to the international community, his hands shaking as he read out from a big piece of paper. At one point, his voice faltered and he appeared on the verge of breaking down. Elyssar didn't even try to hold back the tears that ran silently down her cheeks.

Paul reached out and squeezed her hand. "As an outsider I know I can never understand what you're going through, but I'm here for you," he said.

He took her in his arms and she silently thanked God for giving her this source of comfort when she was so far away from home.

At the same time in Dubai, Rouba was pacing the living room in her suite. It had been over four hours since Majed had sent her the briefest of texts:

"*Found out where she went,*" it said. "*On my way there.*"

He'd been unreachable since, leaving Rouba with only the option to pray as hard as she could and drive herself crazy waiting for his call.

She shrieked when her phone rang.

"We found her," Majed exclaimed, jubilant.

Rouba's tears flowed. "Thank God! Where is she? How did you find her?"

"She used her credit card to buy a plane ticket from Boston to Los Angeles and then used it again to check into a hotel," Majed said.

"Did you locate the hotel?"

"Yes, it's near the house. I'm there now."

The "house" was their US summer residence in Los Angeles.

"Did... did she check in alone?"

Rouba didn't want to alarm Majed even more, but she was worried to death that Hiba might have run away with someone.

"Yes, she's by herself. The investigator confirmed that with the hotel staff."

"Have you seen her?"

"Not yet," Majed replied. "I'm waiting for my lawyer and a child psychologist to arrive. I don't want her to run away again if she knows we found her. So I will let the psychologist talk to her first, and the lawyer will let me know what to do in case she resists going back with me."

Classic Majed behaviour. He hired people to do his work for him, even when it came to parenting his own children.

"I think you should be the one to initiate contact. No matter how good the psychologist is, Hiba doesn't know him or her. You are her father."

Majed paused to consider her idea. "You're right," he conceded. "I will be the one to get in touch with her. But I will ask the therapist to be ready to intervene."

"She knew you would trace the credit card. She's probably expecting you."

"Yes, but let's play it safe."

Rouba took a deep breath. "Majed, I know it's not any more my place ...," she hesitated, but she really needed to say this to him. "But while you're there, you need to have a good heart to heart conversation with Hiba. This stunt was her way of getting your attention."

Majed went silent. "I... I'm not sure I can do that."

"It won't be easy but you have to," Rouba replied. "Your teenage daughter just ran away to the other side of the world. You can't let this pass without getting to the bottom of the issue. You found her this time, but we need to make sure this never happens again; either with her or the other kids. This is the biggest warning you could have received."

"You know I'm no good at this." He sounded genuinely anxious.

"Yes, you are. You have it in you. Remember when we first met? We spent hours on the phone, sometimes talking throughout the night. You used to be able to discuss everything openly."

Majed reflected for a few seconds, then said: "Can you be there too? You have such a good rapport with the kids."

Rouba closed her eyes. Yes, she had a good rapport with the kids, they were *her* kids and she loved them more than she could say. But wouldn't her intervention cause more trouble at a time Majed and she were going through a divorce? She took the time to make sure her voice wouldn't shake when she spoke. "You know there's nothing more I want to do right now than have a talk with Hiba," she replied. "But I'm oceans away. Also, the person she really wants to speak to is you."

"I could call you and leave the phone on while she and I talk, so you'll be able to listen. We won't tell her about it."

Rouba wasn't convinced. For as much as she wanted to be there for Hiba, she had to face the fact that she wasn't part of this family anymore. By getting involved now she would make the separation even more difficult on the kids later. The earlier Majed learnt to deal with them on his own, the easier it would be for everyone to adjust.

"Rouba, I just need to know you're there," Majed insisted.

Rouba sighed. Majed was clearly not ready for a serious talk with his daughter. Maybe by listening in on the call, Rouba would ensure he didn't shy away from it.

"OK, I'll be happy to listen in," she replied.

"Thank you," he said.

It was so heartfelt, Rouba cried her heart out when he hung up.

On the opposite coast to Majed and Hiba, Elyssar was congratulating herself at her shoe selection for Miami: she had just picked two sky-high wedges that provided the perfect lift she would need on the pool.

She headed to the men's section of the store. "Paul are you here?" she asked, going into the fitting area.

"Yes," he replied from behind a curtain. "How are you getting along?"

"I found two gorgeous pairs."

"Let me see." He emerged from one of the dressing rooms... butt naked!

Elyssar looked around; thankfully, no one else seemed to be there.

Paul walked towards her as if it were the most normal thing on earth. "Nice."

He looked appreciatively at the black pair.

She gave him an uneasy smile, trying to keep her eyes on the shoes. But a whole crowd of naked Pauls stared at her in the mirrors: naked Paul from the back, naked Paul from the side, naked Paul from the front....

"I'm not sure about this pair," he said, examining the green wedges.

"Oh. I love them."

"Why? Are you planning to colour coordinate with Kermit The Frog?"

"It's a good colour for the beach. I have a brown bikini and a tan kaftan that would go great with them."

He shrugged and, in the mirror, the other naked Pauls shrugged with him.

"You have good taste so get them if you want to. Just don't forget that it's a very fancy hotel. People there are extremely stylish."

He gave her a light kiss on the lips and she looked around again, worried about security cameras or someone walking in on them. Didn't you get arrested for kissing naked people in public? She imagined the police storming in and arresting them, à la George Michael's bathroom incident. Imagine having to call her father with that kind of news: *Hi Daddy, I've been jailed in New York for lewd behaviour. Can you please bail me out?*

The salesman appeared behind them. Elyssar jumped away from Paul.

"Are you OK with the denims you tried on?" The young man

did not seem to take notice of his customer's getup, or lack of. "Or should I get you some more models?"

Paul stepped into the dressing booth and came back out pulling on a pair of jeans and zipping them up. He was going commando. Elyssar felt her face catch fire.

"These seem nice. What do you think?" he asked the salesman.

"Umm... err...I'll leave you guys to it," Elyssar said, running out of the dressing area. She felt like laughing at herself for acting like the quintessential easy-to-offend Arab, but she couldn't help it. Paul *literally* hanging out in his birthday suit had shocked the hell out of her.

She looked at the green pair of wedges in her hand. Too bad Paul didn't like them, because she did. His words came back to mind. *Everyone is extremely stylish there.* Did he mean that she had no sense of style? Was she going to look out of place at that hotel? Better exchange them for something else; she headed back towards the shoe section.

She really hated this Miami thing. Starting with her un-fabulous beach body to doubting her own dress sense, she'd done nothing but fret about this vacation from the minute Paul had suggested it. To hell with it. She couldn't change everything about herself. She went ahead and bought the big green wedges with big green dollars.

Chapter 19

Majed called as Rouba was getting ready to go out for a swim. She'd sequestered herself in her suite for nearly forty-eight hours now, surviving on room service, news reports from Lebanon and updates on the phone from Majed.

"The counsellor is very happy with Hiba," he said. "She's made a lot of progress. Her assessment is that we'll be done with only a few more sessions."

He'd turned into a completely different father following the incident. As agreed with Rouba, he'd had a tête-à-tête with his daughter. Hiba had been very direct, accusing him of negligence towards her and her siblings, and telling him they felt that he didn't think of them as human beings, but as pets he kept to maintain his social image. They had grieved over Rouba's departure and he'd refused to even talk about it, behaving as if she'd never entered their lives.

Rouba had cried several times as she listened through Majed's phone, unbeknown to Hiba. She shared the responsibility with Majed: she'd been too concerned about her own predicament to fight harder for the kids.

"Hiba is glad that the rest of the kids are coming," Majed said. "And we're getting ready to..."

"The other kids?"

"Yes, I've organized for Mary to bring them all here. The psychologist wants to have a talk with them too."

"Makes sense," Rouba said.

"We're getting the house ready. Hiba has been doing most of the work."

"It will do her good. She loves to prepare for vacations," Rouba replied.

She and Hiba had flown together to Los Angeles several times over the years to prepare ahead of time for the family's summer stays.

"Yes, she's very excited," Majed replied.

"Has the psychologist or 'shrink' said how much more time she'll need?" Rouba asked.

"Not yet, she will have an initial session with each of them and then give me an assessment."

"So you'll be there for at least a couple of weeks."

"We'll probably take a full month," he replied. "I want the kids to have their time with the psychologist but also to enjoy their vacation."

A month! Rouba hid her disappointment. She rejoiced to see Majed get so involved in his children's welfare. Especially considering that a week ago the idea of organizing a holiday for them hadn't even crossed his mind. Yet this new plan meant that she would have to wait for several more weeks before she could resume the divorce proceedings. "I'm happy it's working out," she said, pushing her selfish thoughts to the side.

"Me too. We all need the break."

She'd never heard of Majed talk of a break before. Work and life merged in his mind.

"I will find a furnished apartment to stay in Dubai until you come back," she said.

"Isn't it easier for you to be in a hotel?" he asked.

"For a whole month? It would cost an arm and a leg."

"My office will organise it for you."

"It's fine." Rouba hated it when he tried to get his people to organise her life. "I'll find something for myself."

"As you wish."

Now that the crisis with Hiba was over, it was time to re-open the topic of her residency and the divorce. Majed owed her an explanation – as well as a fix – for the situation. But he sounded so exhausted that Rouba decided to delay opening the topic until their next conversation.

She forced herself to exchange a few more sentences with him without revealing her frustration, and they hung up. Rouba pressed her forehead against the glass of the bay window and stared at the sea below her. The sun had started to set and the soft waves and pale blue water looked inviting. But it would be so lonely to swim there all by herself.

She went to bed, used the fancy wireless tablet to close the black-out curtains and fell into a deep sleep.

In New York, a crisis of a different kind had just been resolved as well.

"All hail the Lipomassage. I am now a believer." Elyssar said to Reem on the phone. She was walking back to the hotel from her final "body perfecting" session in a renowned skincare centre.

"Really? It works?" Reem replied.

Elyssar told her sister about the treatment. She'd had five massage sessions in all and a body wrap in the past few days. The staff had measured her before and after each treatment and she'd actually lost several centimeters around the thighs, hips and stomach. She was even convinced her cellulite was less visible.

"Did you lose weight?" Reem asked.

"Not much, but my clothes feel less tight. I can go a dress size smaller now. Cellulite miracles happen when you believe."

"So is my big sister Miami ready?"

Elyssar groaned.

"No. The thought of being there still terrifies me. But at least I won't feel like a freak-show round the pool. On a good note, though, I've lost my appetite completely. I can go all day on one salad."

"You're starting to sound like an anorexic teenager. I hate to sound old world, but American size six is considered slim," Reem replied. "And you barely have any cellulite. No one can see it unless they're checking you out with a magnifier. When did you get so insecure?"

"Since I found out that I'm going to be thrust in the midst of world-class models in their natural habitat."

Reem chuckled. "I have a sneaky feeling Paul will have already noticed you're not a model. I don't think it will come as a shock to him when he sees you in a bikini."

Elyssar stopped to take in her surroundings. She'd almost gotten used to being in New York, but every now and then, a small detail reignited her excitement. Right now, it was the sight of two women competing to get into a taxi. "Let's change subjects," she said, "I'm tired of obsessing about my big fat ass. What's the latest in Rantour?"

"Lots of action here. We've had to set up a demarcation line between Uncle Najeeb and Aunt Hala."

"Is he still giving her a hard time for watering her lawn?

"He's physically monitoring the water tank levels. He makes us take showers with buckets all around us so he can collect the water to irrigate the garden."

Elyssar giggled. "Who would have thought Uncle Najeeb would turn into an eco-warrior?"

"There's barely any stock of fuel remaining in the country. We've had to reduce the power generator time to two hours a day."

Elyssar's heart pinched. Her family's living conditions were degenerating quickly.

"Emm Kemel is driving us crazy," Reem continued. "The humming just doesn't stop. An urban legend has spread, saying that spy planes can see through walls. We've heard that some people are bathing with their clothes on."

Elyssar laughed. "They must be abstaining from sex as well. That should be listed under war crimes: pressuring people into abstinence."

"Believe me, no one is abstaining. Emm Kemel or not, people have nothing else to do. We're going to have a baby boom in nine months."

Elyssar laughed. "That's the people's way of saying fuck the war."

The next day, Rouba was dressed the part of the power-divor-cée in a new black pantsuit and purple heels for her meeting with Majed's lawyer. She had pulled her hair backwards and gelled it. The lawyer, a young Kuwaiti man by the name of Hazem Makhti, had sent her a short email the day before, asking to meet her at the Shangri-La hotel in Dubai. He hadn't specified what they'd be discussing, but she figured he wanted to get the divorce procedures moving while Majed stayed in the US with his kids.

She found him already waiting for her in the lobby. Hazem stood up to shake her hand with much gallantry. Rouba had met him a few times before; he'd received his law degree from Harvard and always wore suits instead of the traditional deshdasha. He had a tendency to showcase his American accent by plugging as many English words into his conversation as he possibly could.

Hazem hailed the waitress to signal they wanted to place an order.

"I hope you're enjoying your stay here," he said.

"Yes, I like Dubai a lot," Rouba replied, fighting the urge to launch a diatribe against Majed for her residency cancellation.

"I hear that you fled Lebanon by land. How was that?"

Rouba just wanted to get down to business, but decided to follow his lead and play civilized. She gave him the top line story: taxi, long road, could have been dangerous but they got lucky and made it safely.

To her relief, the waitress came back with the coffees.

"Would you like sugar?" Hazem asked.

Rouba nodded; he poured the sugar and handed over her cup.

"Mrs Al Riyyad," he said his face now serious, "I called you to this meeting on behalf of your husband."

"Yes?" The lawyer's slightly theatrical demeanour didn't do much to put her at ease.

"As you know, we had to postpone the divorce hearing in court because of your absence when the war in Lebanon started."

She nodded. Why not tell her something she didn't know?

"Now that you're here, we could have had it re-scheduled."

"Yes?"

"But my client... your husband, has asked me to put it on hold."

He stopped and looked intensely at her. Rouba stared back, at first not understanding what he said, then sparkles of anger speeding up her heart rate as she started to realize where the conversation was headed.

He took a short breath. "Mrs Al-Riyyad, your husband is asking you to reconsider the divorce."

"There is nothing to reconsider, I will pursue it as planned."

Her words came out ice cold.

Hazem seemed to have prepared for her reaction. "As you know," he cleared his throat, "under Kuwait's Islamic laws, a wife is able to request a divorce only if she acquires this right when contracting her marriage but..."

"I didn't ask for that clause to be added when I married Majed," she completed.

He acquiesced, an empathetic expression in his jet black eyes.

"Can I know why my husband has taken this decision and why he's asked you to inform me instead of telling me about it himself?" Her voice remained calm.

"As you know he's been attending counselling sessions with his children," Hazem replied. "And he's reached the conclusion that the decision to divorce was rushed. He would like you to reconsider."

"He thinks that forcing me to stay in this marriage is the way to get me to change my mind?"

"He does not look at it this way. He just believes that your family deserves another chance."

Rouba silently counted to ten before she trusted herself to speak again.

"As you know, when we started the divorce proceedings I didn't hire a lawyer because I thought things would be smooth," she said. "But in view of this new development, I will have to."

"Of course. That's your right," Hazem consented.

"You didn't answer my question: why did he ask you to inform me instead of telling me himself?"

Hazem squirmed on his seat. "He knew this would be difficult news for you to hear," he said, "and he felt that it would be better for the future of your relationship if... somebody else came into the picture to inform you."

Rouba stood up to leave. "Well, you can tell him that there is no future to our relationship so that's one less thing for him to worry about."

"Mrs Al Riyyad, I may be stepping over my limits as your husband's lawyer by saying this," Hazem replied cautiously, "but I do urge you to take some time to re-think your decision."

Rouba shook his hand and turned towards the entrance. She took a few steps then turned back to look at him. "Is that why he cancelled my residency?" she asked

Hazem nodded.

"I will get in touch as soon as possible to give you my lawyer's details," she said before heading out.

As Rouba was stepping out of the Dubai hotel, Elyssar was stepping into airport security at JFK airport. She mouthed "I'm sorry" to Paul across the hall. They'd just checked in for their afternoon flight to Miami and apparently, the system had "triple SSS'd" her. The letter S had been printed on her boarding pass three times, signalling to the security staff that she was required to undergo a thorough check.

She'd never been stopped at an airport before, and it was all the more embarrassing because Paul had to wait on the side for her while dozens of people cruised through the scanning machines.

That's what I get for having a Lebanese passport, she thought. I should have applied for Canadian immigration like everybody else..

A young woman made her take her shoes off and go twice through the metal detector.

"Now, Ma'am, can I ask you to go there?" the woman said, with the extra polite tone that authorities apply when they know they're being horrible to someone.

Elyssar moved in the direction that the woman indicated and found herself a few meters away standing by something that looked like a vertical MRI scanner.

Another staff member gestured for her to go in. "Follow the instructions," he said.

She stepped in, spreading her feet as indicated by a design on the floor. Then she extended her arms to the side, following the written directions on the wall. The lights flickered as she heard a small blast and found herself swept by a brief, but very strong, gust of wind, making her shriek in terror.

The wind died down and she stood there, still holding out her arms. The man outside the machine signalled that she could step out and sit on the side while they opened her luggage. A man and a woman checked the contents of her purse, then opened her laptop, wiping it with what looked like a white paper towel.

"You can go now, Ma'am," the woman said.

Elyssar put her shoes back on, collected her luggage and joined Paul a few meters away. "Sorry about this," she whispered.

He took her hand.

"No, *I* am sorry that you have to go through this in my country."

Elyssar sighed. "It wouldn't happen if some people from my side of the world hadn't earned us the privilege of being profiled at every airport." Relieved to have come through unscathed, she giggled and poked him on the ribs, "Anyway, you have to admit, I do look like a terrorist."

Paul laughed.

"You're my hot little Lebanese terrorist," he said, pulling her close to plant the most terrifyingly sexy kiss on her lips.

Chapter 20

In Dubai, Rouba dropped the last bag of canned foods into the special charity container at the gas station.

"I got a mixture of the relief items that your agency asked for on their website," she told the volunteer who stood nearby. "Canned foods, baby formula, basic clothing items and blankets. Is there anything else you need?"

"Thank you so much," the young man answered. "Everyone's been so generous we've been flooded with donations. But I have noted your contact details and we'll call you if anything else is required."

Rouba waved goodbye and got into the SUV she'd rented for the week. After all the days she'd spent watching the war coverage and obsessing about her botched divorce, it felt good to be outside and doing something productive. This morning she'd gone to a yoga class, then to a supermarket to pick up the goods that she'd just delivered for the relief efforts in Lebanon.

She'd also moved the day before to a furnished apartment. She kind of missed the glitter of Burj Al Arab, but at least the new place felt real.

Putting the music on full blast, she sang along as she drove up the Sheikh Zayed Road highway. She didn't have a destination in mind, but thought she'd go for a drive since the smouldering heat wouldn't let her walk anywhere and she didn't want to go back to the apartment just yet.

Of course, Majed had to choose this time to call her.

"I was actually having a nice day for a change," she said as she answered the call; "I should have guessed you would call to ruin it."

"Glad to deliver on your expectations," he replied.

"Should I assume that you have no bad news to tell me today? You seem to never have the guts to deliver it in person."

After leaving the meeting with Majed's lawyer, Rouba had called several attorneys in Kuwait who all confirmed what Hazem said: as a woman under Shari'a law, she simply had no right to ask for a divorce. Her husband could even legally force her to return to the marital home.

"Why haven't you answered any of my calls in the past two days?" Majed asked.

"Why haven't you given me my divorce?"

"Rouba, we need to talk," he said after a brief silence.

"That's rich coming from you. Anyway, why should we, you've taken all the decisions already: cancelling the divorce, getting me thrown out of Kuwait..."

"I didn't get you thrown out of Kuwait. I simply blocked you from entering because I had to ..."

Rouba pulled over to the side of the road so she could get off the hands free and squeeze her phone like it was Majed's throat. "Whatever the reasons, it was the wrong thing to do and you know it. You abused your power. Did you call your minister friend and ask him to do this? You had me treated like a criminal." She'd sworn to herself not to give him the pleasure of seeing how hurt she was, but she was unable to hide the anger in her voice.

"You're right..."

"You owe me an apology."

"I apologize."

"And you shouldn't have sent your lawyer to tell me you've changed your mind about the divorce," she continued, not stopping to take a breath.

"I did that because I knew my suggestion would make you angry, and since I couldn't be there in person I thought that Hazem would make a good alternative."

"You can't delegate your marriage, Majed."

"I'm sorry."

Feeling her fury begin to evaporate, Rouba smiled. She'd just hit a new personal record: getting Majed to apologize twice in the same conversation. The fact that he sounded genuinely contrite represented the icing on the cake. Still, the admission of guilt didn't really help, she needed tangible concessions.

"OK, here's the deal," she said. "Since we have to get out of this stalemate I will accept I have to talk to you. But first you have to get me a new visa to Kuwait and promise that regardless of the outcome of the discussion, you will grant me a divorce immediately if I ask for it."

An uneasy silence followed. Rouba knew Majed didn't like anyone dictating their conditions to him.

"Majed," she said, "I will not discuss anything more with you when you've put me in such a corner."

Majed weighed her request some more, then said: "I will get my office to start processing a new visa for you."

"Good."

"And I will come to Dubai," he went on. "This will only work if we do it face to face."

"OK. In the meantime, no more bad surprises, please. Let's try to make this a happy divorce."

Elyssar's whirlwind romance was going strong in Miami. Paul had obviously had a lot to drink by the time she met him at the Delano's lobby bar that evening. He'd been waiting for her to get ready for dinner, and seemed to have gone through quite a few glasses in the forty-five minutes he'd been there.

Between unpacking and getting ready for dinner, Elyssar hadn't had the chance to go round the hotel since they'd arrived to Miami in the afternoon, but what she'd seen so far was impressive. For instance, this lounge bar, with its upholstered rose-colored walls and Venetian chandeliers was a sophisticated yet somewhat relaxed spot for chatting and drinks. She suspected, though, that some of the patrons were also here for the people-watching.

"You look beautiful," Paul said when Elyssar joined him.

"You like my dress?" she said, turning around to show off the strapless Diane Von Furstenberg he'd bought her this afternoon after his trip to the gym.

"This ass would look hot in anything," he replied, gaping at her behind.

She smiled. He brushed her cheek with his hand.

"Has anyone ever told you that you have the most beautiful smile? In fact it's as if you don't smile, you... beam. You're like a ray of sunshine."

Elyssar smiled some more.

"I'm so glad I met you, we're perfect together, don't you think?" he said.

"Michelle the matchmaker asked me if I wanted to meet anyone else and I said no. You're the only one I want to be with."

Elyssar's stomach flipped with delight.

"Ellie, don't go back to Lebanon, stay here with me." He carried on with that suddenly serious face that drunken people get. "I've been thinking, and I want you to know that..." he paused for dramatic effect, "no matter what happens, I love you."

Elyssar couldn't remember a moment in her life when she'd felt happier. She jumped into his arms and hugged him very close without saying anything. God knew she'd fallen head over heels in love with him too, but she was just not ready to say it yet. It was much too early and she knew that things had a habit of going terribly wrong. She really wanted this one to work. Throughout her single years and the countless relationships that never went anywhere, she'd always thought that God had something special in store for her and every ounce of her body screamed that Paul was it.

As she held him tight, she told herself that nothing on earth or in heaven could possibly feel better than this.

In Lebanon, the rest of Elyssar's family had very different priorities to deal with. Maya looked on as the children busied themselves around the kitchen. Because of the wide range of ages, Reem had found it difficult to use books and traditional learning methods, so she'd decided to organize what she called extra-curricular activities. She'd delegated Maya to run today's session which focused on learning the names of foods and kitchenware in French.

Since the displaced group had arrived in Rantour, each family in the village had cooked extra portions that were taken to the school at meal times. But this morning, Maya had picked ten students to cook a dish of chicken and rice to take back to their families. Maya's mother, normally more possessive about her kitchen than a medieval lord about his fiefdom, had found it in her heart to lend them the facility for half a day.

The exercise resulted in one of the biggest messes Maya had ever seen, but the outcome actually looked edible. Now each of the children would have to carry a laden platter on the thirty-minute walk back to the school. She would have loved to drive them there, but the fuel shortage forced her to include a little exercise in the activity.

"How is it going?" Reem said as she walked in.

Maya smiled. "I'm very proud of them. The food looks good and they've insisted on cleaning and reorganizing the kitchen before they leave."

"I've asked Dana to join us," Reem said. "I'm worried about controlling ten children on the road. If the three of us walk with them, they'll be safer."

Maya nodded as she wiped down the cooker with a damp cloth. "By the way, didn't the Mayor promise last year that he would build a side walk?" she said, "I remember seeing it plastered on posters everywhere."

Reem shrugged.

"Yeah, he'll promise it again next time he runs for re-election."

Maya nodded in agreement as she turned towards the students.

"Bravo, kids, the food you've cooked smells heavenly," she said in French. "Now are you ready to offer it to your parents?"

Hussein, the oldest boy in the group put his chin up. "I won't take it to my parents."

"But you've just cooked it especially for them," Maya said.

He shook his head. "We don't need to take food from here," he said. "My father will get some for us."

"Your family would love to eat the food you've cooked for them," Reem said.

"*You* paid for it," Hussein replied. "We're not poor to accept charity. Yesterday, my father bought us sandwiches because he said we can't accept food from people every day." His eyes swelled, and the other kids looked like they could start crying too.

"You have a point," Reem said. "You can leave the food here if you want. My family and I will be glad to eat it since all of you put in so much effort to make it. But if you think this is charity, it means we could never accept any invitations from you."

"Why not?" he asked.

"Because you're mixing up hospitality and charity," Reem said. "If Rantour is bombed one day and we had to run away to the South, we wouldn't be able to eat at your house."

"But you would be our guests," he said, starting to see her point.

"So will you accept our invitation today?" Reem asked. "Or do you not want to be our guest?"

Hussein smiled. "I will accept your invitation. And even without a war, one day you will come with your family and have lunch with us. My mother cooks the best *frakeh* in Lebanon." His face lit up so much at the idea of hosting them that Maya felt like giving him a huge hug. She restrained herself knowing that such contact between females and males, even if they were children, wouldn't sit well with the habits of the conservative southern Lebanese.

Chapter 21

Elyssar and Paul greeted the staff as they walked past the reception counter at the Delano Hotel. The faux-tanned man sitting at the concierge desk showed his whitened teeth in lieu of a smile. If the amount of Botox lifting his eyebrows to the top of his forehead was any indication, he had a few years to go before his cheek unfroze enough to manage a smirk. When Elyssar and Paul had checked in the day before, he'd had honey colored eyes; today he'd selected purple lenses that matched his polo shirt.

Paul held the glass door open for Elyssar as she stepped out into the pool area. She could barely hide her excitement at the idea of spending the day here. Paul had woken up early to book two sun beds. Apparently, you had to reserve them by eight in the morning for the pool attendants to hold them for you until eleven. After that, it was impossible to find a seat here but you could walk to the beach which, while open to the public, offered Delano guests exclusive access to chairs and towels.

The sight of the swimming pool took Elyssar's breath away. It was rectangular, lined by palm trees from one end to the other, with water flowing freely over the sides of the pool. As Elyssar had read in the hotel brochure, the pool was part of a lush orchard that featured special design "vignettes" to lend it a surreal feel. It took her only a few seconds to spot the design elements in question: an oversized chess board and an antique day bed.

"The pool has underwater music and separate areas for floating and meditating," Paul said.

Elyssar followed as he made his way through the maze of white loungers and chaises-longues.

"These are the ones I booked for us," he said.

He pointed to two adjacent lounge chairs. They were made like beds, with a fitted terry cloth sheet that wrapped around the cushion. Paul took a seat on one of them, Elyssar followed suit on the other.

Paul smiled at her. "Do you like it here?" he asked.

"This place is an architectural masterpiece," she replied.

Paul leaned on his chair and opened the newspaper he'd brought with him.

Now was the moment Elyssar had been dreading: taking off her caftan and exposing the cellulite. The sight of other hotel guests sunning their Pilates perfect bodies didn't help. She took a deep breath and removed the caftan. She was wearing what she hoped was her most flattering swimsuit: a black bikini with a push-up bra and a full coverage bottom featuring a golden buckle at the front to give it a hint of sophistication. She sat down as quickly as she could to reduce butt exposure time; to her relief Paul was reading his paper and didn't look up. She opened the novel she'd bought at the airport.

"There's coverage about Lebanon in the newspaper, if you want to read," Paul said.

"Maybe later," Elyssar replied. She'd texted with Reem this morning and her sister had reassured her that everyone in the family was fine. That was all she needed to know. Right now, she was in Paul Paradise and she didn't want any war reports to spoil it.

Paul's phone rang; he took a look at the screen and jumped to his feet.

"Hiii," he said as he moved away, phone glued to his ear.

Elyssar watched him walk to the other side of the pool. He seemed engaged in the conversation, smiling nonstop and running his fingers through his hair. She tried to turn her attention to her book, but only managed to stare at the first page without reading a word. She had never thought of herself as the jealous type, definitely not one to panic every time her boyfriend got a phone call, but her intuition never failed and right now it was telling her that something was up. Paul had just used his sexiest "*Hiii*" to answer this call, the same "Hiii" he used when he picked up Elyssar's calls.

She looked again at him; he'd climbed on a stool by the bar, still talking on the phone.

Trying to shake the feeling, Elyssar grabbed Paul's newspaper and turned the pages, looking for the coverage about Lebanon. *Violence, attacks, Israeli army...* she couldn't focus on the full text, but scanning through the words was more than enough to give her the picture. So much for spending a worry free day.

Paul reappeared by her side.

"Do you want to go for a swim?" he asked.

Elyssar forced a smile.

"Maybe after I'm done reading this," she said, holding up the paper.

"Can you keep my phone in your bag while I swim?"

She nodded. Paul dropped the phone in her bag and got into the water.

Elyssar sat up, staring at the bag. Only God knew what had taken over her but she *had* to know who this call was from, and the only way to find out was to check his phone log. While she was at it, she should inspect his messages too.

She wondered how best to do this. From the corner of her eye she could see Paul swimming with his back turned to her, trying not to get his hair wet. Maybe she should go to the toilets to spy on him in privacy. Her eye wandered around the pool ... and landed on the naked breasts of a woman who'd just taken a seat across from her. Model alert! The creature was young, tiny and her even colored skin was shining in the sun without the hint of an imperfection. The only thing she was wearing was an impossibly small bikini bottom, well, "thong" was a better word for it. Elyssar glanced towards Paul. Sure enough, he was staring at the topless woman. So were most people around the pool, both men and women, and who could blame them? Elyssar sighed. There it was again; this newly acquired lack of confidence. Reem was right, she'd never had such low self esteem and it was exhausting.

OK, back to business. She grabbed Paul's phone and placed the beach bag on her lap to hide her arms from his sight in case he turned in her direction. She worked her way through the menus to reach the messages. Once inside his inbox, she saw several of the texts that she herself had sent to him. There were also messages from his daughter, and a few from his assistant, Melinda. His biggest SMS correspondent was someone by the name of Nataly D.

Elyssar opened Nataly's latest message; it read: "*yeah*". Her heart beating fast, she opened the next message; all it said was "*really?*" Ms. Nataly didn't seem to like long messages.

Elyssar glanced in Paul's direction. He'd reached the middle of the pool, keeping his head well above water. She closed the inbox and opened the sent folder. Again, Nataly figured as his most prominent text correspondent.

Elyssar clicked on the last message he'd sent to Nataly: "*Another day in paradise, thinking of you.*"

Elyssar's hand shook so much she had to put down the mobile phone. She wiped her fingers against the towel. Part of her didn't want to read any more, but curiosity got the better of her and she grabbed the phone again, clicking on the next text message: "*I miss you so much, wish you were here. Oh ma cheri I adore you*".

"*Cheri*" lacked the letter "*e*" at the end. Let's hope Nataly knew French and would be unimpressed by the poor spelling.

Still working the keypad as fast as she could, Elyssar moved to the call log, checking the last dialled number. He'd called the office multiple times today but, sure enough, Nataly's name appeared on the list. Elyssar checked the time of the call and made a quick mental calculation. He'd placed it yesterday during the time he said he'd be at the gym... Or maybe even while he was out shopping and came back having bought her the Diane Von Furstenberg dress. Her heart pumped so hard she worried it would make her bikini top slide off her chest.

From the corner of her eye, she saw Paul swim back in her direction. She put the phone on standby mode and threw it into the beach bag, pretending to take out a magazine in the same movement.

His hair still dry and flashing his most alluring smile, Paul came out of the water and walked towards her. He hadn't noticed a thing.

Elyssar wasn't the only one having relationship problems. In Rantour, Maya said a silent prayer as she dialled the hotel's number. She didn't yet know what she would say but figured she'd make it up as she went along, the objective being to buy more time before confirming or cancelling the wedding in September. Maybe they would find it in their hearts to give her a short extension.

After what seemed like an eternity, the operator connected her to Gabriel, the Food and Banqueting manager, whom she'd met a few times. He sounded happy to chat with her, asking about her stay in the mountain and making jokes about the political situation.

He doesn't sound stressed, she thought. Maybe they've decided to just keep their agenda as is. "Gabriel," she said, "I'm calling about my wedding date. With the diplomatic efforts underway, there may be a chance that the war will be over soon, so I wanted to get a few extra days before I come back to you with a decision."

Pause on the other end of the line. A silence that she interpreted as a sign that Gabriel was considering her request.

"Maya," he finally said in a cautious voice, "Maybe I misunderstood what he said, but Ziad called me an hour ago to tell me the wedding's been cancelled."

On the Delano's poolside, Elyssar shot a side glance towards Paul. He was lounging on the chair, newspaper in hand. At least a half hour had passed since she'd read the messages in his phone, but her heart was still beating in a frenzy as a million thoughts went through her mind. Should she confront Paul? How would she explain looking in his phone? And most importantly, what should she do about their relationship?

Elyssar stared into the distance, noticing for the first time the way in which the end of the swimming pool morphed into a wading area. Emerging from the water were a silver coloured table and two chairs. They were now empty but someone would soon snag them to enjoy lunch in this unusual setup. Funny how an hour ago Elyssar found the atmosphere here to be so exhilarating but now it contrasted painfully with her own state of mind.

"Ellie?"

Paul's voice pulled her out of her thoughts. "Are you OK?" he asked.

She nodded.

"You seem upset," he said, looking at her with concern.

He was picture perfect with his toned torso, indigo swimming trunks and round sunglasses. Elyssar drew a short breath. Maybe she could forget about the entire episode. After all, nothing in the messages indicated he was actually in a relationship with this woman. But she couldn't hold herself back.

"I saw your messages to Nataly," she blurted out.

Paul sat up.

"You did *what*?"

"I looked in your phone and saw your messages to Nataly," Elyssar repeated.

He stared at her in silence. Heart thudding, she held his glance.

Paul stood up. "Let's talk upstairs," he said, frowning.

They each slipped their clothes back on. Carrying her shoes, Elyssar walked barefoot behind Paul as they made their way towards the hotel building. They paced through the lobby, barely responding with a nod to the staff's salutations. Elyssar kept her head down in the lift. She didn't trust herself to look at Paul's face right now. She would either erupt into screams or break down crying.

Paul opened the room door and indicated to her that she should enter first. She dropped her bag on the floor and sat on the side of the bed. Paul closed the door and paced the room, running his fingers through his hair.

"You've been planning to do this all along haven't you?" he said, "To go through my stuff?"

Elyssar shrugged. He could try to turn this against her all he wanted; she still had the right to an explanation. "No I haven't. But assuming this was my plan, the fact remains that these messages *were* in your phone," she said.

"Only a woman would do something like that," Paul said, "freaking women!"

Elyssar had to call on each civilized atom in her body to stay poised when all she wanted to do was hurl every object in the room at his head. She kept quiet.

He came to a standstill and turned towards her. "OK," he said, "what do you want to know?"

"You've told me several times that you're not involved with anyone. So explain the situation with this woman."

He stared at her for a few seconds, as if trying to decide what to say. "I met her during my trip to LA. It's a date that a friend of mine has been trying to set up for months, but the timing never worked out until last week."

He looked at Elyssar. She raised her eyebrows without saying anything, prompting him to tell her the rest of the story.

"It was a great date," he confessed.

"How many times did you see her?"

"Only once."

Her intuition told her he was saying the truth. In a way, things could have been worse, she could have discovered that she was vacationing with a married man.

"Why didn't you tell me?" she asked.

"Look, let's be grown up about this. We don't know how things will go between us. You live so far away. I wanted to keep my options open. Everyone does. If you had someone in Beirut, I would be OK with it."

Struggling to control her anger, Elyssar forced herself to stay seated and kept her voice under control. "Well, *I wouldn't* be OK with it," she replied, "Anyway, the point is that you lied."

Paul walked to the window and looked outside. "This is terrible, I haven't really liked anyone in years and now I meet two people at the same time..." he moaned.

"I don't understand the duplicity. I never pressured you to say the kind of things that you've been telling me, just like Nataly probably never asked you to say you adored her after the first date."

Paul turned to face her. "Can we forget about this? We're in Miami, and we're having an incredible time. Can we put this behind us and focus on the two of us instead?"

Elyssar shook her head. "No." She stood up. "I need to go home." It had just hit her that she was in a strange country with a strange man; and she was so far away from all that was familiar.

"Ellie, you know you can't go home..."

"I'll go to Dubai. I can catch tomorrow's early flight from New York."

Paul started to pace the room again. "I can't believe you went through my phone and now we're ending up in this mess," he yelled.

Elyssar swallowed hard. "I'm happy that I did. I guess someone up there is watching out for me and wanted me to know about all of this."

"Yeah, right. You people have to bring God into everything."

There was a silence, as his words hung in the air between them. Realizing his mistake, he tried to reach for her hand, but she pulled away. "Ellie, we're so perfect together, please don't ruin it."

"You said you loved me."

"I meant it."

"Yeah, you tell different people all kinds of things and you mean it every time, don't you?"

He didn't reply.

"I need to take a shower," she muttered.

"Why don't you do that? It will help you clear your head. And I'll go to the gym. We'll talk some more after we've both calmed down."

Elyssar went into the shower as soon as Paul left the room. She stood in the burning water until her skin hurt. Finally she found the strength to get out. She needed to get organized. She slipped on a beach dress and went to the guest service desk downstairs.

"I need to book some flights," she said, sitting down in front of the concierge with the purple lenses.

He turned towards her, the color of his contacts making him look like a glossy eyed reptile. "Is that for two people?" he asked.

"Only one."

"Business or First?"

"Economy, please."

His silicone filled lips coiled in disgust. For a second she thought he would tell her that his contract protected him from having to book cattle class tickets. Under different circumstances, she would have found the snotty attitude funny. She took a piece of paper from the pad in front of him and listed her travel route preferences to Dubai.

"I will leave my credit card with you."

He sneered at the measly MasterCard Gold she handed it to him.

No black Amex from this guest, honey, she thought as she walked away.

When they'd first arrived at the hotel, the lobby's soaring ceiling, combined with the forty-foot curtains, the multitude of mirrors and the eclectic furniture, had taken her breath away.

"The lobby is meant to look like the Gates to Heaven," Paul had explained. "The curtains blur the boundaries between indoor and outdoor."

This was a long way from heaven as far as she was concerned and now she found all of it irritating. The sheer white curtains billowed in the wind, threatening to block her escape and she hated the pretentiousness of the Adirondack chairs and the faux-fur beds.

She slipped into the elevator and walked back to the room. In the light of Paul's revelation, the two hundred square feet that she had called "the ultimate coolness" only yesterday in a text message to Rouba, looked like a sterile hospital room.

"An apple a day…" a sign read by the door. She looked at the green apple that the staff refreshed every day as the design item to constitute "the only splash of colour" in the room; she flicked it with her index finger and it rolled off its wall-mounted hook, landing at her feet. A kick sent it spinning under the granite desk.

She hauled her luggage from the walk-in closet. It seemed like only five minutes ago when she had teased Paul about his Louis Vuitton suitcases as they checked in at the reception desk.

Opening her suitcases, she dumped everything in without folding. Next came the shoes, and she resisted the temptation to just throw them in too. Instead, she put each pair in its own carry case and crammed them on top of each other.

She closed the bag and looked around the room for a final check. Nothing left except the dress that Paul had given her the day before. Picking it up from the floor, she laid it on the chair lounger.

"I'm done here," she said aloud.

Elyssar called the bell captain to ask for help with the luggage. She'd barely put the phone down when she heard a knock on the door. She gasped, this was it… She was really about to leave, leave this room, this hotel and Paul behind. Pushing back the tears, she opened the door to a chiselled young man who belonged more on a magazine cover than behind a bellboy cart.

"Checking out?" he asked.

"Yes."

She watched him load the luggage, lifting each piece horizontally with both hands, as if he were pumping weights. Maybe it was his way of keeping his muscles working when he wasn't at the gym. Maintaining pecs like those was a twenty-four-seven job. Once done, he nodded at her pushing the cart in the direction of the service lift.

Elyssar took a deep breath and stepped out of the room, closing the door behind her. When she reached downstairs, she texted Paul. *"All checked out and leaving for New York in a few hours and Dubai tomorrow a.m."*

The bell captain stored her luggage and gave her the receipts. Elyssar's head was killing her and she craved a latté like crazy. She left the hotel to look for a coffee shop on the main street.

Paul called as she was walking up the road. "I just got out of the gym and saw your text," he said. "Did you really leave the hotel?"

"Yes."

"Where are you?"

"Walking around, trying to get a coffee somewhere."

"Come back, we'll have lunch," he begged.

"I'm not hungry."

"Ellie, I thought we agreed to talk some more..."

"I didn't agree to anything."

She heard him grunt. "Then we'll have a drink," he said.

"No, thanks. I may never come back to Miami. I want to see a bit of the city before I leave."

"You know you can stay. Please stay..."

Elyssar snapped, finally losing her temper and raising her voice.

"Why? To hear more lies from you? How could you? How could you lie like that, telling me over and over how perfect things are between us?"

She carried on striding up the street, oblivious to the stares of people around her.

"I'm so sorry, Ellie. Let's try to fix this."

"Remember what you told me a few days ago? You said that everyone is a player until they meet someone. I wasn't this someone for you."

There was a long pause before he spoke again. "You seem to have made up your mind..."

She kept quiet.

"I will call you to check that all is well with your flights."

"Fine," she said as she hung up. She didn't need him to check on her, but couldn't be bothered arguing any further.

What was wrong with her? Why had she allowed herself to fall so hard for Paul? She should have known all along that he was too good to be true with his romantic declarations of love.

Elyssar stopped walking and looked around her. Damn Paul, she'd been so upset she'd probably walked past several coffee shops without noticing. Her head threatened to detonate any second and her body was screaming dehydration. Spotting a supermarket nearby, she went in, going straight to the cold drinks section. She quenched her thirst with a bottle of lemon-flavoured water before she'd even reached the cashier to pay for it.

As she stood in the line, her eye fell on a display of Miami souvenirs. She always bought a magnet when she visited a new city and this time would be no different. She picked one that said "South Beach Miami" in a thick blue font. God knew she would never need the little plastic triangle to remind her of this trip, but maybe one day she would be able to look back at the experience and laugh.

After the supermarket, she walked in the direction that she assumed would lead to the beach. After a few minutes, she took a turn and found herself on Ocean Drive. It was a moderately hot day, and the activity had started. Teenagers crossed the road wearing shorts and carrying beach gear. Many of them spoke with an American accent, but most were conversing in fast-paced Spanish. Under different circumstances, Elyssar would have loved to join in the fun and spend the day on the golden stretches of sand. At least the atmosphere here wasn't as pretentious as the one around the Delano's pool.

She decided to stop in one of the little shacks serving alcohol along the road; alcohol would be a better fix for her state of mind than the caffeine she was craving. The place consisted of a bar and a few stools. It was empty, except for the bartender and a lone customer at the far end of the bar.

Elyssar perched herself on a stool at the other end. "Can I have a glass of rosé, please?" She watched the barman's biceps bulge back and forth as he fetched a glass, and a bottle, poured her drink and placed the glass in front of her. "The Only The Beautiful Work Here" rule seemed to apply all over South Beach, not just at The Delano.

After taking a sip, she pressed her forehead against the chilled glass.

"You're gorgeous."

She turned in the direction of the person who'd spoken. The older man was looking at her from his seat on the opposite side of the bar. His paternal smile made his words acceptable. He had the typical look of a Florida retiree with his T-shirt, shorts, slippers, silver hair and wrinkled, sun-kissed complexion. With a stab of pain, she realised how much she missed her father.

"Thank you," she said with a smile.

The old man raised his bottle of beer and she reciprocated with her glass. He pointed to the stool next to him, inviting her to sit down.

"Rough day?" he asked as she climbed on the seat near his.

She nodded, not trusting herself to speak for a moment.

"Whatever it is, you shouldn't waste this beautiful sunshine thinking about it."

She drew a deep breath, giving herself a shake.

"You're right. I'm on the world famous Ocean Drive, I should be having a great time."

"You look Brazilian but you sound French," he said, peering at her.

She smiled. "Not really."

"Italian?"

She shook her head again.

"Spanish?"

"Lebanese."

He looked at her with renewed interest but didn't comment. They drank in silence for a while then he asked:

"Man trouble today?"

"What else could it be?"

He thumped his bottle against hers.

"Here's to Lebanon."

"Here's to Lebanon," she repeated. "And to kind strangers in Miami."

Chapter 22

Elyssar wasn't the only one with man trouble. Back in Rantour, Maya stared out of her bedroom window, too numb to cry. She couldn't remember how she'd ended the conversation about the wedding venue, and her attempts to call Ziad had gotten her nothing but his voice mail.

The skirmish about the wedding had been one of the biggest in their relationship, but she would have never imagined it would lead him to this, to cancelling the wedding without even having the decency to warn her, and then switching off his phone to avoid her calls. Was this the same man she'd known and loved for so many years? He'd jumped on the first opportunity to call the marriage off...

Raising her hand, she gazed at the ring on her finger, remembering Ziad down on one knee when he'd given her this ring a year ago during a walk in the cedar forest of North Lebanon. Their engagement period had been great and the wedding preparations had been sailing smoothly before this war came up. And now it was all over...

The tears flowed at last, as she took the ring off her finger and threw it out the window. The platinum shone briefly in the sunlight then disappeared behind the rose bushes. The bushes that had died because Uncle Najeeb wouldn't let her mother water them.

Maya turned away and headed towards the bathroom, wanting to sink herself in the biggest, hottest bath on earth.

Elyssar was pressing her fingers against her temples as she came out of passport control at Dubai airport. It felt as if her head would roll off her body and explode if she didn't hold it in place. She pictured the headlines: "*Alcohol as the new explosive belt. Female Lebanese terrorist in wine-induced suicide bombing. Scores killed and injured...*"

The fourteen-hour flight from New York had tested her hold on sanity. Stuck in an economy micro seat, she'd been too upset to eat anything throughout the journey, but made up for it by downing one small bottle of wine after the other. The flight attendants had started giving her a worried look every time she asked for a new drink, as they took longer to deliver the bottles. On two occasions they brought her water as well, and made sure she drank it before handing her the wine.

She waddled towards the luggage belt, looking at the endless flow of suitcases. They all looked the same to her blurry eyes. How would she ever identify her own bag?

As she turned on her phone, it beeped with two messages. One of them was the standard text welcoming you to a new country. The second came from Paul.

"You were the best time I ever had..."

He just liked the sound of his own cheesy statements. She ignored it. Another bleep.

"I'm so pissed off with you... why did you leave me here with all the memories? Why did you leave?"

Pissed off? He was pissed off!

"I am pissed off with YOU !!!." she wrote back, her fingers threatening to crush the keys as she typed one exclamation mark after the other. *"Couldn't you have told me the truth?"*

"You are wrong about that," came the reply. *"You only hear what you want to hear, see what you want to see."*

His answer didn't make any sense. He probably had nothing better to say.

"Believe me," she wrote back. *"Seeing those messages was NOT what I wanted, nor what I expected."*

He didn't reply. She put her phone away and looked again at the luggage conveyor. Watching its circular movement made her nauseous. She turned her back for a few minutes but when she looked again she couldn't tolerate the sight of the revolving multicolored suitcases. On impulse, she decided to leave without her luggage.

The hot, humid air that hit her as the automatic door opened onto the sidewalk left her breathless. Two giant fans hovered over the taxi row, blowing cool steam on the waiting passengers. On previous visits to Dubai, Elyssar had found them effective. Although they increased the already insane humidity level, they brought down the temperature. But right now it felt like the fans were cutting through her brain. The wind they generated was too strong, the people around her were too loud, the sun was too bright... She closed her eyes behind her sunglasses.

Her turn finally came to step into the air-conditioned taxi. As the car pulled off, a new message arrived. Paul again.

"You're such a quitter."

She wished she had the will power to cut him off completely by not replying, but she found herself texting back:

"What should I have done? Stayed & behaved like nothing ever happened, knowing that while you're telling me about our blissful time together, you're also messaging another woman 2 say u long 4 her?"

"You think you've got all the answers... you could have stayed, you weren't even willing to stay until I came back from the gym...you couldn't wait to leave."

She started to key in another angry reply, but a terrible thought came to haunt her. What if he was right, what if she should have waited? Maybe she should have listened to him and taken the time to talk this over before hopping on a plane and getting the hell out of there.

"I admit that my decision to leave immediately may have been a little rash." Her eyes welled up as she wrote the message. *"But I was extremely hurt... Actually, I am still hurt and will be for a long time."*

She sent the message then typed another one through her tears.

"What really hurt is that you didn't think what we had was worth a whole hearted shot. Not even for a few days."

"You are partly right about that," he answered. *"But I disagree that my heart wasn't in it... you think even I could fake all that?"*

Wiping her tears away, she typed: *"All I know is that I spent the last 2 weeks living for the moments I would be with you. And then to read these messages when I thought you were as happy to be with me as I was to have this time together..."*

"I spent the last two weeks feeling the same and then I messed it all up," he replied. *"Self preservation perhaps. I'm sorry sweetheart I never wanted to hurt you, not ever."*

She cried even more. *"I know you didn't,"* she typed.

"No matter what happened, I love you."

"Madam...Madam?"

Something white wiggled at the tip of her nose. She looked up and saw the taxi driver, his arm twisted over the front seat to hand her a tissue, his worried eyes staring at her in the rear view mirror.

"No problem, Madam," he said in a Pakistani accent. "Only little more traffic. Go quickly after the bridge."

Elyssar looked out the window and saw that they were gridlocked in traffic over a bridge. The poor man thought the congestion was causing her to cry. She took the tissue with a grateful nod. "No worries." She smiled through her sniffles. "I'm absolutely in no rush to get anywhere. I couldn't care less if we were stuck in traffic forever."

In Rantour, Maya was lying in bed, getting ready for an afternoon nap when she heard voices outside her window. Another heated discussion, what now? She sat up and listened.

"I need to talk to you," Uncle Najeeb's voice barked somewhere in the shared garden behind the villas.

"What is it, Dad?" Maya heard Dana reply.

"You need to speak to your cousin."

"I've been doing nothing but speak to my cousins all summer,"

Dana joked.

"It's Maya," Uncle Najeeb said. "Her water consumption is out of control. She just used up a whole cubic meter for a bath!"

Maya went to the window and peeked from behind the curtain, spotting them nearby. Dana must have been on her way back from Reem's house when Uncle Najeeb met her halfway.

Maya saw Dana give her father a look of disbelief. "How do you know it was her, or how much water she used?"

"We share a water pump with them," he replied. "When I hear it working, I know someone in that villa is taking a shower. I know it was Maya because she's home alone. I measured the level of the water in the tank when she started and then again afterwards."

Maya had to stop herself from opening the window and yelling at her uncle. How dare he invade her privacy?

Dana seemed to share her feelings. "Dad, you can't spy on people like that," she retorted. "She's free to shower as she pleases."

"No she's not," Uncle Najeeb bellowed. "We'll soon have to start buying expensive water tanks from private companies if we keep going like this. You better talk to her if you don't want me to do it myself."

Dana shook her head. "OK, OK," she said. "You're right. She should watch her water consumption like the rest of us. I'll talk to her. But for God's sake, don't say anything yourself. You've already had a fight with her mother over water. We're in the midst of one war; no need to start another one in the family."

Maya sat back, tears covering her face. Couldn't she catch a break anywhere? Even her therapeutic bath had turned into a conflict. She dropped on to her bed and grabbed her iPod, thinking she'd play her list of slow songs to put herself to sleep. As she started to scroll down the menu, the battery warning appeared.

"*Recharge battery*" flashed before the player shut down.

"I have no electricity to *recharge battery*, you stupid machine!"

she yelled.

She tried to turn the iPod back on but the same text re-emerged. "*Recharge battery*". A partially bitten apple took over the screen and then the iPod went completely dead.

Damn fruit company!

With all her strength, Maya threw the iPod against the wall, relishing the sound of the crash and the sight of the hundreds of little pieces of plastic flying across the room.

Chapter 23

Miles away in Dubai, Rouba woke up to Elyssar's text message at seven-thirty in the morning.

"*Are you still in Dubai?*"

The message came from Elyssar's Lebanese mobile number, not the American line she'd been using the past few days.

Rouba replied: "*Yes, where are you?*"

"*Dubai,*" Elyssar texted back.

Rouba stared at the single word on the screen. This had bad news written all over it. What was Elyssar doing in Dubai? Rouba dialled her friend's number but no one picked up. She resorted to another text. "Why did you leave America?"

Elyssar must have had her phone nearby but didn't want to have a normal phone conversation. She answered the text on the spot.

"*I found out something about Paul. I couldn't stay.*"

What had she found out? Was he into drugs? The mafia? Did he beat her? Did he…? Rouba made another attempt to phone Elyssar. Again, no one picked up.

A knock on the door interrupted her panicky chain of thoughts. She opened the door to find a puffy-eyed Elyssar standing outside. Without saying a word, Elyssar walked straight into the living room and collapsed on the couch. She grabbed the remote and zapped until she got to a music channel.

Shocked and unsure what to do or say, Rouba stood, holding the door open. For a second she wondered how Elyssar knew her address, then she remembered she'd mentioned it by email when she'd rented the flat. At least Elyssar looked safe; no bruises or bumps.

"Don't you have any luggage?"

"I couldn't be bothered to wait for it at the airport," Elyssar replied.

"So you intend on just leaving it there?"

"They'll take it to the lost luggage area. I'll pick it up tomorrow."

Rouba closed the door and sat on a chair, waiting for her friend to speak.

"We need to get me intoxicated," Elyssar said.

"You're already intoxicated," Rouba said, knowing the signs. "But let me check what I have."

She headed towards the kitchen but Elyssar was faster and got to the fridge first. She opened the door and took out a bottle of pink champagne.

"It's the only alcohol in your fridge," she said.

"It's all I have," Rouba answered. "I bought it at the airport, thinking I'd be celebrating my divorce."

Elyssar unwrapped the cork and popped it open. A little champagne spilled on the floor but she ignored it. She took a long gulp straight from the bottle, then another. "I really need this," she said.

Rouba pulled herself out of her state of bewilderment and fetched a glass from the cupboard, holding it out.

Elyssar shook her head and, still holding the bottle, headed back to the couch. She let herself fall on it so hard, Rouba heard something crack.

"Elyssar, you're freaking me out. Are you going to tell me what happened?"

Elyssar took another gulp without replying.

"Did he harm you? What is it that you found out?

"No he didn't harm me, at least not physically."

"Thank God," Rouba said out loud.

"All men are asses," Elyssar said as she took another gulp from the bottle.

Rouba nodded. "Welcome to my world."

"Isn't this skiing food?" Elyssar said a few hours later as she watched the waiter approaching their table with a fondue set. "Maybe we shouldn't have ordered it."

She had passed out on Rouba's couch after telling her about the events in Miami. She woke up starving so they'd come for dinner in a restaurant that overlooked Dubai's indoor ski slope.

"It's comfort food," Rouba said. "Anyway, we're in a make-believe alpine resort."

Elyssar nodded. "That bubbling cheese sets off the calorie counter in my head," she said, "but I'm now free to go back to junk eating. No more Miami top models on my horizon." She dug her fork into the bread and swirled it in the pot as soon as the waiter finished laying out the table.

"I'm pathetic for being so hurt over someone I knew for five minutes," she said, picking up where they'd left the conversation before the food arrived.

"The Paul thing had all the ingredients of a whirlwind romance," Rouba reasoned. "It would have been impossible for any woman not to fall for it."

"Obviously he didn't feel the same way. Otherwise why would he actively go after somebody else?"

"Because he can," Rouba sighed. "The way the world is today, we have so much choice we can get away with never settling down. We know we can always move on to the next thing."

Elyssar nodded and picked up her glass of wine.

"In Paul's case," Rouba continued, "scores of eligible women probably replied to his ad. His matchmaker can find even more, his friends want to fix him up and if he goes online he can get dozens of hot girls at the click of a mouse."

"Do you think the same applies to us?" Elyssar asked, frowning. "My decision to leave the US without taking the time to have a proper discussion with Paul; your insistence on getting a divorce? Is it because we know we can move on to the next thing?"

Rouba considered her words for a moment. "Yes. Maybe if we didn't have the choice we would have stayed and tried harder."

The very thought of it put a lump in her throat. "Do you think I should have stayed in Miami?" Elyssar asked.

Rouba looked her friend in the eye. "I think you should not have looked in his phone."

"Wouldn't you look in Majed's phone if you had a bad hunch?"

Rouba *had* looked in Majed's phone a few times. Not because she suspected anything but just as a routine check; a little habit she wasn't ready to admit to in front of anyone, not even Elyssar. To Majed's credit, she had never found anything suspicious.

"It's different. You've just met Paul," she said to deflect the question.

Elyssar rotated her wine glass. "He should have been more careful where he left his phone," she said.

That night, Elyssar lay in bed in Rouba's apartment, struggling to sleep. It was late in Dubai time, but too early for her body, whose internal clock was still on US time. Giving up the struggle, she sat up in bed, typing away on her laptop when her phone flashed. She had set it to silent to avoid waking up Rouba in case it rang.

Her heart jumped when she saw Paul's name on the screen. In her imagination, he'd called a million times and she'd been strong enough not to pick up. But now that it was a reality, she couldn't resist the opportunity to hear his voice. She pressed the green button.

"Not asleep yet?" he asked.

"I'm jetlagged."

"I can't get you out of my mind so I thought I would call you," he said.

"Funny, I was just writing to you."

"What is it?"

"I'll email it later."

"I really miss you, Ellie," he said. "Every time I walk into the hotel room, the lobby or by the pool, I imagine what it would have been like if you were still here."

Her eyes welled up. Maybe she could have - should have - stayed in Miami and heard him out. She had run away instead of giving her relationship a chance.

"I told Ashley what happened," Paul said.

"What did she say?"

"That only a woman would go and check someone else's cell phone," he replied. "But she understands that you left. She said it was the proud thing to do."

Elyssar closed her eyes. Talking about this was too difficult when she was still tortured by regret. She changed the topic.

"Have you decided to stay in Miami? Or will you be going back to New York?"

"I'll stay here in Miami. I need the space to clear my thoughts."

Why don't you invite your adored Nataly to join you? Elyssar wondered, her anger at him resurfacing. She kept the thought to herself.

"What are you writing?" he asked. "I'm sure the word "surreal" will be in there."

She smiled. "I'll send it now. Good night."

"Good night, sweetheart."

After they hung up, she re-read the letter she'd just written:

To you, the man beyond my wildest dreams.

I never thought I would write something like this, but from the moment I read that ad in Happenings Magazine, I've followed my heart and it has lead me to you. So I will follow my heart again and send you this message.

I just went over my first letter to you.

"Was it you?" I asked.

Well, now I have the answer... and no, it wasn't you.

I had always hoped to meet a wonderful person who would make me laugh and feel great and loved. But what I didn't know, what I didn't even suspect existed, was someone who could take me beyond what I ever thought life could hold, someone who showed me a kind of passion that poets, books and films have failed to describe. Someone who put the sunshine in my soul and gave a purpose to everything.

But I lost it all. Perhaps out of my own doing.

My luggage is still sitting closed in the hallway. I don't know if I will ever open it. Somehow the best time of my life is locked in that suitcase and I'm terrified that if I open it the memories in every item in there: the "Kermit the Frog" wedges, the black shoes that you said you liked, things that I wore and that you commented on... will evaporate. These memories are all I have left, and I fear that I will manage to lose them too.

Please spend as much time as you can in that beautiful room at the Delano and by the pool bar. A little piece of me is still there and I like to think it is getting to enjoy some extra moments with you.

Elyssar.

She created a new email addressed to Paul and wrote: *"No, the word surreal is not in there".* She added the letter as an attachment and sent it off.

She had to wait a few minutes, but sure enough he replied,

"Oh, Elyssar...," his message said.

She cried herself to sleep.

Chapter 24

At least Rouba and Elyssar had each other for consolation.

"I'm happy so many people came," Rouba said as she and Elyssar each picked up a glass of wine from the tray that a waiter was circulating in the crowd.

Over the past two days, they'd taken part in the preparations for a charity auction, hastily put together by a university friend of theirs to benefit those who had been displaced in Lebanon. The Lebanese community had responded well, showing up in large numbers. Many were residents of Dubai but others, like Rouba and Elyssar, were non residents who had found refuge there as they waited to return home.

The organizers had persuaded a kind hearted hotel manager to provide the ballroom free of charge and several local shops and artists had donated items for the auction.

"And here's a blast from the past," Elyssar said, pointing with her eyes behind Rouba. "Look who's coming our way."

"Let me guess," Rouba said as she turned to follow Elyssar's gaze. Sure enough, the person she expected was coming through the entrance: Najla Roumad in all of her un-spoilt, un-aged, five-foot-ten-inch-greatness: jet black tresses falling like a satin curtain around her face, endless legs and the chiselled, full-lipped face that had made her the most popular girl in school. The same looks that helped Najla's mother land her daughter a billionaire husband straight out of college.

Rouba had seen her name on the confirmed attendees' list and was expecting her to make her grand entrance any time.

"She's coming straight towards us," Elyssar said, hiding her smile by sipping on her wine.

Elyssar had often joked about the unspoken war between Najla and Rouba. It wasn't a war so much as a case of Najla holding a grudge ever since Rouba had been asked to join the modelling club in high school. At five-foot- nine and with her fair skin contrasting with jet dark hair, Rouba had received quite a bit of attention in her teens from local modelling talent scouts; the kind of attention that Najla believed only she deserved.

Although they hadn't seen each other in years, Rouba had heard through the grapevine that Najla was peeved by her marriage to Majed: apparently he had more billions than her own husband and she couldn't forgive that.

"Hiiiiiiiiii," Najla shrieked as she approached them. She highlighted her height advantage by dramatically leaning to give Elyssar a hug.

Najla moved on to squeeze Rouba, who struggled to breathe through the shroud of perfume and longer-than-life hair extensions.

"Rouba and Elyssar, still together. Nothing has changed," Najla said, moving her hair away from her face with a much-rehearsed, ballet-like movement that showcased her long, tanned, French-manicured fingers.

Elyssar and Rouba had never taken Najla seriously, but you could never be too careful in a conversation with her because she spat poison in every sentence. Back in school they'd nicknamed her The Cobra.

"Elyssar, still working hard?" Najla asked, pursing her lips and raising her eyebrows to give Elyssar a "you poor baby" look.

As far as she was concerned, work was something losers and spinsters did. The only measure of a woman's success was the number of digits in her husband's bank accounts.

"I haven't yet succeeded in finding a man to free me from corporate slavery." Elyssar replied.

Najla's nostrils expanded like those of an irritated horse, but Elyssar was too middle class, too unmarried, and not tall enough, to warrant her attention. She turned towards Rouba.

"How's married life treating you?" she asked. "Still in Kuwait?"

She pronounced Kuwait with a bit of disgust. With so many Lebanese living abroad, an implied hierarchy of expatriate cities had developed over the years. Paris and London sat squarely at the top, New York came next and other western European cities followed. Dubai was desirable, albeit "common", because too many people had moved there in the past decade, while the rest of the Gulf countries, as well as Africa and Australia featured at the bottom. Najla divided her time (and that of her three children, four nannies and two drivers) between Paris and Beirut, while her husband ran his trading empire from Zurich.

The conversation was taking a predictable course, and in her current state of mind, Rouba would rather not be bothered with it. Then again, she didn't want Najla to think she'd won.

"Yes, in between flights. I was busy redoing the Paris and London houses this year, but we're almost done."

On familiar territory, Najla went on to complain about the amount of work the redecoration of her various properties around the world had taken, but how lucky she was to have finished her villa on Dubai's Palm Island in time to stay here during this war.

Rouba and Elyssar exchanged openly bored looks. Oblivious, Najla changed topics. "Rouba, any children yet?"

"We have four," Rouba replied.

"I heard your husband has them from a previous marriage," Najla said. "Have you had any of your own?"

"Not yet," Rouba replied, gritting her teeth.

"May God give you that pleasure, some day. It's an incomparable feeling."

Sensing her tension, Elyssar flew to Rouba's rescue. "Oh My God!" she shrieked, pointing to Najla's abdomen. "Are *you* pregnant again? That's wonderful!"

Najla's perma-superior expression vanished and she stared at her own belly in consternation. "No, do I look pregnant?" she said, squeezing her oh- so- flat stomach for any signs of fat deposits.

"Oh, sorry, I just thought, maybe..." Elyssar replied, faking embarrassment. "I must have had too many drinks. Don't listen to me, you don't look pregnant *at all*."

Rouba stopped herself from laughing at how easily Elyssar had scored. Najla looked like she couldn't wrap up the conversation fast enough and pulled away, muttering how much she was looking forward to the auction.

"That was checkmate," Rouba whispered in Elyssar's ear. "Thanks for saving me from her fangs."

"I can only tolerate a few minutes of her at a time," Elyssar replied with a grimace. "I have to admit, I enjoyed pulling her strings, though. She's probably calling her plastic surgeon as we speak to book a second tummy tuck."

With Najla out of the way, Rouba found herself enjoying the event again. She and Elyssar moved between people, catching up with friends they hadn't seen in years. It seemed like their entire generation of Lebanese had found themselves stranded in Dubai this summer.

An hour or so later, one of the student volunteers came on stage to announce the start of the auction.

"I might as well buy a few things," Rouba said. "I'll need them for my single's apartment very soon."

Another student took on the duty of auctioneer as the items were brought out one by one: handcrafted pottery jugs, baby knits, lounge cushions and kitchen towels. They sold out in no time. Rouba bought a series of multicoloured cushions, Elyssar an Arabic coffee set and kitchen towels.

"And now onto our final piece for the night," the auctioneer read, thanking the artist who had donated the painting. "Many of you will love the depiction of this old door: distressed and chipped, sitting against the stone wall of a traditional Lebanese house."

The auction started at two thousand American dollars, the amount climbing quickly. Liking the work and keen to help raise funds for the evening, Rouba was happy to increase the stakes every time someone outbid her.

"Don't look to your five o'clock," Elyssar whispered in Rouba's ear. "The Cobra has raised her head and she's hissing in your direction. She wants to compete with you."

Sure enough, Najla's voice resonated from the back. "Ten thousand dollars," she said, more than doubling the last bid.

Silence followed, no one was willing to go above that.

Rouba raised her hand.

"Is that ten thousand five hundred?" the auctioneer asked.

Rouba nodded.

"Eleven thousand." Najla called out.

Rouba put her hand up again, to the auctioneer's delight.

Murmurs went through the crowd. Rouba imagined the comments that people were exchanging: this was clearly an ego war between two socialite rivals.

"I see what you're doing," Elyssar whispered. "You're evil."

"Yap," Rouba replied. "Since she's so proud of her husband's money, let's get her to put it to charitable use."

Keeping her poise and trying to look determined, Rouba kept raising the stakes until Najla shouted out the number Rouba had been aiming for: twenty-five thousand dollars.

Rouba turned towards her with a smile.

"Congratulations," she said, speaking over the few dozen people who were standing between them. "It's all yours."

Najla smirked. Her eyes were glazed over with the same rush of adrenalin that fighters have in a boxing ring.

"Not only did you help raise a lot of money for charity, but you've probably given this artist the biggest sale of her career," Elyssar said, patting her friend's shoulder in approval. "You've perfected the art of the diva duels, I'm so proud of you."

"So remind me again, why are you divorcing Majed?" Elyssar asked two days later, as she sat on the sofa, sipping a glass of wine.

They'd been watching the news broadcast on Lebanese satellite TV all evening and had downed a bottle and a half of the best rosé wine Rouba had gotten her hands on illegally. As a Moslim, she didn't have a license to purchase alcohol in Dubai.

"You're drunk," Rouba replied.

"OK, so I'm drunk. But that's no excuse for you to avoid the topic."

"You and I talked about it months ago," Rouba replied. "I know you don't agree with my divorce. You've said it clearly and I've noted it. Now let's move on already."

"The more I think about it, the more obvious it is that you're making the wrong decision," Elyssar slurred, ignoring Rouba's words.

"What *I* think is that you need to have some water to dilute all this wine," Rouba said as she stood up to go to the kitchen.

"You're stupid to leave Majed," Elyssar called out, speaking up for Rouba to hear her all the way in the kitchen. "I don't think you even know why you're divorcing him".

Rouba took a bottle of water from the fridge and came back to the living room. "Seriously, why are you divorcing him?" Elyssar asked. "All the reasons you've given me sound like cause for a couple to have an argument, not a divorce."

Rouba knew that Elyssar wouldn't give up until she got her answer. "Because every conversation he and I have had in the past two years has been nothing but an exchange of poison in both directions. We can't stand each other any more. This is not the life I signed up for." She poured water and held out the glass.

Elyssar accepted it without taking her eyes off Rouba's face. "I think you're angry because of the pregnancy thing, and you're taking it out on him."

She blurted the words out as if she'd been thinking them all along but never dared say them aloud. Rouba had gone through great efforts in the past three years to get pregnant, undergoing treatments in several countries and trying in-vitro and other interventions. None of them had worked. Although Rouba knew that she'd been pumped with enough hormones to drive the female population of a small country neurotic, she didn't accept that as the only reason behind the breakdown of her marriage.

"It wasn't only that," she replied. "Everything went wrong."

"Like what?"

"My relationship with the kids. We found out several times that they lied to everyone, including me. They'd tell us they were going somewhere, when they actually went to a totally different place. Not to mention all kinds of other lies..."

"All teenagers do that," Elyssar said. "And no one more than you and I when we were their age. That's no reason for parents to divorce."

"You don't understand," Rouba said. "It's different when you're their stepmother and they don't trust you."

"What I know is that you're the one they call when they're upset or in trouble," Elyssar replied. "Hiba reached out to you when she ran away to the States. Majed's other kids can't go for a few days without calling you or chatting with you online."

Rouba shook her head.

"Stop being so hard on yourself," Elyssar continued. "You have a better relationship with your step kids than most biological parents that I know. They love you and your departure broke their hearts."

Rouba lowered herself onto the couch, trying to hide the tears in her eyes. Elyssar put her arm around her shoulder.

"The signs are everywhere, Roobs. There's a reason why the

universe is conspiring to delay this divorce. Why don't you listen to what God is telling you and take the time to think it over?"

Rouba wiped the tears from her eyes. "Yes, I am angry at Majed," she admitted. "I know it's not his fault that I couldn't get pregnant, but what killed me is that he just didn't care. He was completely detached through the entire process. At the beginning, he went for it to make me happy, at the end to make me shut up."

"He deals with things differently. A fifty-something year-old man is not going to react in the same way as a woman in her thirties."

Rouba shook her head. "It's like he was just doing the bare minimum by showing up at the fertility clinics when he was required to. He became nothing more than a sperm donor."

Elyssar squeezed her friend's shoulders. "I know for a fact that he wanted that baby as much as you did. But he's a bad communicator, he doesn't know how to talk about personal stuff and the two of you let your relationship break down because of that. Just make the effort to communicate and you'll find that I'm right."

Rouba stayed silent.

"He's doing the right thing by giving himself more time to think," Elyssar said. "You should do the same. You two are still madly in love with each other."

Shaking off Elyssar's arm, Rouba turned to glare at her. "So you think he did the right thing by robbing me of my Kuwaiti residency and then taking a unilateral decision about the divorce?"

"Of course not," Elyssar answered. "But he's already apologized. *And* he's a man. You know how stupid they can be where such things are concerned. In his mind, he probably thinks that's the way to show he loves you."

"Since when did *you* become the shrink?" Rouba asked, smiling.

"Since I realized that my best friend is about to make a huge mistake and that single life's a bitch."

Chapter 25

The following day, Elyssar opened the door to Majed. She ushered him into the small living room.

"Should I get you a glass of wine?" she asked.

"No, thanks. But I'll have water if you don't mind," he replied.

On her way to the kitchen, she put her head round Rouba's bedroom door. "He's here."

Rouba was standing in front of the mirror, looking like a performer preparing to go on stage. She nodded.

"I'll get his water and leave," Elyssar said.

Rouba grimaced. "Shouldn't we give him some serious alcohol instead? I like him more when he's tipsy."

Elyssar chuckled. "I offered, but he's pre-empting our tactics. He wants water."

"See? He never ceases to disappoint me," Rouba said.

Elyssar walked up to her. "Listen to me," she said looking at her friend in the mirror. "He's doing everything he can to make this work. You should do the same."

"My life is miserable *with* him," Rouba said.

"But not because of him," Elyssar insisted. "And if anyone can help you fix it, it's Majed."

Rouba nodded.

"Just remember everything we've been talking about," Elyssar said. "Your marriage has gone through a rough patch, but you can get it back on track. Getting divorced is the wrong thing to do, although right now it looks like the easy way out."

"Fine, Dr Phil," Rouba said, straightening her shoulders.

Elyssar gave her one last smile in the mirror and then fetched the water from the kitchen. She laid the tray down on the coffee table in the living room. "I got you two glasses and a bottle, should be enough for the both of you."

Majed looked nervous. "Is she in there getting ready to lynch me?"

Elyssar giggled. "Maybe not lynch you, but probably throw a couple of punches. I say you take them nicely."

Elyssar had always found Majed a little intimidating. Although they'd never had a close relationship, she felt compelled to give him her two cents of wisdom. "Rouba's hurt," she said. "But she loves you a lot. That's why she's so angry."

"I know," he said.

Elyssar smiled.

"Just remember to shout back if she screams at you," she said. "I learnt to do that when we were in high school. If you stay calm, she'll think you don't care and you're disregarding her feelings."

Elyssar grabbed her purse on the couch, waved goodbye, and left the apartment.

Rouba heard the door close behind her friend and felt exactly as she had when her parents used to drop her off for her school finals. Just as though you have to do well for everyone's sake, but you're still left to perform all by yourself. She took a final look at herself in the mirror. She was already a little taller than Majed, but a bit of extra height wouldn't hurt, so she'd put her sky high heels on. The power divorcee suit completed the look.

Taking a deep breath, she walked to the living room. Majed was looking out the window, his glass of water in his hand. He turned around and she saw that he was wearing his striped red and white polo shirt. Rouba had given it to him in the early days of their relationship. He'd only worn it once and said he would never wear it in Kuwait, because the red colour looked "gay".

"So red is not too gay for you any more?" Rouba regretted her words immediately. Majed took the hit without saying anything, but she wished she would have found a more positive way to start this meeting.

"Would… you like some wine?" she asked to fill the silence.

"No, water's fine," he replied.

The pair of them stood there facing each other in the middle of the room. At least the heels worked. Rouba towered over Majed and it felt good. In his jean and polo shirt he looked smaller anyway. He always seemed bigger in his Kuwaiti clothes.

"Did everything go well with my visa?" Rouba asked.

"Yes." He picked up an envelope from the coffee table and handed it to her. "I got you a work visa. I thought you'd be more comfortable with that than a spouse permit."

"Thanks." She opened the envelope and checked the document. It seemed to be in order. "I'll put it away in my room," she said. "I'll be right back." Back in the room, the image the mirror sent her back was quite different from the strong woman she thought she'd seen a few minutes earlier. Now, she just looked tense and severe with her pulled back hair. She also looked a lot older.

This is me in a few years, she thought. Bitter and soul-less.

She put the visa away in the top drawer of the dresser and went back to the living room. Majed had sat down on the sofa.

"Why don't you take a seat?" he asked, inviting her with his hand.

She perched herself on an armchair.

"I want to start this discussion by apologizing again for all the things I did wrong," he said.

"You sound like you're opening a board meeting."

"I know." He grimaced. "I am not good at this stuff."

"No, you're not."

Truth be told, she appreciated his effort but she couldn't stop herself making it harder for him.

"Rouba, the past few weeks have been horrible. I came so close to losing everything: my daughter, my family... you."

Rouba looked at him in silence.

Majed looked down at his hands on his lap. "And that is when I realized that things never had to get so bad; that with a little effort, I could have kept it together."

"It wasn't only the past couple of weeks, Majed," Rouba said quietly. "What happened recently is the result of problems that have been brewing for years."

"I know, and that's why I wanted to talk with you."

Rouba had always thought Majed had the look of a lion with his full head of thick hair and his piercing black eyes, but right now he reminded her of a pleading puppy.

"What are you apologizing for?" she asked, trying to see how much he understood.

"Everything."

That was not an answer. Majed needed to spell out what he thought he'd done wrong so that he could fix it. He must have guessed what she was thinking because he elaborated. "I know what I did wrong with my kids." He sat back and cleared his throat. "We've talked it over with the psychologist."

"So what was it?" Rouba still had her doubts. In his own mind, Majed always did the right thing. That's why he never usually apologized for anything, and when he did, it was just to get out of an argument, not because he felt genuine remorse.

"I never communicated. I thought that my role as a parent was to provide them with food, shelter and education, and that everything else fixed itself by itself. I didn't talk to them when their mother died, I didn't talk to them when I introduced you to the family, and then I didn't talk when you and I decided to divorce."

"That shrink's done some good work on you. I'm impressed."

Majed stood up and poured himself some water. "Would you

like some?" he asked.

"I need something stronger." She went to the cupboard, took out a bottle of red wine and poured herself a glass. "So what's your plan moving forward with the kids?" she asked.

"I will keep making a conscious effort to talk and spend quality time with each of them. I've also agreed with the psychologist that she visits us in Kuwait in three months to make sure things are on track."

"Sounds good."

Majed's kids had been through so much in their young lives, it was good to see the most important person in their life, their father, finally taking notice.

"So now, there's one more member of the family that I have to speak to." He said, focusing his attention on her.

She leaned back on her chair and took a sip of wine. "Speak."

Majed went back to the couch and signalled for her to sit next to him. Rouba shook her head, so he stood up again.

"I've been going crazy since the war started in Lebanon. I couldn't handle the thought of losing you."

"You had already lost me before I went there."

"I mean I was worried about you getting physically harmed. Especially on the day you drove through the border. I was livid with you, yet terrified for you at the same time."

Rouba glared at him, still furious at the memory. "So you decided to punish me by blocking me from entering Kuwait? You weren't worried about me then?"

"I knew you'd take care of yourself at the airport. I had to leave urgently to find Hiba and I wanted to make sure you didn't do anything drastic until we were both in the country at the same time. You were on the flight from Damascus and I couldn't reach you to tell you."

Rouba stayed quiet.

"Also, I had just spoken to your grandmother and she told me about what happened …"

"My grandmother? What does she have to do with anything?"

"We don't have to talk about this if you don't want to…" He hesitated. "You could discuss that separately with the shrink."

"No, I want to discuss it now. But first tell me what you're talking about. I have no idea about what my grandmother could have told you."

Majed cleared his throat. "Well… she told me about the fire."

Rouba looked at him, perplexed. "Which fire?"

He cleared his throat again. "She told me that you got drunk and tried to set your parents' apartment on fire."

"What the hell?!" Rouba couldn't hold back the cuss although she'd made a pledge to herself not to let anything in this meeting cause her to lose her cool. Had Teta gone senile? What fire was she talking about?

Suddenly, it dawned on her. "Oh, she must have been talking about the night I dropped the candle. But that was an accident and it barely burnt a small hole in the carpet."

Majed looked bewildered. "She also said that you cancelled your bus departure…"

"That's not true. Actually, she was the one who answered when the evacuation company called to inform me the day's buses were all cancelled. And when I called them a few days later to follow up they said they never called and…Oh!"

Rouba went silent. She saw on Majed's face that he'd just arrived to the same conclusion as her.

"OK, what else did she tell you?" she asked.

"That you confessed to her that you were having serious thoughts about killing yourself once we received the finalized divorce papers."

Rouba couldn't help but chuckle.

"And you believed such a story?"

"What else was I supposed to do? Drama surrounded me everywhere. On the one hand, I had an unreasonable wife who insisted on taking stupid risks in a war zone, and on the other, a runaway teenage daughter and three more angry children."

Rouba shook her head, smiling. "That explains a lot."

"Well, there's quite a bit more. Let me pour myself a glass of wine. This is going to be one long conversation..."

Elyssar raised her glass in a toast as she sat with Rouba a few hours later.

"Here's to the treacherous Teta," she said.

Rouba had called her back to the apartment after Majed had gone back to his hotel to get changed for the evening.

"And to her suicidal, pyromaniac granddaughter," Rouba replied, raising her glass.

Elyssar hadn't been able to stop herself from laughing throughout Rouba's account of her grandmother's fabrications. "So when will you tell her she's been caught?" she asked.

"Not yet, we need to resolve a few other things first." Rouba stood up to adjust the thermostat. The air conditioning had turned the apartment into an ice cube.

"So let me get this straight: you're planning to have a secret affair with your own husband?"

Rouba smiled. "Everyone has affairs with married men, why shouldn't I?"

"Well, if you put it that way. I guess the fact that he's married *to you* shouldn't be a show stopper."

"You know what? I'm relieved," Rouba said. "I feel like our relationship belongs to the two of us again. When we were officially married, it was like … our life was in the public domain, people had to know everything: where we were planning our next holiday, when we were going to have a baby, why I had a job instead of playing desperate housewife etcetera…"

"So the two you of are going to date again?" Elyssar laughed, but she actually liked the idea. She'd always thought the institution of marriage was too regimented and people should have more flexibility to do it their way.

"I will get my own apartment in Kuwait while we give things another shot. We will let everyone think that there's been an administrative delay on the divorce. This way, neither the kids nor my family will be disappointed if things go south again."

"And you'll come clean if you decide you want to be together for good?"

"Yap."

"Well, as long as the wife never catches you…"

Chapter 26

While Rouba and Elyssar were discussing the future of one relationship, the cousinettes were playing their part in helping another. Reem and Cousinette Dana walked Lara to her Honda SUV. Lara got into the car and turned towards them.

"You look scared," Reem said.

"I'll be fine," Lara replied. "The drive is less than twenty minutes and there's no reason for this road to be attacked. I'll be back in no time."

Reem gave the car a little tap as a gesture of good wishes as Lara reversed out of the garage and accelerated slowly to leave the property with as little noise as possible. The parents wouldn't approve of this mission, so the girls had to keep it under wraps. Reem looked around, expecting someone to appear at a window or from a balcony, asking about Lara's departure. Thankfully, they all seemed to still be on their mandatory afternoon nap. Maya was nowhere to be seen either.

"OK, that's one car safely gone," Reem said to Dana. "Our turn now."

They crossed the garden towards Dana's parents' villa and got into her car, careful to be as silent as they could.

As soon as Dana started the engine, she switched it back off. "I'm out of fuel. We don't have enough for the return journey."

"Oh, no," Reem said. "Do you think we can borrow one of the parents' cars without them knowing?"

"With my father's fuel and water obsession, he'd probably notice if a drop went missing from his car," Dana said. "And to be honest, as much as I've liked revisiting my teens in the past few weeks, stealing cars is where I draw the line."

Reem smiled, remembering how they used to practice their driving by "borrowing" their parents' cars and going for a spin around

Rantour before they were legally allowed to drive. A few cousins used to stay behind to cover for those who had gone astray, but they'd been caught a few times....

"I know what we can use," she said, an evil grin on her face. She got out of the car and headed towards the storage room in the back of the garage. Moving a few boxes around, even an old mattress, she found what she was looking for: a bright yellow bicycle with red streamers coming out of both sides of the handlebars.

"No. Please, no," Dana said, rolling her eyes.

"We're running late and it's the only solution we have," Reem replied. "Yours is in there too."

"We had these bikes when we were twelve years old," Dana cried. "They're too small."

"My mother got them serviced last spring for the cousins' kids. They're in working condition."

Reem got on the saddle and cycled around the garage. Though she felt ridiculously oversized, the tiny mount moved steadily enough. "Are you coming or not?" she asked.

Dana grumbled but went into the storage room and came out a few minutes later pushing a pink bicycle. "Thank God mine has a big Barbie sticker on the front wheel cover," she said, "Otherwise I would have been too embarrassed to ride in front of the entire population of Rantour."

Reem laughed. "I used to envy you for your Barbie bicycle," she said. "That pink basket in the front will come in handy today."

Dana lowered herself onto the saddle. She must have been a very small twelve year-old, because her bicycle was tiny compared to Reem's. She tried to go for a test spin but her knees hit the handlebars so she had to keep her legs wide open to pedal. The cycle zigzagged under her weight. Reem repressed a bout of laughter.

Dana stopped and dismounted. "I refuse to do this," she said.

"It's just a trip to the village centre. Come on, we have to leave now."

Reem pushed her bicycle towards the gate and Dana followed, still grumpy. They mounted when they arrived on the main road. The plan was to first try the local grocery store in Rantour, and if that failed, go to the larger village of Dar-Jesr because it had a supermarket and a semi-proper bakery.

The cycles squealed in protest as the girls pedalled them on the road, but they kept going, ignoring the stares they received. They left the cycles by the entrance of the grocery store and rushed inside. Reem noticed the curious look that the owner, Abu-Firas, gave their red faces and dishevelled heads, but he chose not to comment, greeting them instead with the customary inquiry about their fathers and their health.

"They're fine," Reem replied, leaving Dana to catch her breath. "They send their warmest regards to you and the family."

She exchanged a few more platitudes with Abu-Firas as she looked around. The small shop seemed to be even more under stocked than usual.

"We're not going to find anything here," she whispered in Dana's ear.

"We can't leave without buying anything," her cousin replied. "Abu-Firas would be upset."

Reem nodded and they each picked random items from the shelves: a pack of pita bread and toothpaste for Reem, while Dana bought a loofa and a pack of batteries.

"I told you this would come in handy," Reem said as she lifted the lid of the Barbie basket and placed their purchases inside.

"I will die riding this bike to Dar-Jesr," Dana complained as they set off again on the road.

The sight of her cousin trying to keep her balance on the tiny pink bike had Reem in splits until she ran out of breath half way towards their destination. "I need to stop," she said, struggling to regain her breath as she stopped on the side of the road.

Dana shot her a resentful look. "I'm tempted to leave you behind. Stop laughing at me."

Reem giggled even more and Dana couldn't resist the contagious laughter. "Man, Maya owes us," she said.

They got back on the road, trying to steer their cycles in a straight line. The road to Dar-Jesr was almost completely flat, but they were both sweating profusely by the time they arrived at the supermarket. Reem rushed towards the alcohol rack, then turned towards Dana in despair.

"No champagne," she said. "No alcohol whatsoever, only juices."

They looked at each other, unsure what to do. Reem grabbed a bottle from the shelf. "You know what? It's the intention that matters," she said. "This is sparkling apple juice but the bottle looks like champagne and I'm sure we can get it to spray if we shake it hard enough."

"Who needs real champagne anyway?" Dana replied "Let's try to find a chilled bottle at least." They checked every fridge in the store, but no luck.

"No problem, we'll drink warm non-champagne," Reem laughed. "I'm loving this idea more by the minute."

Now, the task was to find the perfect cake. Reem left Dana to pay for the bottle and headed to the bakery next door. Same problem there; the display was almost empty except for a lonesome English cake.

"With the power gone, we're unable to refrigerate the pastries," the sales lady explained, "You can make an order for tomorrow."

"We need it today," Reem replied. "I'll just take the English cake."

Dana came into the store, carrying the bottle in a plastic bag. "What do we have here?" she asked.

"Dry English cake."

With no electricity for the cash register, the woman scribbled a receipt on a piece of paper and handed it to Reem.

"Please can you pack it very well?" Reem asked as she handed over the payment. "We're going to have an interesting ride back home."

The woman did the best she could, putting the cake into a carton box and then wrapping it in a plastic bag.

"OK, so how do we do this?" Dana asked as they readied to get back on their bikes, each carrying a plastic bag.

"We'll put the cake in the basket," Reem said, "but the bottle won't fit. I'll have to attach it in the plastic bag to the handlebar."

She knotted the handles of the plastic bag together and wrapped them around a handlebar. Dana did the same with the bag of groceries bought from Abu-Firas in Rantour, then she placed the cake in her Barbie basket.

"I'll call Lara to check on things at her end," Reem said.

She dialled her cousin's number.

"So, did you find the stuff?" Lara asked.

"Err, kind of," Reem replied. "Let's just say it's not going to be the most sophisticated catering job. What about you? Is your cargo in the coffer?"

"Reem, don't speak like that," Lara replied. "I'm sure all the phones in the country are monitored. We'll get in trouble for speaking in code, even if it's just for fun. They'll think we're spies."

"You're paranoid," Reem replied. "Anyway, is he with you?"

"Yes, we've just started on the way back."

"Go slowly. Try not to get there before us. We're kind of challenged on the transportation front."

Again, Reem found herself on the verge of uncontrollable laughter when she saw Dana get back on the bicycle, having an even harder time staying balanced because of the extra weight of the bottle hanging on the left side of the handlebar.

This was going to be a party to remember....

An hour later, Reem stood jittering in expectation under the gazebo with the cousinettes and other members of the family as Aunt Hala went into Maya's room to call her outside. They could hear Emm Kemel hovering high up in the sky, but the afternoon's bombings seemed to have taken a break.

Reem's phone rang. She had texted Elyssar earlier to tell her all about their plans. "How is it going?" Elyssar asked.

"Lara has arrived safely with her passenger," Reem replied. "And somehow Dana and I managed to get the cake and drinks. The cake got a little defaced during the trip so we redecorated it using rose petals from the garden."

"How did you do the setup?"

"We used the garden table. Glasses, plates and napkins to one side, the cake in the middle and the so-called champagne bottle on the other side. As decoration, we've cut Aunt Hala's surviving roses and placed them around the gazebo. We're also wearing a rose each in our hair."

"You ladies should start a party planning service," Elyssar said. "I feel so left out. Believe it or not, I'd rather be at Maya's party than Madonna's concert.

"Yeah, right," Reem replied. "You're only saying that because your New Yorker isn't with you."

"Send me pictures," Elyssar said.

Cousinette Lara came up to Reem, looking anxious.

"What are they doing in there? Why won't they come out?" she said.

"The suspense is mounting here," Reem told Elyssar. "I need to hang up."

Dana came to stand with them. "Maya's probably being stubborn and refusing to come out," she said.

They hung around for a few more minutes until Aunt Hala finally came out of the house, followed by Maya. The latter seemed distracted and didn't notice anything until her eyes fell on Ziad standing a few feet away, a big smile on his face.

Maya came to a stand still. She stared at her fiancé, an angry look replacing the initial surprise on her face. Everyone held their breath. They expected Maya to jump into Ziad's arms, so her cold rage came as a shock.

Ziad seemed equally taken aback. His smile disappeared.

"Are you OK?" he asked.

"What is all this?" Maya retorted, finally noticing the setup and everybody watching them both.

"I just arrived," Ziad said. "I came here via Syria. This wedding stuff was getting too stressful so ...."

"You *cancelled* the wedding!" Maya accused.

Reem could almost hear everyone breathe in. *Ziad cancelled the wedding!* This was the first time she'd heard this piece of news. Why hadn't Maya said anything? Aunt Hala looked like she was about to have a heart attack.

Painfully aware that the shock on the faces around him could soon turn into anger, Ziad knew better than to be alone in the midst of a bunch of incensed Awwads. "I wanted to take the pressure off you. I thought that if I took the decision, you wouldn't have to stress so much anymore."

Maya didn't look convinced.

"How did you get here?" she demanded.

"I flew to Damascus and took a taxi from there to downtown Aley because it's the nearest city the cab agreed to drive to. I called your cousins and they organized to pick me up."

Maya darted a black look at the cousinettes.

"Let's go in," Ziad said, grabbing her by the elbow to take her inside the house.

As soon as they were out of earshot, an animated conversation broke out.

"This is why she's been so upset ... He cancelled the wedding!"

"How could he do that?"

"Why didn't she tell us?"

A few minutes later, as if there wasn't enough suspense, Maya stepped out to call her mother. They both disappeared in the house, sparking an even bigger flurry of debate.

"I'm feeling a little awkward," Reem told Dana. "This is a very personal thing. Should we leave?"

"You must be kidding me," Dana said. "I'll die of curiosity if we don't find out what's going on."

Eventually, Maya, Ziad and Aunt Hala all resurfaced together. Maya had her old smile back and was almost skipping with joy as she held Ziad's hand.

"OK, everyone," Ziad announced. "It's all sorted out. Let's have that celebration!"

Reem and the others waited to hear more from him, but Ziad had already grabbed the bottle to open it. It seemed they had to wait for the explanation to come later.

Ziad poured very little in each glass, to make sure each family member had a taste from their lone bottle.

"Toast to the bride and groom," Reem said, raising her glass. "We know this is not very fancy but we thought it would be nice to have this surprise pre-wedding party. The important thing is that Ziad made it here safely and all of us are together to celebrate." Everyone cheered. As Maya took her first sip, she burst into tears.

"What's wrong?" Ziad asked.

Unable to speak, Maya indicated her glass and the cake, as her weeping escalated.

"This drink... is... terrible," she finally managed to say between her sobs. "And the cake is disgusting! It's broken into small pieces. Look at how they've covered it with petals to hide the damage."

Reem and the cousinettes exchanged catastrophe stares while Ziad and Aunt Hala looked at them apologetically.

"You guys managed to throw us a party with almost nothing," Maya continued, now laughing between her tears.

She jumped into Reem's arms.

"You went to all this trouble for me. I love you so much."

Reem held Maya at arm's length to take a good look at her. "So are these happy tears?" she asked.

"Yes," Maya replied to everyone's relief. "I don't care if we never have a wedding. I couldn't have asked for more than this party."

Phew!

Reem raised her glass again and everyone toasted, although one sip of the warm apple juice was enough to put a disgusted look on all of their faces, and force them to abandon their glasses on the nearest table.

"By the way, you smell really bad," Maya teased her cousin.

"Yeah, Dana and I just came back from cycling class," Reem replied.

"You've already had your shower for the day," Uncle Najeeb intervened, "You're going to smell like this until you're allowed to shower again tomorrow."

Chapter 27

The sight in the area surrounding Bercy Arena's entrance did miracles to comfort Elyssar's broken heart. The scene played out like perfect Madonna Land: banners at every lamppost to advertise the show, the star's lookalikes everywhere, official merchandising booths, and young men in baseball caps selling all kinds of gear: posters, T-shirts, key rings...

One of them held a paper sign advertising last minute tickets. Elyssar walked up to him. "I have a ticket I want to exchange," she said.

She'd figured that, out of the misery of this trip, one little triumph was at hand: she would exchange Reem's ticket for another one the next day and attend the concert twice.

He adjusted his visor to take a better look at her. "You want money?" he said in tentative English.

"No, I'd like to exchange it for another ticket to tomorrow's show," Elyssar clarified, switching to French.

"Come with me," he replied.

Elyssar followed the tout as he led her around the corner and stopped behind a garbage container.

"Show me your ticket," he said, throwing a look around to ensure no one could see them.

She took the ticket out of her pocket. "It's a good seat," she said.

The man tried to take it from her fingers but she held tight to the little piece of cardboard.

"Show me what you'll give in return." OK, she officially felt like a drug dealer now, but the situation gave her some kind of a guilty kick.

The tout took out a stack of tickets from his jacket and looked through them.

"This is what I can give you," he said, producing one of them.

She examined it. "Row W is too far behind," she said. "I'm giving you a ticket on row D, I want something closer to the stage."

He gave her a pointed look then went through his tickets again. They haggled some more over seating until he agreed to give her a ticket in row K. But instead of giving him her ticket plus fifty Euros as he asked, she only agreed to twenty five. Thank God for the years spent haggling with shopkeepers in Beirut.

Elyssar handed him the money, placed the new ticket safely in her handbag and turned to walk away.

"Which country are you from?" he asked, following her.

"Lebanon."

"Lebanon. There's always war in Lebanon. I'm originally from Morocco."

The comment about Lebanon bothered her more than she cared to admit but she didn't reply.

"I sell flags, do you want one?" he asked.

"Why would I buy a flag?"

"People show them to Madonna when she's on stage. Maybe if you carry the Lebanese flag she will say something about your country."

Elyssar smiled.

"No, it's fine. Thanks."

She waved goodbye and headed for the merchandise booth. She planned to buy gifts for everyone: Reem, Rouba and the cousinettes, not to mention plenty of mementos for herself.

As she arrived at the booth, she noticed a group standing a few meters away. She had never heard their language before but it sounded familiar enough to make her turn around to take a closer look at the young people engaged in conversation nearby. They appeared to be in their twenties or early thirties, three women and two men; all of that would have been inconspicuous had it not been for the Israeli flag that the two men held stretched between them.

Elyssar turned around and went back to the ticket guy.

"I changed my mind," she said. "Do you have a Lebanese flag?"

He indicated the Israeli group with a nod. "You saw them and now you want a flag? That's how it is, eh? Israelis and Arabs against each other all the time."

"As long as we're not shooting bullets at one another, it's all constructive confrontation," she said. She paid the ten Euros he asked for and carried the folded piece of cloth with care. She needed it to stay clean until the show started.

Elyssar joined the line outside the entrance number marked on her ticket. It felt awkward to be standing alone when everyone was out in groups or couples. Talking about couples, the man and woman in front of her seemed intent on using continual kissing as the way to spend time. Elyssar's mind went back to her own public displays of affection with Paul. Had they caused disgust to everyone else around them, just like the two people in front were grossing her out now?

She looked away and busied herself by reading the newspaper she'd bought on the way to Bercy. Of course, Lebanon was still in the news. *From the Switzerland of the Middle East to the land of killing fields,* the headline read. The article chronicled the current war but also all those that had come before it since the seventies. It concluded by saying that, until the Lebanese got their act together and behaved like one country, they'd be open to civil unrest and the aggression of their neighbours.

A movement went through the crowd, making Elyssar look beyond the still lip-locked couple. The gates had opened; she gave a sigh of relief. Following the orderly line of fans, she found her seat quite easily. She looked around her and down at the stage: her ticket was well worth its black market price, she'd be sitting almost as close as possible to the stage.

Elyssar felt like she had attended this concert many times: the crowd's jubilation, her own jitters and expectations, the sights and sounds... She'd been here so often in her daydreams.

Laughing, she raised her arms to join the Mexican wave every time it reached her, holding the Lebanese flag well stretched above her head. She could see the Israeli group a few rows away.

The cheers escalated and she added her voice to the thousands chanting their idol's name: Madonna, Madonna...

In spite of her excitement, she felt that something was missing. Maybe leaving her family behind was too high a price to pay for a mere concert. Not to mention that she'd gotten her heart shattered in pieces on this trip...

Her nostalgia was short lived. The lights went out, the crowd roared, Madonna descended from the ceiling in a disco ball and Elyssar turned fourteen years old again.

In Rantour, the party was going strong. The cousinettes had gathered around Maya and Ziad on the patio, each holding a glass of water and lime in lieu of real alcoholic drinks: everyone had taken a final look in their kitchens cupboards and cellars, but they appeared to have run out of wine or any kind of spirits.

"So are you going to tell us what's been going on?" Reem asked Maya, "What's this about Ziad cancelling the wedding?"

"He thought he would make things easier on me if he took the decision to postpone the wedding," Maya replied. "He hoped to come here and tell me about it in person."

"But of course, she called the hotel while I was on my way to Lebanon," Ziad added. "When they told her what I had done, she couldn't reach me because my phone was out of coverage while I travelled."

"So I thought that was his way of breaking up with me and avoiding my calls," Maya concluded.

Reem exchanged looks with Dana and Lara. They'd had fears about a possible breakup since Maya had stopped wearing her engagement ring, but they hadn't dared ask her. Reem glanced at Maya's hand, the ring was now shining again on her finger.

"Aw, and he was risking his life to come and see you," Cousinette Lara said. "That's so romantic!"

"Not sure about romantic," Ziad said. "When she first saw me this afternoon I was worried for my life."

Animated conversation followed, everyone debating whether it was Uncle Najeeb, Aunt Hala or Maya who'd looked most homicidal when Maya had accused him of breaking up with her.

"So what are you going to do about the wedding?" Reem asked.

"We're postponing it until the winter," Maya replied. "If the war is still on, we'll just get married without a wedding party. I don't care that much about it any more."

"I'd hate for all of our beautiful dresses to go to waste," Cousinette Dana said.

"They won't," Maya replied. "Worse case scenario, if we can't hold a reception, we'll get dressed up, get our make-up and hair done and hire a professional photographer to take pictures. War or no war, I will lose the weight and I *will* have gorgeous portraits in my Zahy Rammini dress."

Reem's phone rang. The screen told her it was Elyssar calling but Reem only heard loud music and screams when she picked up.

"Elyssar, are you there?" she yelled into the handset.

"Yes," her sister replied, screaming at the top of her voice to be heard over the music. "I don't want to be alone in the concert. Put me on speaker, at least for this song."

Reem did as her sister asked and the music blared around the patio. She recognised the song; it was *Celebration*. The cousinettes smiled. The parents who were lounging around the table a few meters away gave them an inquisitive look but then carried on with their conversation. The expressions on their faces said that they wouldn't bother finding out what their daughters were up to on this occasion.

"Maya and Ziad, this is for you," Elyssar shouted on the speaker. "A special performance by Madonna herself."

"Let's dance," Maya said as she started to move to the music. Laughing, everyone else followed. Even the parents took to the act, clapping and cheering.

With the screams of the crowd in Paris mingling with those of the cousinettes in Lebanon, it was the perfect complement to the day: non-live music to go with the non-champagne at the non-wedding; but the family had found a way to be together and to have a wonderful time.

"So, Paris, how are yaaaaaa?" Madonna asked an hour later as she took a seat on her stage's staircase after a particularly gruelling rendition of *Ray of Light*, one of Elyssar's all time favourite songs.

Still in a trance, the audience cheered.

"I said, how are you, Parrree?" Madonna repeated, prompting the thousands of adoring fans to scream at the top of their lungs.

A young man dressed in black appeared on stage and placed a bottle of water next to Madonna. She took a sip then turned again to the audience.

"Show me your flags."

Oh my God! Elyssar rushed to hold up the flag she'd stored under the seat at the start of the show. From the corner of her eye, she saw the two Israeli men reach for theirs.

"Madonnaaaaaaaaaaaaaaaaaaaaa, look at me!" Elyssar yelled, brandishing her flag although she realized her voice went unheard in the ocean of clamour as hundreds of people raised their national standards.

The five Israelis jumped up and down, trying as hard as everyone else to attract the star's attention. One of the women gave Elyssar a side look.

"Darn it, they outnumber us again," she joked to herself, realizing how childish her behaviour was.

Still, she tried to jump higher and scream louder than them.

"So what do we have here?" Madonna said looking at the crowd right beneath the stage, "Canada; Britain, and... Argentina! Wow, you've come a long way."

In spite of Elyssar screaming herself hoarse, Madonna never even looked in her direction.

"This concert is the perfect example of people from different countries and belief systems living together," Madonna continued. "Now, repeat after me, we want peace, we don't want war!"

The crowd chanted as instructed. Elyssar couldn't help but look again at the Israelis and caught two of the girls staring at her as well. One of them gave her a brief nod; she nodded back. Kind of awkward.

Madonna didn't acknowledge either of their flags. That was another battle neither side won.

Chapter 28

Elyssar couldn't remember a flight when everyone onboard had been so quiet. For the first time in years, she had asked for a window seat, and pressed her face against the casement to ensure she would not miss a minute of the flight over Lebanon. After crossing Syrian airspace, the plane flew low along the Lebanese coastline which was shining like a green jewel in the mid-day September sun.

All onboard held their breath.

Elyssar stored away the newspaper she'd peered at over and over again in the past two days: *UN brokers Lebanon truce, International peacekeepers and Lebanese army to spread along border to ensure cessation of hostilities,* the headline read.

All factions had accepted the deal. After a few days of warfare where each side had unsuccessfully tried to provide a final proof of its military superiority, the ceasefire had come into effect at last. The airport reopened and Elyssar was proud to be onboard one of the first flights back to Beirut.

The aircraft finally landed.

"Welcome to Beirut's Rafic Hariri International Airport where the temperature is..."

The sound of passengers' sniffles and excited conversation deafened the flight attendant's announcement as people erupted into a round of applause.

Elyssar hid her face in her hands, unable to control her sobs. She wasn't sure what she was crying about, but she cried with all her soul.

-THE END-

GLOSSARY

Hummus: A ground chickpea and tahineh, or sesame paste, dip.

Labneh: A strained thick yoghurt dip eaten as savory, with olive oil, and spread on bread.

Teta: Grandmother –diminutive name for grandmother used in some Arabic countries, as nanna, grannie grandma, or grams in English.

Emm/ or *Umm:* Mother, used as Mother 'of' someone, so Emm Kamel.

Abu: Father, used as Father 'of' someone, Abu Abdo.

Force Majeure: A greater or superior force that excuses another party from liability.

Fool moudammas: Fava beans in a lemony olive oil mix served with bread often as a heavy breakfast in the Middle East.

Habiti: A term of endearment made to a female addressee (male: habibi); similar to darling or 'my love'.

Baqlawa: Sweet pastry of Turkish origin consumed widely in the Middle East.

Manakish: A pizza like dough base served with either thyme mix or cheese, usually taken as breakfast.

Abaya: A traditional black outer garment worn by women in some Middle Eastern or Muslim countries as a conservative respectful cloaking to whatever is beneath.

Frakeh: A southern Lebanese speciality, made from meat and cracked wheat.